The Sea House

Caroline Smith

Published by Honeybee Books
www.honeybeebooks.co.uk

Printed in the UK using paper from sustainable sources

ISBN: 978-1-913675-40-0

THE SEA HOUSE

Chapter 1

There it was, the Sea House, perched above the Esplanade facing out across the bay where the Atlantic Ocean meets the waters of the Bristol Channel. After years of neglect, it looked scruffy and down at heel; the paintwork peeling, the windows dull and lifeless. Grass grew out of cracks in the render like an old man sprouting whiskers on a lined and wrinkled face.

My insides churned and I felt a little sick. I took a deep breath, steadied my nerves. "So Gran, I've done it," I said, as I pushed open the creaky gate set into a slate archway and climbed the uneven steps to the overgrown garden above. Daffodils stood tall in the unkempt flower beds and tufts of primroses were just visible amongst the grasses and weeds. Aubrietia was beginning to flower and would soon be cascading over the wall, like a purple waterfall.

Before heading to the house, I crossed the unruly lawn to a quirky hexagonal summerhouse, almost hidden by a wild tangle of honey-suckle and clematis. A rusty stump, the remains of a weathervane, protruded from the roof. Like the house itself, this little garden room lay forgotten and dilapidated, but I had fallen in love with it the moment I saw it and planned to restore it to its former glory.

"Don't get distracted," I said, and made my way to the front door of the house. The key, still attached to the estate agent's fob, was warm in my hand. It turned smoothly in the lock, the door opening into a musty hallway. I picked my way through the usual debris of an empty house – a scattering of post, circulars advertising the latest deals from bargain supermarkets, takeaway menus and the local free newspaper. I shuffled them out of the way and, heart thumping, took the stairs two at a time, to the first floor. I threw open the French windows on the landing, gasping as the chilly air rushed in, and stepped on to the balcony that ran the width of the house. The green paint was faded and flaking but I didn't care. I leant on the rail and breathed in great lungs-full of sea air. The outlook before me brought a lump to my throat - an uninterrupted view of the bay, right out to Lundy Island and the horizon beyond - and tears pricked my eyes. I was home.

I couldn't really believe I'd done it; bought this wreck of a house, and I'd nearly chickened out at the last minute, but family and friends had backed me up – 'it's a once in a lifetime opportunity, Sophie,' they'd insisted. 'You'll never get another chance like this,' they'd said. So here I was, the new owner of this decaying, but fabulous, old relic. The Lord only knew how I'd cope with the refurb – I had a bit of a thing for interior design, but no idea about total renovations. Well, only one way to find out. At Mum and Dad's insistence, one of their surveyor friends had given the place a once over and assured me it wasn't about to fall into the sea anytime soon, and so the deal had been struck.

The view was a real time-waster – how would I get *anything* done? – but I stood for a few moments more drinking it in and gave silent thanks for my good fortune. Eventually I tore myself away, leaving the windows open to clear the stale air, and moved on. I peered into the two large bedrooms at the front of the property, where others before me had woken to that same timeless view, then hurried along the landing to a third smaller bedroom with another impressive outlook towards the headland of Morte Point, then peeked inside the scruffy bathroom. That avocado suite would *have* to go. I opened windows as I went, exposing the rooms to a blast of fresh air. I gave a cursory glance into a built-in cupboard on the landing – nothing hiding in its darkest recesses. I re-traced my steps down the stairs.

In the living rooms, sun streamed through the full height windows. I threw my arms wide and turned my face to the warm glow, allowing the intense coastal light to sear my eyelids. I wheeled round and round like a spinning top, whooping with delight. "If they could see me now!" I laughed as I twirled.

I made my way to the kitchen. At the back of the house with windows facing east, it was cooler, darker and somehow less welcoming than the rooms at the front. I felt a stab of disappointment that it didn't feel like my grandmother's. Her warm and cosy kitchen had wrapped itself around me like a comforting duvet. Instead, this empty space felt stark and cold. Suddenly I was prodded by a finger of doubt. Would I really be able to pull it off – replace the flat roof with a vaulted ceiling, studded with skylights? I had visions of the room flooded with light. I shrugged off my doubts; only time will tell, I thought as I mooched about opening and closing cupboards and drawers, turning taps on and off, sneaking a look inside the oven, before hurrying back to the sunnier side of the property.

I peeped into the cupboard under the stairs on my way past. The previous owners had made a thorough job of clearing the house – no broken furniture or faded curtains left dangling from sagging curtain rails – but I ran my hand across a shelf at the back of the cupboard anyway, just to check it was clear. It wasn't. I lifted down a book, an old leather-bound photo album, and took it into the living room for a closer look. I eased the stiff pages open, still full of photos held in place by sticky backed photo corners made brittle with age. A sudden beep from a horn and a knock on the door made me jump. The album would have to wait.

***

I was so relieved to see Nick as he embraced me in one of his huge bear hugs. "Wow, what a stunning place, what an amazing view! When can we move in?"

I laughed, planted a kiss on each cheek then repeated the ritual with Will. "My goodness, you're here already, I didn't expect you for ages. Come in, come in, welcome to the Sea House."

The removal van was small - there wasn't much to bring – and I had hired Nick, an actor friend with a side-line in shifting furniture, and his mate Will, to transport my belongings from West London. While they unpacked the van, I unloaded kettle, mugs, tea and coffee from the car. I suddenly realised how thirsty I was, not having had a drink since a brief stop on the M5 earlier in the day. I ran the cold tap into the deep Belfast sink for a minute to clear the pipes, then downed a mug of water in one before filling the kettle. I knew from previous moves that the best way of getting the job done was to keep refreshments flowing in the general direction of the removal men. Nick and Will were no exception. They shoved, yanked, hoisted and heaved my belongings up the steps while I directed operations from the front door, until furniture and boxes were unloaded into more-or-less the right rooms. Table and chairs were dumped in the middle of the kitchen; the box marked 'unpack first' was found and wine glasses, plates and cutlery unloaded. I lifted a cool box on to the table and produced a picnic of bread, cheese, cold meats, olives and a bottle of bubbly. "Well, you've got to do it in style, haven't you?" I said, grinning broadly. "Welcome to the Sea House, home sweet home."

"Cheers!" said Nick as we raised our glasses and clinked them together.

"That'll do for me," said Will. "What a great place you've got here, Sophie, a real gem."

The grin spread across my face "I'll drink to that!"

***

Will returned to London the day after the move but Nick had promised me three days' work, so long as he didn't get a call for an audition, in which case, he declared dramatically, he would have to 'love me and leave me bereft'. We unpacked boxes, constructed flat-pack furniture and made sure the kitchen was fully functional. We worked out the idiosyncrasies of the boiler, plumbed in the

4

washing machine and gave the Aga a quick once over. Once alight, a comforting warmth spread through the room. I set my grandmother's carver at the head of the chunky pine table and placed a bright patchwork cushion on the seat. I could see her so vividly sitting in that chair and wanted to hold on to the memory and not forget the unconditional love and guidance she had given me. I had used colours in the patchwork inspired by India – deep greens, oranges, reds and purple – in homage to her's and grandfather's life there, before they returned to London in the 1950's.

After three days hard slog the house was looking in fairly good shape in a bare bones sort of way, and we were exhausted. There were rugs on the floors but no curtains at the windows. I didn't mind the living room windows being bare, I wasn't overlooked, but we rigged up temporary drapes in the bedrooms using throws strung across wooden poles, with ropes and big brass hooks for tie-backs. "I don't know why you're bothered about being seen in the buff, Soph, you'd be a sight for anyone's sore eyes!" I turned and caught a wicked glint in Nick's eye as he headed off down the stairs.

I found him in the garden, gazing out to sea. A tad under six feet, with thick sandy coloured hair and hazel eyes, he could easily have played the part of a surfer-dude. My heart jumped as I watched him soak up the magic of the place. I sensed it touched his soul as it did mine.

"Come here my most gorgeous girl." He pulled me over and put his arm around my shoulders. "Come and look at this view; it's almost as ravishing as you."

"Idiot!" I laughed. "Come on, let's celebrate getting the house in order – fish and chips are on me!"

"Hey, you sure know how to treat a man. Let's go."

We wandered arm in arm into the seaside village. It was March; the last few days had been bright and sunny, the sea sparkling like crystal, but a biting north easterly wind cut through to the bone. The evenings were drawing out and we stopped to admire the sunset for as long as we could bear, before being forced on by the bitter wind. Burnished oranges and golds were reflected in the windows of the houses and hotels that stood above the Esplanade and the sky itself seemed to be on fire as the sun sank towards the horizon. We sighed contentedly and moved on.

We made a beeline for the nearest fish and chip shop to get out of the cold and were soon hurrying back up the hill with supper tucked inside our coats to keep it, and us, warm. We settled at the kitchen table chatting between mouthfuls of cod and chips and swigs of Prosecco.

"So, what next my 'ansome?" asked Nick, slipping into a pseudo-Devon accent, "and 'ow's I s'posed to get along without 'ee?"

"I'm sure you'll manage. Think of all those nubile young starlets just waiting to get their hands on you."

"Seriously, Soph, I'm going to miss you." He looked straight at me, his eyes holding mine.

"Me too," was all I could say, our deeper feelings left unsaid. I felt a pang of something – doubt, regret, sadness? It reminded me of the unease and loneliness I'd felt at being dropped off at school at the beginning of term. Was this a reaction to leaving my home of the last five years, the fear of Nick returning to London, or the scale of what I'd taken on? Nick sensed my change in mood and knelt in front of me, taking my hands in his. "You'll be fine. You're going to love it here. It's so 'you'. You never really were a city girl. Besides which, you won't be able to keep me away from the place. You'll probably see more of me here than you did in town."

My heart swelled with fondness. Nick always knew how to bring me out of the doldrums, sensed my wobbles, my need for reassurance. "Sounds good to me," I said, and Nick placed gentle butterfly kisses on my lips and forehead before moving away, scrunching up the fish and chip wrappers and chucking them in the bin.

By the time we'd cleared up the debris of the take-away and were sitting in front of the un-lit fire – mental note to get the chimneys swept - cradling mugs of coffee, the status quo of our frustratingly platonic relationship was restored. Before I curled up next to Nick on Grandma's worn leather sofa, I unearthed the photo album from under a pile of discarded paper packaging.

"What's that?" asked Nick.

"I don't know, a photo album. I found it under the stairs."

Nick blew across the cover unleashing a cloud of dust. The leather was dry and cracked with age, the pages rigid. The photos were fading and curled at the edges. In the first, a young girl, maybe three or four, was captured spade in hand on a beach, looking shyly up at the camera. In the next, the girl, now a few years older, was snapped holding hands and giggling with a smaller girl – the family resemblance was clear to see. The years moved on as the pages turned and the girl grew. We watched as a stocky young boy joined her, the pair, side-by-side poking out tongues at the photographer. Then they were teenagers, holding hands and smiling fondly, the girl's head resting on the young man's shoulder. A blank page followed, then the girl was with another man. Her look was different, the innocence gone and instead a more measured smile. And then, on the final page, just one with the girl holding a baby.

Tucked in beside the photos were small scraps of material, so tiny and delicate they felt like they might turn to dust in our fingers. But there was no mistaking that they were from the clothes the girl was wearing in the pictures, until the last one where there was a tiny, knitted booty. "Who *are* these people?" I fondled the fabric remnants. "And why put bits of material with the pictures? It's as if the photos themselves weren't enough, like they wanted a more tangible memory. It kind of makes me sad." We continued to pour over the album. "D'you think these later ones are wedding photos? They're sort of dressy but informal. Here, look, she's hitched up the dress and he's rolled up his trousers for the beach."

"Waste of a good tux' if you ask me. Looks like the beach across the road. And this one with the baby is taken outside the front door. They must've lived here."

"Annoying there are no captions; I so want to know who they are. And why is the album even here?" I returned to the first page and leafed through again, as if I would find the answers on second looking. "When d'you think they were taken? '60s, '70's? I'm loving those blue gingham hotpants," I felt the little square of material tucked in beside a photo of the two girls together.

"Somewhere around then - the era of free love and flower power." Nick gave a wistful sigh. "Must've been great growing up then, living down here. Such freedom. I could've been a real beach bum with a VW camper van and a surfboard." We leafed through the album again before reluctantly setting it aside.

"So what are your plans when you're back in town?" Nick would be leaving in the morning and I hardly dared ask the question, trying to delay the stomach-churning anxiety that I knew was going to hit with his departure. Nick pulled out his i-phone and checked his calendar. "OK, Wednesday I'm driving Will and his band to Birmingham, staying overnight to see the gig, then bringing them back. Friday I've got an audition for a short film; next weekend I'm going to see the parentals and then I'm back at college for a bit before Easter. How about you?"

There it was, as soon as Nick uttered the question, insides in knots again, confidence plummeting at the thought of being on my own, but I tried to sound assured as I answered. "Hmm, where do I start? BT are coming to install broadband tomorrow and I'm going to get on to the builders about the quote for fixing up the house. Oh my days, Nick, I've never spent so much money in my life."

"That's because you've never had so much money. It's no more than you deserve Soph."

"Maybe. I just feel so guilty; that I shouldn't have so much. Anyway, where was I? Builders, Penrose and Son, came in with the best price. Hope they're OK. And I'm going to start looking for a job. Could take a while to find something down here."

"Packed programme then. Hope the natives are friendly."

"Why not come down for Easter?" I asked suddenly. "See how I'm getting on." I tensed as soon as I'd uttered the words. What if he couldn't make it, didn't want to come; when would I see him again?

"Yay! Thought you'd never ask. I'd love to. Just so long as no work comes up, in which case I'd have to ...."

"Yep, I know, love me and leave me bereft."

"Damn it, am I so predictable?"

"Yes, but I love it." I laughed, feeling suddenly lightheaded. But our laughter quickly died away with the knowledge that this was our last evening together. I felt unexpectedly self-conscious and fussed with the cushions to hide my discomfort. There was so much left unsaid, feelings unexpressed. "Don't know about you but I'm done in, need my bed," I said awkwardly as I got to my feet. Now wasn't the time to open my heart to Nick. He got the message and, ever the gentleman, accepted my insistence that we keep things safely platonic.

"Yep, me too, gorgeous girl," he said, and gave me a lingering hug before scooping up the coffee mugs, dumping them in the kitchen and heading up to bed.

Chapter 2

Charlotte - 1976

The girls were walking the rugged coast between Tintagel and Boscastle; the steep and rocky paths that had been their playground since childhood. "Hang on Charlotte, I've got a stone in my shoe," said Verity, wobbling on one leg and reaching out to her sister to steady her.

"Oh come *on*. We'll be late!" answered Charlotte impatiently, pulling away and continuing along the path.

"Oh, well thanks for your help!" Verity said sarcastically, as she swayed precariously before regaining her balance. "What's the rush anyway? Johnny'll wait; he worships the ground you walk on."

Verity was right - Johnny adored Charlotte. He had lost his heart to her when the Tremayne family arrived at Trethevy some seven years ago. Charlotte had attracted boys like bees to honey with her 'come-on' smile and mischievous nature and could have had the pick of the bunch; Johnny never really understood why she had chosen him. Now, at twenty, Charlotte had blossomed like an exotic flower into a tall, exquisite beauty, with long blond hair, deep brown eyes and a tiny but distinctive birth mark on her face in the shape of a butterfly. In contrast, Verity had an innocent prettiness with a heart shaped face and large hazel eyes. Her hair hung in tight ringlets with stray curls refusing to be controlled by hairbands or elastics. She was smaller, more petite than Charlotte, and looked younger than her eighteen years.

"Hurry *up!*" said Charlotte. She turned and waited with arms folded.

"I don't know what all the fuss is about," Verity puffed, running to catch up. "So he's leaving his job. Big deal."

"Shut up Verity. You sound just like dad. Johnny's got plans."

"Yeah, well he'll have to make something of himself if dad's ever going to approve."

"Why does it even matter? Dad's such a snob. Mum loved Johnny, fisherman's son or not."

"She did," agreed Verity. "She loved everyone." The girls walked on in silence, arms linked, immersed in thoughts of their mother. Charlotte was transported to hot summer days, racing through impossibly narrow lanes to seek out secret coves in Lizzie's Triumph Herald convertible, roof down, the soft air buffeting their hair into tangles. She could almost smell the hot pasties they'd wrapped in towels to keep warm in their beach bags, ready to satisfy their hunger after a swim in the crystal clear waters of the Cornish sea.

Verity's recollections were more tranquil, of woodland walks and hours spent in Lizzie's studio where they painted together. Lizzie had watched with delight as her younger daughter's talent flourished. Their childhood had been idyllic, if sheltered. While other families took package holidays to Spain and Greece, Cornwall had offered the Tremayne family everything they wanted. In their memories, summers were sunny and hot, it never rained, and lazy days were spent on golden sandy beaches.

"There they are," said Charlotte, as they reached the headland above Boscastle and watched the fishing boats come in on the tide. The mournful cries of seagulls were magnified as they echoed around the deep rocky inlet that formed the entrance to the harbour. Lobster pots were being unloaded and stacked on the quayside. The girls waited while Johnny shook hands with his brothers and climbed ashore, leaving them to clean and secure the boat. He shed his oilskins and ambled over to the girls. "Is that the best send-off you're going to get?" asked Charlotte indignantly. "No good luck banners and streamers?"

"It's a fishing boat, not a farewell party in some fancy office," replied Johnny, smiling, as he gave Charlotte a kiss. "Anyway, I don't want a fuss. The family's upset enough I'm leaving the firm ...." He turned to look at his brothers, Matthew, Mark and Luke, who raised their hands in a sort of final salute. He felt a twinge of sadness – they were a close-knit unit and were still known locally as the 'gospel boys', despite Johnny having added 'ny' to his name some years earlier to avoid the relentless teasing at school.

"Come on then," said Charlotte impatiently, as she pulled Johnny along the harbour wall. "Let's celebrate. Where shall we go for a drink?"

"We've got to be back by nine remember, or dad'll be on the warpath," said Verity.

"Nothing new there then. Bloody hell Verity, we're grown women and he still treats us like kids. We've got time for a drink."

"He's just over-protective since mum died, you know that. Needs to be in control."

"You're right there, Verity," said Johnny. "Come on, we'll have a drink then I'll take you home."

They piled into The Wellington. Johnny went to the bar while the girls found seats at a table in the window. It was quiet in the pub, this early in the season. Visitors rarely arrived in large numbers until Easter. Johnny nodded at an old boy in the corner, sucking on his pipe and watching languidly, as a bunch of American tourists discussed the next day's itinerary on their European tour.

"Isn't he gorgeous?" said Charlotte, as she gazed at Johnny. "And he's given it all up just for me. No more worrying when he's night fishing."

"Yeah, well, I hope you're as committed to him, Charlotte."

"Of course I am! I adore him, you know that. I'll show dad this is for real."

"That's what worries me, that you're just trying to prove a point to dad."

Johnny returned with the drinks. "Here you are girls - two bitter shandies."

"Thanks Johnny."

"Yes, thank you my darling," said Charlotte, as she planted a kiss on Johnny's lips and looked daggers at Verity.

Verity watched as Charlotte snuggled up to Johnny. She often felt she was the older sister, the sensible one. Charlotte was impetuous, spirited - some said a wild child - but so engaging that everyone loved her. She got her way in most things while Verity, quieter and more reserved, lived in her shadow, often watching enviously from the sidelines. She hoped Johnny wasn't being led a dance. He'd been in their lives since they moved to The Mill House at Trethevy. He'd looked out for them when they were the new girls at school. She remembered how he'd shown them the special places: the beach at Trebarwith Strand, where they watched golden sunsets behind Gull rock; Rocky Valley, where he held them tight as the sea pounded into the steep river gorge, and most magical of all, St Nectan's Glen, where they stood together beneath the magnificent waterfall, screeching as the icy cold water splashed against their skin. She worshiped Johnny, but he only had eyes for Charlotte.

Johnny had been there for them when Lizzie died, and Charlotte had clung to his quiet strength, while Verity was left to comfort and care for their father. Before she knew it, Johnny and Charlotte were an item. Verity knew they were lovers. She'd overheard them talking about their first time together and jealousy had gripped her heart.

"What? Barnstaple? That's miles away! Why on earth have you got to *live* there?" Charlotte exclaimed. Verity jumped out of her thoughts.

"You know why. My uncle's business is there. It's our future," replied Johnny patiently.

"But I didn't think you'd have to *move* there."

"Course I do. I can't travel there every day. I've got to make a go of this, get qualified, not least to get your dad on side." Johnny spoke in a soft Cornish accent, but with a determination to match Charlotte's.

"I don't care about dad, I just want to be with you." Charlotte had a steely glint in her eye. "S'pose I'll just have to come too."

"Look, just give me time to find my feet and somewhere to live."

"And how long will that take?"

Johnny turned to Verity for back-up, but she was checking her watch. "Come on you guys, time we were making tracks. If dad gets in a lather, it won't help your cause."

"Damn him, he's so bloody difficult!" said Charlotte, as she stormed out. Johnny drove them home in his old Land Rover. They made it just before nine. "See you tomorrow at The Gathering - last party before the Emmets arrive," said Johnny.

"OK," said Charlotte dismissively. "Pick me up at 10.00."

"See you tomorrow, Johnny, thanks for the lift," said Verity.

***

When Johnny called for Charlotte the next morning he was greeted by Verity. "She's not here, Johnny. She had a massive row with dad last night and has gone to the glen. You'll find her there."

"Suppose I don't need to ask what it was about? I don't get why he's so against us being together. Would it help if I told him my plans?"

"I don't know, probably not right now. He's not exactly approachable. And he's gone to church in Tintagel. I can't be doing with the service, but I'll take a walk there later to put some flowers on mum's grave."

"See you at The Gathering then. I'll go and find Charlotte."

***

Charlotte wandered through the wooded valley alongside the river and her temper subsided. The glen was working its magic. Trees were in bud, leaves starting to unfurl; catkins danced like

14

lamb's tails in the gentle breeze and daffodils swayed in the soft air. Clumps of delicate yellow primroses peeped out from the woodland undergrowth. The sound of the river and the birdsong; the dappled sunlight shining through the trees all worked their charm, so by the time Charlotte reached the top of the valley and climbed down to the waterfall she felt soothed and at peace. She went to the place where she had left a stone in memory of her mother, set on a small shelf in the rock face of the gorge, and withdrew it. She paddled through the shallow water to stand at the base of the waterfall and lifted her face to the sun as it shone through the spray, casting an ethereal glow. It was here that she felt the presence of her mother most intensely; where she came when she wanted to feel her closeness and comfort. As she stroked the smooth stone on which she had painted Lizzie's name, she could almost feel her mother's arm around her shoulder and imagined them examining the stone together, laughing at the rough paint job Charlotte had made of the lettering.

As the sun disappeared behind a cloud and the temperature quickly dropped, the image faded, and Charlotte felt alone and abandoned. Suddenly tears came and she welled up with anger and frustration at her father's lack of understanding and his unwilling-ness to see things from her perspective. She knew Lizzie would have seen things differently. But as she looked at the stone again, trying to recapture the moment with her mother, she felt a rush of guilt for giving her father such a hard time - the man her mother had truly loved. Sobs wracked her body and grief penetrated to the depths of her soul. Charlotte offered up a silent prayer, seeking forgiveness and resolution, and eventually her tears subsided. She waded back to the shore and replaced the stone in its sacred place. There were many stones - some stacked into small cairns - and other keepsakes in the cracks and crevices of the rocky gorge, left by erstwhile travel-lers and pilgrims who had journeyed to this healing place.

As Charlotte climbed out of the gorge, Johnny came towards her down the rocky steps. She ran to him and he wrapped her in his arms as she wept again. Johnny stroked her hair and lifted her chin to meet his eyes. "I love you, Charlotte. Whatever happens, I love you. Do you want to tell me what happened?"

Charlotte brushed her tears away. "I was telling dad about you going to Barnstaple and how I was going to join you in a few weeks, and he went on and on, saying I didn't know what I was doing, didn't know my own mind, that I had latched on to you when mum died. He just went on and on." Johnny held her tightly and she felt safe and assured by his strong body. She knew she had to find a way to be with him, no matter what her father said. Eventually she shook herself off and her resolve returned. "I'm fine now. Come on, let's go and find the others."

"Hey, that's better, that's my girl." And he swung her round into a tight embrace as their lips met. "Mmm, sweet girl," he said as they drew apart. She smiled up at him and without words he led her to the Land Rover parked above the Hermitage. He took a rug from the back and Charlotte gave him a knowing look.

"Johnny, we're not at the beach yet."

"And I don't want to share you yet." He took her to their secret place, a densely wooded glade they had found some weeks before and where they had first made love. Now they lay on the rug and stared up through the budding branches and new spring growth, to the sky above.

"Think how this will be in the summer, completely hidden, completely secret, completely ours," said Charlotte, as she nuzzled Johnny's neck. "Even when the glen is full of tourists, we can be alone. No one would find us here." She paused. "Except in the summer you won't be here..." She leant up on one elbow and stared hard into Johnny's eyes, ready to start pleading to let her come to North Devon with him. But Johnny started kissing Charlotte so she could do nothing but stop talking and start responding to his loving caresses. They made love urgently, holding on to the precious moments they still had together.

Later, they went to the beach at Trebarwith to join The Gathering. These get-togethers were an established part of the local youngsters' lives. They had started some years before, when a group of teenagers held a party on the beach before the season began, and the tourists, known locally as Emmets, arrived. They had changed with the times, from picnics in wicker hampers and games of French cricket, through the era of flower power and free love - guitars strummed Dylan-like; joints shared around driftwood fires - to what they were today. Charlotte and Johnny joined their friends, some sitting amongst the rocks, drinking and talking, others dancing in the sand to the music of Queen and Abba - bodies gyrating and voices belting out the lyrics of 'Bohemian Rhapsody' and 'Fernando', as they played loudly on a cassette recorder propped in the rocks. Another group played with a Frisbee at the water's edge.

Johnny sat with his arms around Charlotte and she leant into his sturdy body, basking in the afterglow of their love making and mellowing to the sound of James Taylor, as it drifted across the beach on a cool breeze, mixed with the heady fragrance of wood smoke and patchouli oil. As Charlotte relaxed Johnny was filled with a sense of nostalgia, a feeling that this was the beginning of the end of those heady days of the late '60s and early '70s of which he had been a part; that now it was time to grow up and take responsibility. He was overcome by an unaccountable feeling of foreboding.

Chapter 3

Sophie - 2015

I wandered around aimlessly. Nick had returned to London and I couldn't settle. My heart ached for him. I'd insisted we stay 'just friends' after my last disastrous relationship, and Nick hadn't wanted to impose the precarious lifestyle of an actor on anyone, so we'd agreed to keep it platonic. But now I was worried. I mean, *I* was certain we were meant for each other but was Nick? What if I'd lost the chance, if he thought it was too much effort to invest in a long-distance relationship, if he met someone else? A hot rush of panic surged through me.

It was bad enough knowing I could no longer call him and arrange to meet for coffee (right now, I didn't know *anyone* I could meet for coffee). But what if I didn't have Nick at all? I felt small and alone, adrift in this new life. "Come on, come *on*, got to learn to stand on your own two feet. You *can* do it! Nick won't let you down," I said. I suddenly realised it was becoming a bit of a habit, this talking to myself. Nick would think I was losing the plot!

I gazed out of the window as a weather system streamed in from the Atlantic. The bright, sunny weather was gone; the wind had strengthened from the West bringing milder, wetter air. The euphoria of the last few days was blown away and I was slipping into the doldrums. I tore myself away from the window and forced myself to pick up my 'to do' list. I had to start *doing* and stop dwelling inside my head.

By lunchtime, as promised, BT had installed a phone line and broadband was set up. "Tick," I said, smiling with a sense of achievement. I was re-connected to the outside world. I received a text from Nick. *Missing you already gorgeous girl.* My doubts and fears subsided.

Spurred on, I curled up on the sofa with a cup of tea, my laptop and the phone. I rang the builders to discuss the work on the house. The conversation didn't go quite as anticipated.

"Penrose Senior speaking."

"Hi, I'm Sophie Chapman. I'm ringing about your recent quote."

"Righto me dear. Which quote was that then?" He spoke with a gentle West Country accent.

"It's for the work on the Sea House in Woolacombe."

With that, the line went quiet; then a few clicks and I was connected to another, female, voice. "Miss Chapman, could you hold for just one moment please?" Before I could reply, irritating canned music was assaulting my ears.

"Hello? Is that Miss Chapman? Sorry about that. Rob Penrose speaking. I understand you were calling about the Sea House estimate?"

"Um, yes, I'd like to accept your quote and arrange for someone to come and discuss the work in more detail?"

"Oh right. Good. I could come on Wednesday at 11.00, or it'll have to be next week. Busy time with the holiday season coming up."

"Wednesday will be fine, thanks."

"See you on Wednesday then. Bye," and the phone went dead.

Blimey, I thought. That was short and to the point. Hope I've chosen the right men for the job. My confidence started ebbing again and I forced myself to focus. Right, what's next on the list?

I looked up a local chimney sweep and gave him a ring. He sounded friendly enough on the phone. "Name's Cole," he said, and was quick to spell it. "That'll be C-O-L-E," he chuckled. "Always spell it out maid. Saves any muddle." We made a date for the chimneys to be swept.

I was cracking on with my list but, as I replied to emails from well-wishing friends, I wondered how many relationships would endure across the miles. When I emailed the new phone number to my parents, loneliness stabbed at my heart. Suddenly I was that small girl again, watching the car drive away at the start of a new school term. They were so far away. I was desperate to show them my new home, to gain their approval all over again.

I put the list to one side and, back inside my head, fretted about whether I would fit into the local way of life. I was deep in thought when a knock on the door made me jump. A smiling couple, perhaps ten years my senior, were on the doorstep. "Hello. We're Mark and Anna Sanders," said Anna, as Mark thrust out his hand. "We live at the top of the lane. Our house is Tamarisk. Welcome to our little corner of Devon. It's good to see the house lived in again - it was empty for such a long time. How're you settling in?"

"Sophie Chapman, good to meet you," I said as we shook hands. 'I'm doing fine thanks - was just thinking I must get to know people. Will you come in for a cup of tea?"

"No, we won't stop now, we're just back from work," said Anna. "Thought we'd pop by and say hello. We're having some neighbours over for lunch on Easter Saturday and wondered if you'd like to come? A lot of the houses round here are holiday lets, but there's a small group of us that live here full time. It would be a chance for you to meet them."

"That'd be great, thanks." My stomach lurched at the thought. "Oh, my friend Nick may be down from London that weekend. Would it be OK if I brought him along?"

"Of course. The more the merrier," said Anna with a smile. "We won't keep you now. See you on Saturday week. Come about 12.30. If you need anything before then, give us a shout."

"Great, thanks. See you then." Well, there you are, I thought, I'm a local already.

I wandered into the village to stock up with supplies and check out the jobs advertised in the post office. They were mainly seasonal positions working in cafes and cleaning holiday lets. I ambled over to the counter to buy some stamps.

"Morning m'dear. On holiday are you?" said the rather rotund, rosy cheeked, post mistress.

"Hi, no. I've just moved into the Sea House."

"Oh have you, my lovely? Well welcome. Hope you'll like it here. I'm Mary Webber. Me and my husband run the post office. Such a nice house, the Sea House, but such a tragic to-do all those years ago. Shame of it was, she was so young."

"I'm sorry, I wasn't aware…" I started to reply, but Mary Webber was on a roll.

"They said t'was suicide, but her body was never found. She had a young baby too, and that dishy French husband of hers, poor man. Never got over it so they say, and he upped and left. Some said t'were murder, but I don't know. A chef he was, and they said he could be temperamental. But murder? That's a bit rich. They never really solved it." She paused to take a breath and caught my surprised expression. "Well, that was all a long time ago and what that house needs now is to be brought back to life again. T'was such a happy house once, so they say. Been closed up far too long."

"Well, I'll do my best," I said rather feebly. "Nice to meet you, Mary. I'm Sophie Chapman. See you again. Thanks for the stamps."

My head was reeling as I left the post office. Mary's ramblings sounded like something out of a novel – 'young woman inherits broken-down house and uncovers shocking secrets.' Goose bumps ran up my arms. Hang on, I told myself, this is real life. Things like that don't happen in sleepy Devon villages and I'm not going to get in a state on the say-so of the local postmistress. Then I remembered the photo album. Was it the young woman with the baby who had been murdered and had the baby perished with her? Mary hadn't said. I *had* to find out more about the people locked inside the pages of the album. I popped into the local store and bought bread and milk, before a wet walk home. As I climbed the steps to the house, I wondered whether its grisly past was the reason it had been on the market for over a year. Maybe its reputation had proved too much for other would-be buyers. I peeled off my dripping waterproof and hung it on the back of the kitchen door, made a coffee and sent a text to Nick. *Call me when you've got a moment, something's come up.*

I retrieved the photo album from the living room and settled in the kitchen, which felt cosy from the warmth of the Aga. I flicked through the pages again. "Are you the girl whose life ended so tragically?" I asked the pictures. "Who are you; what was your name?" I studied the images again, happy young people suspended in time, and wondered if one of them had perished here. I shivered, suddenly cold in the warm kitchen. When Nick rang later that evening, I told him of Mary Webber's revelations.

"My goodness Soph, sounds like the plot of a whodunnit."

"Yes, but what if they're the people in the album, the only photos left of them? Or maybe it was left here by mistake and someone's longing for its return? Oh, I don't know. Sounds ridiculous but I *so* want to find out."

"Whoa, hang on. That's all a bit far-fetched, isn't it? Might have nothing to do with it at all. And you don't even know the full story. Doesn't sound like Mary Whatshername was sure of all the facts. Why don't you ask her more about it?"

"Mmm, may do. But I don't want her to think I'm snooping about, when I've only just arrived."

"Sounds like she'd be only too pleased. You must be the talk of the town, taking on the house with a grisly past."

"Oh Nick, don't!" I groaned.

"So, apart from tales of murder at the Sea House, how're things?"

"Fine. Bit of an emotional rollercoaster to be honest, and I am talking to myself rather a lot. Does that sound normal? Sometimes I think I'm going a little bit crazy!"

"Aha, you know what they say? First sign of madness. I knew it, you've finally cracked, Sophie Chapman!"

"Funny! You know what they also say? Takes one to know one! Any news of Easter yet? Can you get away? We've been invited to a lunch party at the neighbours."

"Sounds good. Yep, I'll be there, try and stop me! I'm seeing the parentals this weekend, so at Easter I'm all yours! Feeling the need for some 'us' time. Have I told you how much I miss you?"

A warm glow spread through me, knowing Nick would be back soon. The thought of him visiting his parents stirred a longing to see my own, but they were on the other side of the world enjoying their holiday of a lifetime, and it would be months before I saw them again. I was used to being without them: my father had been in the military and I'd been packed off to boarding school at the age of ten – the memory of being lost in a new school building, the noise and smell of the corridors, could still tie my stomach in knots - but now I longed to share my new life with them, and not just on Skype. They loved travelling and within a year of retirement were off. I was different; maybe because of my itinerant childhood I had longed to put down roots. The last five years with my grandmother were the longest I'd spent in one place. Then, with her passing, the house had been sold and the inheritance allowed me to buy the Sea House. At last, I could stay put.

***

Wednesday dawned grey and damp, a veil of drizzle obscuring the horizon, but with the weather front moving away to the East, brighter conditions were forecast to follow. Rob Penrose was due at 11.00 and I paced around awaiting his arrival. What would he be like? Would he see how naïve I was? I hoped West Country builders were scrupulous. He arrived on time and was friendly enough, in a 'call me Rob' sort of way. He said he could start the repairs to the roof and render after Easter. "You'll have to have scaffolding. Most of our pre-season stuff will be done by then, so we should have a few clear weeks when the boys can crack on. Weather permitting, should take four to five weeks. How does that sound?"

"That's great," I said. "I expected to wait much longer."

"We want to get it done while we've got the chance of some decent weather. Did you want me to look at the kitchen roof while I'm here?" We discussed the drawings and the timeframe for this, much larger, project. "Right, that's about it for now then. Lovely place you've got here. I'll just do a bit of measuring up while I'm here, if that's OK?"

"Yes, sure. Would you like a coffee?"

"Thanks. White, no sugar."

When I returned with the coffee, the sun was peeping out from behind the clouds and Rob was sitting on the old, lichen covered bench set against the house. He was miles away, deep in thought.

"Penny for them?" I asked. I handed him a steaming mug and perched beside him on the damp wood.

"Thanks. I was just thinking how much I love it here, got a real connection to the place. This is where I surf now, but as a kid I always went to Croyde. Dad wouldn't come here; still won't to this day. We had massive rows about it when I was young. In the end I just waited till I could drive and then came with my mates instead. Shame really, it's such a great place."

"It is. I came here a few times on holiday and fell in love with it. When I started looking for property in Devon and this came up, I couldn't believe it." The penny suddenly dropped. "Oh, was that your father who was a bit, umm, offish, when I rang the other day?"

"Uh yes, sorry about that. Hope he wasn't rude. I've never found out what it is about Woolacombe and I've given up trying. Anything for a quiet life." Rob was silent for a moment and his expression closed. He drained his coffee. "Thanks for that. Time I was off. I'll let you know when the scaffolders are due."

"Thanks Rob. Bye." As I walked back to the house, I thought he seemed vaguely familiar, but couldn't grasp a connection.

***

I eased out of the chair, stretched and groaned. I'd spent hours bent over colour boards, planning the design for my living room. I was thrilled to see it coming to life; the colours and patterns weaving together into a seaside theme. I was a complete amateur at interiors but had found a natural flair with my first makeover at my grandmother's house. I'd moved in with grandma after splitting from my last boyfriend. We'd been together for about three years, that last six months of which I'd spent in denial that things weren't as they should be, but when I accidentally picked up his phone as a message pinged in, I had to accept that regular weekends away with his mates had, in fact, been weekends with my best friend. I was heartbroken and distraught, but grandma provided a sanctuary, - somewhere to lick my wounds and recover.

I was determined it would be a temporary arrangement, but she offered me the top floor of her three storey Georgian house to do with as I pleased. She loved my revamp of the dated interior and we got along so well that I stayed for five years. As my heart healed, her own began to fail and eventually she made the difficult decision to move to a nursing home. She insisted I stay on at the house and when she passed away a few months later, I remained until it was sold, helping my parents sort through a lifetime of possessions, before learning that she had left me the proceeds of the sale in her will. So now I wanted to honour grandma in the renovation of The Sea House. What a shame she would never see the place that was mine, only because of her benevolence.

25

On a trip to Barnstaple to pick up materials for the colour boards, I had registered with an employment agency and was waiting to hear about a part-time job with a holiday letting company, Devon Dwellings. This could work, I thought, keep me in the job market and give me time to concentrate on the house. I wasn't particularly career minded. While school friends had taken a gap year, done university then stepped on to the career ladder, I'd completed a business course and started temping. It suited me - I liked the challenge of moving from one job to another and didn't get bored or stuck in a rut.

My mind was full of design ideas, job possibilities, Penrose senior's aversion to this place and talk of murder at The Sea House. I needed to clear my head. The fine weather had returned, so I packed a picnic and set off to Morte Point. The resort was filling with visitors, the small winter population swelling by the day, but I soon left the crowds behind. I puffed my way up the steep hill and off along the coastal path. The headland was emerging from the muted shades of winter, the cliff top grasses donning a fresh spring coat, and the gorse was at its most vivid yellow. Further out towards the point, bright green shoots of bracken uncurled into the sunshine. Cushions of thrift clung to the cliffs, seeming to grow out of the rocks themselves, with splashes of pink appearing against the grey slate. I stopped to eat my lunch overlooking Morte Stone, a rocky outcrop separated from the point by a treacherous channel, the site of many shipwrecks. Despite the perilous reputation of the rocks below, my concerns melted away as I took in the view and inhaled deep breaths of the salty air.

Invigorated, I headed on towards Rockham Bay, across grassland carpeted with primroses, then took an inland path to Morthoe. Suddenly, a small dog bounded up to me before tearing off and disappearing into the gorse, and when I crossed the lane in Mortehoe into a field, he was there again, tail wagging furiously. "Great, that's all I need," I said. "A loose dog in a field of sheep." I crouched down, gave him a pat and as I fondled his ears, noticed his collar had no tag. He was a small Collie-cross with a shiny brown and white coat, unusual orangey-brown eyes and a white blotch on his nose. "OK Smudgey-nose, if you insist on coming with me you're going on a lead." I found a scarf in my rucksack and threaded it through the collar. We passed a few walkers as we continued through Twitchen Farm and Combesgate Valley, but none claimed him. I arrived home with a new companion.

After a round of phone calls to the council and dog warden, I found I was lumbered with my canine chum for the weekend, until he could be collected and taken to the pound on Monday. Fatal, I thought. I'll be totally in love with him by then. Nick was his usual laid-back self when I told him about Smudge. "Cool Soph, are you going to keep him? It'll be good for you to have a dog, - bit of security, bit of company when I'm not around."

"Because this is the crime capital of the South West isn't it? And I'm completely hopeless without you," I laughed, but I knew he was close to the mark. Smudge *was* a comfort curled up next to me on the sofa. I nattered away to him, reassured by his closeness.

"Can't wait to see you next weekend," said Nick. "Have you found out any more about murder at the Sea House? Sounds like an Agatha Christie."

"I called in at the post office yesterday, but it was Mrs Webber's day off. I can't believe it was really murder, I think she was speculating. You can imagine how much gossip would've gone on at the time."

"The place would've been rife with it. Gotta go now gorgeous girl - lines to learn for an audition. It's for the part of Macduff. Can you believe this company is taking 'Macbeth' on tour around the Highlands and Islands later in the year? Talk about taking coals to Newcastle. Must've heard about my brilliant voice work. Och aye, that'll be it, ma wee bonny lassie."

"Good luck with that then. See you on Friday. Can't wait." Absence really does make the heart grow fonder, I thought, as I hung up. My mind wandered back to our first meeting about two years ago. I'd worked as a temp at a London drama school where Nick ran voice workshops on an ad hoc basis. He found himself caught between the role of reluctant babe magnet to the young, star-struck girls, and foil to the old luvvies who spent their days at the school in one associate role or another. After a particularly gruelling session, Nick came to the office for a note pad. "Hi, I'm Nick. I've nearly been eaten alive by a bunch of hormonal first year girls!"

"Oh OK, I'm Sophie. And I'd love to be eaten alive by a bunch of first year boys!" And so it began, a friendship which had blossomed but, by mutual agreement, hadn't progressed to anything more.

***

I was waiting for the dog warden when my phone rang. "Hi, is that Sophie Chapman? Jo Williams here from Devon Dwellings. The agency emailed me your CV. Any chance you could pop in for an interview sometime this morning?"

"Oh, hi. I'd love to, but a stray dog adopted me at the weekend, and I've got to wait in for the dog warden. Is this afternoon any good?" I could feel this job opportunity slipping away.

"'Fraid not, I'll be out at some of our properties." A slight pause, and then, "Tell you what, I'll be coming your way. Could I call and see you at home? I really need to get some cover for Sandy, she's had to go off suddenly."

"Um, OK. What time? I'm sure it'll be fine."

"About 1.00, is that OK? I know where you are in Woolacombe."

"Fine, see you then, thanks." Jo hung up before I could ask any more about the position on offer.

I changed out of my scruffy jeans and sweatshirt into a pair of navy chinos and white blouse. As I applied a brush of mascara, I noticed freckles appearing on my nose and a healthy glow on my cheeks. The clean Devon air was having a good effect. I stared at my reflection and pondered what to do with my hair. I fixed it up with a colourful headband, leaving a few strands framing my face.

That'll do, I thought. I smeared on some lipstick and wondered how I'd keep my chinos free of dog hair until Jo arrived. I needn't have worried; the warden turned up just after I'd changed. He explained the process – if Smudge wasn't chipped or claimed within seven days, I could have him. Smudge gave me a heart-breaking look, his tail well and truly between his legs, as he was led away. Just as I feared, I was smitten.

Jo arrived on the dot of 1.00 and I took her through to the kitchen. "Sorry, let me move those," I said, gathering up the colour boards scattered across the table.

"Don't worry. Are these yours? There wasn't anything about interior design on your application, I thought you were admin. Do you mind if I have a look?" She started leafing through the boards.

"Yes, I am, just admin that is. These are for my own use. I'm refurbishing the house."

"Wow! They're so good, you're a natural. I love the seaside influence. You could be really useful to us. As well as the cottage bookings we help people bring their properties up to scratch. Visitors expect so much more these days, and some places need to be brought into the twenty-first century. Would that interest you?"

I could hardly believe what I was hearing. "That sounds great. I've wanted to take the design stuff further but never had the chance, and I've got no formal training. I'd be happy to do either, or both, but only part time."

"That's all we want. We're very flexible. There's often more to do out of season when owners are sprucing up their cottages and clients are booking for next year. Sandy works up to three days as and when we need her but is off for the foreseeable. We'd start you on two days and see how it goes. Could you come for a trial, so we can see how you get on? Shall we say Thursday?"

Blimey, no hanging about. Here's a woman who knows what she wants, I thought, as Jo breezed out as coolly as she'd blown in. I watched as she drove off in her Land Rover Discovery, emblazoned with the company logo. If only I had a smidgen of her self-confidence.

I was itching to call Nick and tell him about the job offer but knew he'd be tied up with the Macbeth audition. I'd visit Mary Webber instead. I had to find out the name of the tragic girl from the Sea House. I thought about taking the photo album with me, but didn't want to jump any guns. One step at a time, I'd start with getting a name.

"Hello m'dear, how're you settling in?" said Mary, as I entered the post office. She was busy stocking shelves with Easter eggs and sweets, her ample bosom brushing the lower shelves as she placed the most expensive eggs on top.

"Fine thanks. I was just wondering, Mrs Webber, if you knew the name of the girl you said had died at the Sea House."

"Oh yes, dear. Didn't know her myself of course, we moved here in late '77, a while after it happened but t'was still talked about and the house was all closed up. She was called Lottie Dupont. Her chef husband was French you see. Did I tell you that? Ran the cafe on Barricane Beach in that long hot summer of '76. My word, t'was a scorcher, I remember it well. Water shortages and standpipes. Tempers got frayed that summer, I can tell you."

"So this all happened in 1976 did it?"

"No dear, 'twas early '77, February I think. Silver Jubilee year."

I was about to ask more, when a gaggle of children burst into the shop and Mrs Webber saw an opportunity to shift some Easter eggs. I chose one filled with Smarties for Nick and left the money on the counter. "See you again soon."

"Bye dear," said Mrs Webber, as the door closed behind me.

30

Chapter 4

Charlotte - 1976

Gerald Tremayne's forebears were clergymen. It was said his ancestors had close associations with John Wesley himself. His father was a Methodist minister and Gerald grew up in a routine of church services and religious festivals. He developed a strong faith but did not feel called to follow in his father's footsteps. After qualifying as an accountant, he secured a position with Truro City Council, a job for life.

Gerald considered himself well-grounded and reasonably success-ful, if a little dull. Until he met Lizzie. She came to work as a clerk and was, quite simply, the most beautiful girl he had ever seen - deep brown eyes set in a heart shaped face, blonde hair twisted into a chignon and an hourglass figure, shown to its best in a snug fitting jacket and pencil skirt. In a moment of madness, Gerald asked Lizzie for a date and to his amazement, she accepted.

She was perfection. Professional and circumspect at work, away from the office she showed him a life he hadn't known. She taught him to walk barefoot in the sand, skinny dip in the sea, light drift-wood fires on the beach and watch the sunset over the ocean. She called him Gerry – his name had *never* been shortened before! - but didn't mock or scoff at his buttoned-up ways. She loved his tight sandy coloured curls and hazel eyes, which reminded her of a teddy bear.

Gerry's family loved Lizzie's generous spirit and welcomed her into the fold. They were married by Gerry's father and began their life together in Truro. Charlotte was born in 1956 and Verity, two years later. Gerry loved his daughters beyond measure and watched with wonder as Lizzie performed tiny miracles every day with the girls, teaching them to treasure all she loved – sea swimming and rock-pooling; walking the cliffs and headlands; sketching Cornish landscapes - and so when Gerry could afford to move them to the north coast, to the Mill House nestled in the wooded valley at Trethevy, he felt he had provided well for his family.

Gerry's deep-rooted religious beliefs drew him to worship at the parish church in Tintagel, perched on the cliffs outside the small town, overlooking the legendary ruins of King Arthur's Castle, where he gave thanks for the blessings of his family. Lizzie found her spiritual solace on the wild and rugged cliffs, standing high above the powerful seas pounding the rocks below – it was here she connected with her maker.

The following ten years were idyllic, despite Gerry's long commute to Truro. Returning each day to his little piece of heaven and the delights of his family made it worthwhile. Then, when Lizzie was diagnosed with cancer, his world fell apart. He struggled to manage the demands of his girls, now teenagers, and the needs of his wife. Charlotte sought comfort from Johnny, a local fisherman's son, while Verity slipped into a caring role, providing practical and emotional support for her parents. She grew up fast and developed a maturity way beyond her years. When Lizzie passed away, Gerry reverted to the rigid ways of his upbringing, the only way he knew how to cope.

He became angry at Charlotte and the blossoming relationship with Johnny – why couldn't *he* provide the love and care for his daughter that Johnny did? His attitude towards Johnny soured but this only strengthened the growing bond between the young lovers. Verity was left to play the part of peacekeeper, stepping in to diffuse the tension between Charlotte and her father. From the kitchen, she heard another row in full swing.

"What d'you mean, you want to live with Johnny? Absolutely not."

"But dad, that's what people do now, live with each other before marriage."

"I don't care what other people do. No daughter of mine is going to live in sin."

"Live in sin? This is 1976 dad, not the dark ages. I'm old enough to make my own decisions. You can't stop me."

"And how do you think you're going to support yourself? I'm sure Johnny won't be making enough to keep you both."

"How d'you think? I'll get a job. I'm perfectly capable of picking up work. There's bound to be seasonal work in North Devon."

"And that's all you'll get with no qualifications. Why your mother didn't insist you take a secretarial course, I'll never know."

"Don't bring mum into this," shouted Charlotte, her eyes filling with tears. "This has nothing to do with her. Unlike you, she'd be OK with our plans. She was so fond of Johnny. God, I wish she was here," and she burst into tears.

Gerry's heart was breaking at his daughter's distress, but he couldn't help himself. "That doesn't mean she'd want you going off and living with him, 'specially while he has so few prospects."

"There you go again. You sound like a dinosaur. He's training to be a master carpenter; you should approve of that!"

"And when he's qualified will be the time to think about your future together."

"That'll take years. I'm not waiting that long. I'm going as soon as we've got a place to live. I don't bloody well care what you say."

Gerry sat opened mouthed. Swearing was *unheard* of in the Tremayne household. Verity walked into the room. "Supper's ready you two, if you can stop shouting at each other for five minutes." She turned and left. Gerry and Charlotte were too pent up with their own anger and frustration to notice Verity's red eyes.

Later, Charlotte told Verity her plans. "Johnny's coming home this weekend and I just know he'll have found somewhere for us to live. I'm going to work my notice at the tea shop and go with him."

"Oh Charlotte, dad'll go spare. Are you sure you're doing the right thing?"

"Don't you start. I love Johnny. It's simple. I'm going, and no one is going to stop me."

"Well, I hope you know what you're doing." Verity knew there was no point in arguing. If only mum was here, she thought. She could always talk Charlotte round.

***

Johnny and Charlotte had arranged to meet at their secret place in St Nectan's Glen. It was the end of April. Trees were in full leaf in the sheltered valley, clad in the fresh bright greens of spring. The woodland floor was a carpet of bluebells, and the scent of wild garlic was in the air. They came together, young lovers hungry for one another, after weeks apart.

"I've missed you so much, Charlotte, I'm only half alive without you." They kissed again, gently at first then with a growing intensity as their bodies moved together in the rhythm of love.

"Johnny, you're amazing." Charlotte lay, eyes closed, with her head resting on his chest. "We'll be able to do this in our own place soon. Have you found somewhere?"

Johnny manoeuvred so he was leaning on one elbow, looking down into her deep brown eyes. "I think it's best I stay with Uncle Jim for now. If you come directly, we won't be able to spend much time together and we'd have no money." Johnny watched as Charlotte's face clouded with disappointment. "I'm so sorry love, I'll come home every couple of weeks. By the end of the summer, we can be together."

She wriggled from under Johnny and sat up, pulling her blouse around her naked body. "No Johnny. I've got to come with you, I can't stay here. I've told dad I'm going and my life's hell, now he knows. Why do you have to be so bloody sensible? You're as bad as

34

dad. Why can't we just go for it? Please Johnny, take me with you," she sobbed, as her hopes fell about her in tatters.

Johnny pulled her into a tight embrace. She wanted to pull away but needed to feel Johnny's strength and comfort. "You know I want you with me, but we've got to do it right. Trust me and it'll work out sooner than you think."

Charlotte listened to his rational words but was already thinking how she could make things happen for herself. What was to stop her moving anyway? Her life had been put on hold when Lizzie was ill, but now she was filled with a sense of purpose, a sudden longing to spread her wings. Excitement bubbled up inside, she wiped the tears away and dazzled Johnny with one of her smiles.

"Hey, that's better, that's more like my girl. It'll all work out, I promise."

"I know it will, I know." Charlotte's head was already spinning with her own plans. Before long they were laughing and tumbling again in their secret woodland glade.

***

Johnny returned to Barnstaple early on Monday and Charlotte started her shift at The Copper Kettle. She worked as a waitress and helped with the baking - her scones were reputed to be some of the finest in Tintagel. She had formulated a plan - she would take a week's holiday; go and see what Barnstaple had to offer. If it all worked out, she would find work and somewhere for her and Johnny to live. She thought of how she would surprise him when everything was set up.

Charlotte was tired of fighting with her father. She was all too aware of how her tempestuous behaviour would have upset her mother and she felt guilty about the grief she was causing in the Tremayne household. With a definite plan in place, she explained calmly that she was taking some leave to look for work in North Devon. "Dad, I'm twenty. I need to spread my wings. I'll see what's available there,

35

I may be able to get work with accommodation then I can be close to Johnny. But not living in sin," she said with a wry smile.

"You're right Charlotte, you need a change of scene, it'll do us both good. But don't rush into anything. How long will you be away? Where are you going to stay?"

"Only a week dad and don't worry, I'll find a B&B. I can't stay with Johnny, there isn't room for me at his uncle's." But Charlotte knew that if things worked out as she wanted, she wouldn't return. Gerry gave her a hug and the tensions of the last few weeks melted away, but he couldn't bring himself to relax completely, such was the feeling that he was losing another of the women that made his life worth living.

Before Charlotte left, she visited the glen and waterfall. She took the stone from its place in the rock and sat on the shingle shore as she told Lizzie her plans. "I know you'll understand why I need to do this, why I need to be with Johnny. I love him mum and I've just got to be with him. I know you're at peace here and I've made my peace with Dad." She shed a tear as she replaced the stone in the rock face, wondering when she would return.

Verity and Charlotte clung to each other as they said their good-byes. "You are coming back, aren't you?" Verity tried hard to keep the tremor from her voice.

"Course I am. I'll probably find nothing more than a few new beaches to explore," Charlotte said with a determined cheeriness.

"Take care of yourself." Verity was dreading this. They had become so close as their mother faded away and she felt the responsibility for their still-grieving father rest heavier on her shoulders.

"I'm only going for a week for goodness' sake. It's only seventy miles up the road. I'll be back soon."

But Verity wondered if she would.

***

Charlotte set off in Lizzie's Triumph on a bright and breezy morning. April had been an exceptionally dry month and today was no different; fluffy white clouds scudding across a brilliant blue sky. As soon as she reached the A39, Charlotte was overcome by a thrilling sense of freedom. She realised just how much her confidence had been knocked by Lizzie's illness – the family's world really had fallen apart. So now is the time to build it up and start living again, she thought. Today is the first day of the rest of my life. She stopped in Bude, just because she could. She sat for a while on the beach and watched the comings and goings: young couples strolling hand in hand; families arriving laden with windbreaks, picnic hampers, buckets and spades; dog walkers throwing sticks and determined surfers braving the waves.

Before continuing Charlotte put the roof down and felt the familiar exhilaration of the wind whipping through her hair. The little car ate up the miles and soon she crossed into Devon and reached Bideford Bay. She noticed the changing scenery – gone was the rugged, wind-swept Cornish landscape, replaced by rolling hills and deep wooded combes, then the wide river estuaries of the rivers Torridge and Taw.

Oh goodness, here already, thought Charlotte. Unease gripped her. She had arrived in Barnstaple and for a moment completely lost her resolve. The plan that seemed so plausible and simple in the safety of her childhood home, was suddenly overwhelming. She considered seeking out Johnny's place of work but immediately thought better of it. What if he's not pleased to see me? What if he's angry or embarrassed with me turning up unexpectedly? Oh my gosh, what've I done? The sound of a car horn behind her made her jump and she realised she'd stopped by the side of the road with no indication.

She parked the car and wandered round the small town. Her worries dissolved, and she became absorbed in exploring. She found a busy pannier market leading off Butchers Row, an aptly named street with at least eight shops selling meat and game. Why, she thought, would you need so many? She mooched about the market, captivated by all that was on offer. How Lizzie would've loved this, she thought, with a pang of sadness. She could see her mother rooting through the stalls, emerging with some treasure or other for her studio. Charlotte bought a small wooden box which she knew Lizzie would've chosen. It felt like a talisman, a charm to carry with her into her new life.

Charlotte reached the river where hotels and guesthouses beckoned, but she felt restless. This wasn't her journey's end. She needed to continue. She returned to the car and drove along the River Taw to Braunton, then climbed through pretty villages to the high point of Mullacott. After a moment's hesitation she turned towards Woolacombe, just because she liked the name. As she drove into the seaside village, a steep combe falling away to her left, she saw glimpses of sand dunes and breaking waves. And far out in the bay, an island. Her heart soared; this was so like the beaches she loved to visit with her mother. She parked the car as soon as she could, ran on to the sand and kicked off her shoes. It stretched away for miles: golden sands, rocky outcrops, grassy dunes and dramatic headlands to the north and south. This, she knew, was where she should be. She bought an ice cream from the Hockings van. "Do you know if there are any summer jobs going here?" she asked the lad in the van.

"There's probably loads," the ice cream seller replied, handing over a '99. "'Specially in the hotels and guest houses; they're always wanting staff. Have a look in the windows, that's usually how they advertise. A pretty girl like you should find a job easy enough."

Charlotte wasn't sure if she was being chatted up by Ice Cream Man. She raised her eyebrows and smiled coyly. "Righto, I'll do that, thanks." She took a lick of the creamy cone. Mmm, nearly as good as Kelly's Cornish, she thought. She walked along the Esplanade peering at the various notices. Some establishments looked more salubrious than others. At the top end of the village stood the

Watersmeet Hotel – no posters stuck in windows there, more likely a place that would put an ad in the local newspaper.

She re-traced her steps and saw the impressive Bay Hotel tucked away behind the beach. A board in the entrance announced, 'Staff wanted, apply within'. This looks like the kind of place, she thought, but decided to tidy herself up before making enquiries. She returned to the car and quickly brushed her hair, wiped the remains of ice cream from the corners of her mouth and applied a little lipstick. She wriggled out of her jeans into a floaty summer skirt, which looked pretty with a cheesecloth blouse. Right, here goes, she thought, and felt a thrill of anticipation as she entered the hotel. A young man in a smart uniform stood behind the desk. "I'm enquiring about the staff vacancy," announced Charlotte assuredly.

"Hang on, I'll get the manager." The young man blushed, taken off guard by Charlotte's confidence. "Would you like to wait in the lounge?"

She took a seat and waited. It was a full ten minutes before anyone appeared and she'd almost given up. At last, an impeccably dressed man approached, with a look of surprise as he saw Charlotte. "Hello I'm Mr Bramdean, hotel manager. I'm slightly confused. Are you here about the advert in the Journal? I wasn't aware we'd arranged interviews yet."

"Um, no. I saw the board outside."

"Ah, that's just for casual kitchen staff, dish washers and veg preppers and the like. If you don't mind me saying, you don't look as if that's the sort of work you'd be looking for."

"Oh I see." Charlotte's hopes dipped, but immediately she saw an opportunity. "Could I ask what the advertised job is for?"

"It's for a live-in breakfast head waitress and part time receptionist, but we haven't closed the advert yet."

Charlotte gave Mr Bramdean one of her most disarming looks. "Is there any chance you would consider me for the position, as I'm here? I have waitressing and reception experience in the holiday trade in Tintagel. I don't have references with me, but could get them very quickly."

"Well, I'm not sure…"

Charlotte knew she needed to grab this chance while she had it. "How about if you give me a trial for a few days while I'm staying here? If you don't like me, you haven't lost anything. You'll still have the newspaper ad."

Mr Bramdean was amused by Charlotte's directness and after a few seconds summing her up, went with his gut feeling. "Go on then. I'll give you a three-day trial and then make a decision. Have you got a black skirt and white blouse? We can give you a white pinny. You'll need to be here from 6.00 for the breakfast shift until 11.00, then back for two hours on reception from 1.00 to cover lunch time. The rest of the day will be yours."

"That sounds perfect, thank you so much." Charlotte could hardly believe her luck. "I appreciate the opportunity. Yes, I've got something I can wear. Shall I start tomorrow?'"

"Yes, although if you can spare an hour now, I'll get Mike to show you the ropes on reception." Mr Bramdean returned to his office, wondering how he'd had his arm twisted so easily.

Charlotte was over the moon, and more than a little pleased with herself. Mike showed her the booking, registration and filing systems. She was a fast learner and, by the time she left, had grasped how they liked things done at The Bay Hotel.

Charlotte booked into a small B&B not far from the hotel. She threw herself on the bed and willed her racing heart to calm. Oh good grief, I've done it! I've got myself a job *and* accommodation! OK, so it's not in Barnstaple, but this is much more exciting! Wait till I tell Johnny. And dad. The excitement turned to a stomach-churning anxiety at the thought of explaining her impulsive decisions. She climbed off the bed, leant against the window and stared across the beach. This is *my* life to do with as *I* please. She stuck her chin out defiantly and decided not to contact anyone till after her trial period. No one was expecting to hear from her for a few days anyway.

***

The hotel ran like a well-oiled machine. Mr Bramdean took great pride in his business. His attention to detail was second to none. He glided round the dining room adjusting a table setting here, tweaking a flower arrangement there, so that everything was in perfect symmetry, whilst always keeping an eagle eye on the guests, ready to respond to their every need. This extreme sense of order was new to Charlotte - in comparison, standards at The Copper Kettle left a lot to be desired - and she quickly came to appreciate how important they were to Mr Bramdean. She watched and learnt. Her vibrant character and sunny disposition were popular with the guests and at the end of day three, not only was she offered the job, but also had a sizeable stash of tips.

"I'm impressed with you, Charlotte, and would like to offer you the position. I must say I'm particularly pleased with your attention to detail."

Charlotte smiled demurely. "Thank you so much for giving me this opportunity Mr Bramdean. I won't let you down."

"I'll show you your accommodation in the staff quarters and you can continue from tomorrow. You will have one day off a week in the high season, usually a Monday, but until the school holidays start, you will also have Sunday afternoon off." There didn't seem any room for negotiation and Charlotte wasn't about to push her luck, so accepted the terms. Her room was small and at the back of the hotel. Well, I wasn't going to get the deluxe suite with sea views, was I? she thought. She was so pleased to have the job she'd have slept in a broom cupboard if necessary. Wait till I show Johnny. A frisson of desire raced through her at the thought of their naked bodies entwined together. She moved her belongings from the B&B and placed the small wooden box on her dressing table.

***

Armed with change she walked through the village to a phone box. Her heart was in her mouth as she dialled her home number. She prayed that Verity would answer. "Hello Verity, it's me."

"Charlotte! How are you? Where are you? Is everything OK? Are you having a good time, have you seen Johnny?"

Charlotte told Verity of her arrival in the little resort. "It's a fab place with a lovely beach. I haven't seen Johnny, but I've got a job and it's got accommodation."

"Oh. So you're really going then. What is it and when do you start?" Verity's voice was shaking with emotion and Charlotte knew she had to be quick before she lost her resolve.

"The thing is, I've started so I won't be coming back. It's working in a lovely place called The Bay Hotel, in Woolacombe. They took me on after a few days' trial. Verity, will you tell dad? I know he'll go mad because I'm not coming home. Listen, my money's running out. I'll write to dad and explain and if you need to contact me look up the number of the hotel in the telephone directory."

"Oh no, Charlotte, please don't go! Do you have to do this?" but the pips were already going, then the line went dead.

Tears streamed down Charlotte's face. She stood rooted to the spot in the phone box. What've I done? she thought, squirming with guilt at leaving Verity to tell their father. But she couldn't face talking to him just yet. She took a deep breath and dialled the number of Johnny's uncle. Johnny came on the line sounding worried, "Charlotte? Are you alright? I was going to ring tomorrow, is everything OK?" Her heart melted at his voice.

"Johnny, everything is fine, in fact more than fine," and she filled him in on the events of the last few days.

"My goodness, you *have* taken things into your own hands. Are you sure you'll be all right?"

"Of course I'll be all right," she said indignantly, put out by Johnny's assumption that she wouldn't be. "I'm so excited to show you the hotel. It's lovely here and the beach is amazing. You'll have to come over on Sunday; I get the afternoon off. And I've got my own room Johnny," she added suggestively.

"I'll be there, try and stop me. Ring me on Saturday and we'll arrange where to meet. Or can I ring you? Have you got a number?"

"No I'll ring you. I'm not sure if I'll be able to use the hotel phone. My money's going, I'll have to go. I love you, Johnny."

"And I love you, Charlotte. I can't believe you're just up the road, what an amazing girl. See you on Sunday."

***

It was early evening. Charlotte wandered along the Esplanade to look at a small beach separated from the main sands by an outcrop of rock. She climbed down to Barricane beach and found a tiny cafe set on a concrete platform. It was little more than a garden shed with a hatch cut into the side. How appropriate, she thought, as she noticed 'Le Shack' painted on a rough piece of driftwood nailed to the door, which was padlocked shut. She was alone on the beach and mooched about looking for shells. She picked a couple for her dressing table. After watching the sun sink towards the horizon in a blaze of orange and gold, she made her way up the steps and very nearly collided with someone running down. At the last moment he noticed her and stopped in his tracks. For the briefest moment their eyes locked and Charlotte felt an explosion of something so visceral, it made her gasp.

"Zut alors!" he exclaimed. "Pardon, excusez-moi Mademoiselle. I did not mean to startle you. I 'ave left my 'ouse keys at le café." His accent made Charlotte go weak at the knees.

43

"Oh that's all right. I was just leaving. Not the café, I mean, the beach. The café's closed." She blushed, her words tumbling out as gibberish. She was flustered and unable to move. Should she squeeze past or wait for him to pass her?

Charlotte's obvious embarrassment amused the Frenchman. "Pardon Mademoiselle, let me introduce myself, Claude Dupont." He extended his hand and looked deeply into Charlotte's eyes, a smile playing on his lips.

"Charlotte Tremayne," she squeaked.

"Enchanté. May I call you Lottie?" He took Charlotte's hand and gently lifted it to his lips.

Chapter 5

Sophie – 2015

We were well into Easter week and the quiet seaside village was transformed into a thriving resort. I liked the contrast and felt the buzz as it braced itself for another season. Mr Cole arrived to sweep the chimneys. He seemed as old as the hills, but his rosy complexion extended up to his shiny bald head, which looked as if it had been polished vigorously until it gleamed. He had a band of thick white hair around the base of his head and a bushy white beard, so he looked more like Captain Birdseye than a chimney sweep. I wondered if it would be so white once he'd swept the chimneys. His smile reached to his twinkling eyes, still a clear blue, despite his apparent age.

"Morning Maid. Not so bright 'smorin', 'tiz proper dimpsey." While I was struggling to tune into Mr Cole's broad Devon accent he continued. "Tidn't proper, this 'ouse not bein' lived in for so long, an' all. Not since that maid died over yonder," and he nodded towards Morte Point.

"Did you know her then?" I asked, my interest immediately piqued.

"Not really, no, can't say as I did. Knew 'im, the Frenchie. Cleaned the chimneys for 'im, but the maid were 'ere and gone in less than a year and it weren't long after 'e shut the place up and left. 'Twere let out then for many a year, then closed up again."

"Do you know how she died?"

"Can't rightly say as I do. T'was all sorts of talk, rumours and the like. I think 'twas more 'n likely 'er lost 'er footing and fell. They'm

45

rough old paths out along. 'Twas no body found, only some clothes, so no one really knows the truth of it to this day."

I was about to question him further when the phone rang. It was Rob Penrose confirming that the scaffolding would be erected next week. By the time I returned to the sitting room, Mr Cole was folding up his dust sheets. "There we are m'dear. That'll see you right 'til next year. Be off to my next customer over Morthoe now."

He seemed in a bit of a rush, so I didn't like to delay him with more questions. I paid him and saw him to the door. His white beard was streaked with soot. "Proper job. See you next year. Cheerio maid." And off he went down the steps with his brushes in a bag on his shoulder.

I wandered into the kitchen and made a coffee, thinking of what Mr Cole had said about Lottie's body never being found. What a tragedy. I wonder where Mr Dupont went. And the baby - Mr Cole didn't mention the baby.

Now that the chimneys were swept, I was eager to make a start on the decorating and couldn't wait for Nick to arrive on Friday so we could begin. I looked at my to do list and crossed off 'chimney sweep'. The next job was to ring the dog warden. I found myself hoping Smudge hadn't been claimed. "No, no one has been in touch about a missing dog with Smudge's description and he's not chipped. If he's not claimed by the end of the week, he'll go to a re-homing centre or you can have him if you still want him," I was told.

"OK, yes I still want him, couldn't bear to think of him going to a rescue centre. I'll call again on Friday if you're open."

"Yes, someone will be here. Good Friday or not, dogs get lost every day. But you'll have to collect him on the Saturday. That will be a full seven days since you found him."

"Righto. I'll be in touch at the end of the week." I came off the phone with some misgivings. Did I really want a dog? Would he be a welcome companion or an unwanted tie? If I didn't have him, how

46

long would he have to spend at a rescue centre? I'd run it past Nick when we had our daily catch up.

***

"Why are you even asking?" said Nick when we spoke later. "Of course you should have him, you've always loved dogs. Why wouldn't you?"

"Yes I know, just needed some reassurance. We'll be able to pick him up on Saturday if he's not been claimed. So, how did your audition go?"

"OK I think. Now I just have to play the waiting game, you know how it is. Did I tell you I've got some radio work lined up? Recording at the Bristol studios so will be nearer to you, my gorgeous girl."

"Mmm lovely." I was loving the sound of Nick's voice on the phone. He seemed so close, and I couldn't wait for him to be back here and to feel his strong arms holding me and his body next to mine. "Suddenly I'm missing you like crazy. Just as well it's only two more days 'til you're here or I might have to jump in the car and drive all the way to London for a squeeze."

"And you'd be welcome any time and the thought of it is making me twitch, if you know what I mean. Watch out on Friday, that's all I can say Sophie Chapman."

***

Thursday was my first day at Devon Dwellings and I was looking forward to getting to grips with a new job and getting to know Jo. She was a fine looking woman, perhaps five years my senior, tall and elegant. Her face was long and thin and her brown eyes soft and smiling. She wore her thick, straight hair in a choppy cut that looked like it had been hacked with a pair of garden shears, but which she carried off with style. She wore leggings tucked into boots, topped with layers of tunic, jacket and scarf, which suited her

47

tall frame. When I arrived at 8.30 on the dot, she was already in the office with the coffee machine on. Over our first cup of the day, she explained that I should start by learning the holiday cottage booking system. If that went well, I would get into the marketing side of the business, using my design skills to encourage owners to upgrade their properties where needed. "I liked your style the moment we met, Sophie, and think we could make a good team while Sandy is off. I was really impressed with your colour boards and would like to see more. It'll be good to have some new ideas. But first things first, let's get you going with our high tech, if temperamental, booking system. Typical bloody IT, love it when it's working, a nightmare when it buggers about."

Jo was bright, energetic and self-assured, and her enthusiasm was contagious. By the end of the morning I had mastered the system and felt like I'd known her forever. Over a lunch of sandwiches delivered by the local bakery, Jo and I chatted about my move to Devon. "…and so I was lucky enough to buy The Sea House. But the place has some history. Apparently, a young woman called Lottie, who lived there in the '70s, committed suicide off Morte Point. And when I moved in, I found an old photo album with what I think is pictures of her, her husband and baby. Damn it, I should've shown it to the sweep yesterday. He would've known if it was them; he's been doing the chimneys for years. I completely forgot. Anyway, after the tragedy it seems Mr Dupont, the girl's husband, shut up the house and left. Since then, it's been let out or left empty over the years. I can't understand why the old album was left there. And apparently, according to Mr Cole, the sweep –"

"You're kidding?"

"What? No, that's his name. C-O-L-E. Mr Cole the chimney sweep, although he looked more like Captain Birdseye! Anyway, where was I? Oh yes, he said her body was never found."

"Intriguing. What're you going to do with the album?"

"I don't know. I can't throw it out but don't know what else to do with it. I guess the first thing is to check out if it is the Duponts in the photos."

"Mmm, how very Miss Marple. You must keep me informed. I might ask some of my clients out your way, although most of them with holiday properties don't live there of course, but there are a few old timers who would've been around in the village back in the '70s."

The afternoon went quickly and by the end of my first day, it was like I'd been there for years. We agreed I'd do a Wednesday and Thursday and review after one month. My design boards would be done at home and charged by the hour. It suited me perfectly and I couldn't believe how it had all fallen into place. I'd have time to do my own thing and work on my design skills, and the idea of being paid for what had only ever been a hobby, was more than I could have hoped for. We agreed an hourly rate and I went home with a light heart.

**

I woke early on Friday but couldn't settle to anything and knew I wouldn't until Nick arrived. I grabbed my scruffy Barbour jacket and set off across the beach. It was a bright sunny morning, but the forecast for the weekend was mixed, with rain expected on Monday. No surprise there, I thought, it's a bank holiday. The tide was out, the golden sands washed clean by the sea, and Lundy Island was standing high in the bay. As I walked along the beach, the island appeared to be moving across the water with me; an illusion created by its position between the headlands of Baggy and Morte Points.

I strode out towards Putsborough Sands at the southern end of the beach, crossing the stream that ran down to the sea. I walked for about an hour, enjoying thoughts of Nick and his imminent arrival. As I turned and started the trek back, my thoughts turned to Lottie Dupont and her tragic end. I decided I'd take the photo album and show it to Mrs Webber after the holiday weekend. I felt sure she would recognise the family, even though she hadn't lived here at the time. She seemed to know enough about the events of '76/77 and I wasn't due to see Mr Cole again for a year, so couldn't ask him. Mary Webber was my only hope.

As I approached the Sea House, I saw Nick drawing up in his VW Golf. I ran along the Esplanade and into his arms as soon as he was out of the car.

"God I've missed you Sophie," he said as he took me in his arms.

"Me too," I whispered into his ear, as I became folded into his embrace. He pulled away and looked deeply into my eyes. I held his gaze and our lips came together. No more friendly pecks on the cheek; time apart meant we needed more. Eventually we drew apart and realised we were still on the pavement in full view of goggle-eyed passers by.

"Wow, what a welcome," said Nick, as he unloaded his stuff from the boot. He took my hand as we climbed the steps to the garden.

"Give me your bag. You'll have to move your car into the lane and tuck it in front of the garage. You have to pay on the road now the season's begun."

I left Nick moving his car and took his case upstairs. I hesitated before putting it in the spare room. The temptation to put it in my room was huge, but I knew if we crossed that line there would be no going back and our relationship would change forever. Was I ready for that? I still wasn't sure. I went down to the kitchen and put the kettle on. Nick came in, swept me up in his arms and swung me round.

"Put me down you idiot, you'll drop me." I squealed.

"I'd never drop you Soph, you're much too precious. Have I told you how much I've missed you?"

"I have to say, the feeling is entirely mutual," and we kissed again, our tongues tingling together sending little shocks shooting through my body.

Then Nick pulled away. "Sorry Sophie, I know it's against the rules. Just couldn't help myself, you are so bloody gorgeous and I've missed you so much. Let's have some coffee."

"Does it matter?" I said, as I moved away. "We're adults, we've both been around long enough to know how we feel. Are we being too cautious?"

"I don't know. Maybe. I'm just so afraid of it spoiling everything between us and I couldn't bear to lose you. Let's just enjoy the weekend, shall we?"

"OK, if you insist. No taking me on the kitchen table then?" I laughed as I poured water into the cafetière.

"Don't tempt me, sexy girl," and then the 'phone rang.

It was the dog warden telling me Smudge hadn't been claimed and that he was mine if I wanted him. "We can pick him up at 9.30 tomorrow in Barnstaple. That'll be early enough for us to get back in time for Anna and Mark's lunch party."

"Great, can't wait to meet the little pooch."

We spent a lazy day gently savouring one another's company after our time apart. We were both especially tactile; a touch here, a peck on the cheek there, the stroke of a hand, as if checking the other was really there. We wandered down to Combesgate beach and sat on the rocks, where it was warm and sheltered in the sun, and watched the waves breaking on the shore, both captivated by the ceaseless motion of the sea. I leaned against Nick, his arms folded around me, and he kissed my hair and nuzzled my neck. We talked and laughed and watched other people on the beach going about their seaside business.

"What a great place for people watching. I could base a few of my characters on some of these," said Nick observing the assortment of visitors to the beach in every conceivable shape, size and state of dress.

We stayed on the beach until the sun disappeared behind a bank of cloud, then made our way back to the house, where we cooked up a dish of chicken with garlic and mushrooms in a creamy white wine sauce, which we ate with pasta and salad, accompanied by a chilled Pinot Grigio.

Nick raised his glass. "To us, Sophie Chapman, and to the little addition to our family tomorrow."

"I'll drink to that, Nick Brewer."

***

I slept badly: a night mixed with regret that Nick hadn't shared my bed and dreams of Smudge chasing sheep on Morte Point, so when Nick brought me a cup of tea in the morning, it took me a few moments to come round to his soft voice.

"Cup of tea, sleepy head."

"Mmm thanks." I rolled over and opened one eye and there he was, looking drop dead gorgeous with his thick sandy coloured hair, all tousled and sticking out at angles, wearing only pyjama bottoms. I groaned with pleasure.

"Come on lovely lady, if we're going to get this dog and get back in time for lunch, we'd better get a move on. It's 8.30 already. I'll take a shower while you come to." I must have slept better than I thought.

Three hours later we were on our way back from Barnstaple with Smudge curled up at Nick's feet in the footwell of my Rav4. He was beside himself with excitement, so we drove to Crow Point, to give him a run on the beach. It was empty apart from a few other dog walkers - this stretch of coast where the rivers Taw and Torridge meet, overlooking the seaside villages of Instow and Appledore, was rarely crowded. Having expended some energy, Smudge was happy to enjoy the ride back to his new home. Nick and I did a quick change and I put an old blanket in front of the aga for Smudge, gave him a chew and prayed he'd be content to stay put while we were out. We grabbed a bottle of red from the wine rack and set off up the hill, to get to know the neighbours.

Mark and Anna were gracious hosts and their two children, Hannah, twelve, and Reuben, fifteen, were easy going in the company of assorted guests. Reuben was well into his surfing and offered to give Nick a few lessons and Hannah was delighted when I told her about Smudge, and asked if she could take him for walks.

We met a variety of near neighbours; some were longstanding incomers and others true Devonian locals. Nick's natural charm, and his association with the so say glamorous world of theatre, had him surrounded by a group eager to hear about any connections, tenuous or otherwise, to the great and the good of the acting world. I slipped away into the kitchen to re-fill my glass and found Anna at the sink.

"Do you want a hand?" I asked, as I picked up a tea towel.

"No not at all, it'll go in the dishwasher, I'm just rinsing a few glasses. I'm so glad you and Nick could come. He's lovely, you've got a real gem there. How're you settling in?"

"Fine, I love it and I've found a part time job in Braunton so couldn't be better. How long have you and Mark lived here?"

"I was born here. My parents owned this house, and their parents before them. It's been passed down through the generations since it was bought by my grandparents in 1950. I went away to university and then worked in London, met Mark and we moved here in 1998 before we had the children. We've been so lucky - my grandparents had great foresight and bought a bungalow to move into in their older age so the house could be passed on. My parents are now in the bungalow in Braunton and so it goes on. My grandparents loved it here so much and wanted every generation to have the opportunity to bring their children up in this wonderful place. And it is great for the kids, so much of the natural world on their doorstep, it gives them a fabulous start in life."

My mind was racing. "Does that mean you were living here when the Dupont's lived at The Sea House?"

"You've heard about that then? Didn't think it would be long before the gossip reached you. Yes, I was about five when Lottie lived there." Anna had a slightly wistful expression as she continued, "She was so pretty; long fair hair that hung almost to her waist and she had a little butterfly birthmark on her face that I found fascinating. As a little girl, she seemed to me like a princess. She used to babysit me sometimes and we would play in the summerhouse in her garden, or she would take me to the little café on the beach, Her French husband, Claude, ran it and he'd give me crêpes or a chunk of French bread with a slab of chocolate inside it."

"So you were around when she died?"

Anna's face clouded. "Yes, it was my parents who were the last people to see her alive."

"Oh my Lord, did they see her jump from the cliff? Is that what happened? Mrs Webber, in the post office, said there was talk of murder."

"There were lots of rumours at the time, but it wasn't murder. They reckon it was suicide. Mum and Dad were walking back from Morte Point, the weather had turned, and they passed Lottie going in the opposite direction. They had spoken to her briefly, warning her there was a storm coming, but she insisted she wanted to carry on, said she was trying to get the baby off to sleep. Mum called to see her the next day, but there was no one in and as the days passed, she got really concerned and alerted the police. Anyway, she was never seen again. Claude was in London; in the winter season he was a chef in a top West End restaurant. They searched the cliffs, but her body was never found; just an old jumper of Claude's she'd been wearing."

I was going to ask Anna more when Mark came into the kitchen and whisked her away to mingle.

"Hello, I don't think we've met. I'm Sarah and live up the hill in Morthoe at 'Seabreezes'," said a hale and hearty woman in her sixties, as she thrust out her hand, and the moment to learn more about Lottie was gone.

After a couple of hours, we said our goodbyes and left, once I'd promised Hannah I'd let her walk Smudge sometime over the Easter holidays.

"Great neighbours," said Nick as we walked down the hill hand in hand.

Chapter 6

Charlotte - 1976

Charlotte was on cloud nine. Never had she felt such a visceral attraction. Claude Dupont filled her every thought, and she raised her hand to her mouth to relive the moment when he had kissed her. Since that evening, she'd returned to Barricane Beach whenever she had a spare moment, in the hope of encountering Claude again. As the days went by and there was no sign of him, she became desperate to see him again, so consumed was she by this charming Frenchman. Le Shack remained closed, and she almost began to wonder if she had imagined the whole thing, but then she remembered the gentle sweep of his lips across her hand and knew it had been for real.

It was early summer, and May was following the same pattern as April, dry and warm. Visitors to The Bay Hotel were enjoying day after day of sunshine; no wandering around aimlessly in damp anoraks this year. Charlotte loved her job, had made friends with the other young people working at the hotel and was well thought of by Mr Bramdean and the more senior staff. Her confidence was growing, and she was relishing the sense of independence and freedom that she had so recently acquired. But her mind was constantly on Claude Dupont and she was determined to find out more.

"Do you know when Le Shack on Barricane Beach opens?" she asked one of her work colleagues, as a group of them sat on the beach wrapped in towels, watching the sun go down after a refreshing swim.

"It'll open at Whitsun, end of May, and then stay open for the summer, usually 'til September, depending on the weather. The guy who owns it is a real dreamboat and he's got a sexy French accent. All the girls round here have got a crush on him."

Charlotte felt a pang of irrational jealousy but didn't give anything away "Mmm, I know. I bumped into him the other week when I was on the beach. He's gorgeous."

"Yes, he's good at bumping into pretty girls, so I've heard. He does amazing French food there, moules, crêpes and things. Very sophisticated; a bit posh for hereabouts if you ask me, but it seems to be doing OK."

***

Johnny came to visit Charlotte most Sundays and they spent happy hours walking on the beach and lying in the dunes planning their life together, but Johnny sensed that Charlotte had changed.

"What is it my lovely? You don't seem quite so enthusiastic about our plans. We should be able to get a place together by September. I can't wait."

"Neither can I Johnny, but let's just enjoy the summer first." She didn't know what else to say and felt guilty that she didn't feel the all-consuming desire for Johnny as she had, only a month or so before.

"You seem different Charlotte. Are you OK?"

"Yes of course I am," and she bent to kiss Johnny as they lay together in a private dip in the dunes, hidden from passers-by. Her passion was re-kindled, but her thoughts were not only of Johnny, as they made love amongst the banks of sand and marram grass.

And then, one Sunday towards the end of May, Charlotte saw Claude again. Johnny had returned to his family in Cornwall for the weekend and Charlotte guiltily looked forward to having Sunday all to herself. She packed up a picnic, a flask of tea, a book, coconut oil, a towel and her bikini and headed for the beach. It was a baking hot day, not a cloud in the sky, and the sea a glistening blue. As she looked across the sand the air seemed to shimmer in the heat. There was no breeze and little surf, and the people that came and went appeared lackadaisical in the warmth of the day. Le Shack was closed but she noticed a sign had been pinned to the wooden hatch 'Opening on Saturday.' Her heart jolted. Only a week to go and I will see him again, she thought. She was amazed at the sense of anticipation she felt, mixed with disappointment that she wouldn't see him today. She decided to spend the day on the beach anyway, so spread her towel on the sand and her body with coconut oil and read and sunbathed the day away. She was conscious of admiring looks from young men as they passed her by and was pleased with the way her tan was developing, turning her skin golden brown. She was more aware of her own self than ever before and felt aroused by the hot sun and soft air on her sun-baked body.

Eventually, as the evening sun slipped towards the horizon, Charlotte packed up her belongings, pulled on her shorts and turned to head up the beach. And there was Claude sitting at one of the tables on the platform below the café, smoking a cigarette and watching her as she made her way across the sand. Her heart leapt so high she thought it would break through her chest. She attempted to walk nonchalantly towards him, not quite knowing whether to speak or walk on past, but as she approached, Claude stood and made his way towards her. And then she tripped, dropped her bag and watched as all her bits and pieces scattered on the sand. He was there in a flash and helped as Charlotte, cheeks burning with embarrassment, collected up her beaching paraphernalia. As she stood, Claude once again had an amused twinkle in his eye.

"Ah Lottie, let me assist, are you OK?" He'd remembered her name!

"Yes I'm fine, what an idiot. Thanks," Charlotte replied breathlessly, as she looked again into those deep brown eyes.

"Come, sit with me mon petit papillon. Do you smoke?" Claude said, as he offered her his packet of Gauloises cigarettes, and they took a seat at one of the tables. Charlotte shook her head as Claude lit one for himself and she inhaled the uniquely French smell of the tobacco.

"Papillon? Doesn't that mean butterfly?" asked Charlotte, dragging up her school-girl French from the deepest recesses of her brain.

"Mais oui. Pardon, but you 'ave that beautiful butterfly mark on your face; it makes me wish to call you papillon. I 'ope you do not mind?"

Charlotte flushed again. She wouldn't have minded if he'd called her l'escargot, so flattered was she that he had made up a name for her at all. "No, of course not Claude," she said, and watched as he smiled at her use of his name. "You're opening up next week then? If the weather stays like this, you'll have a good season."

"Ah, you English. Always you talk of the weather. Mais oui, it will be good for business. Would you like a coffee? We can go inside and make one, a special espresso for you before we open for the season, no?"

Charlotte was dumbstruck at the charm of this man, so forward, so sure of himself, and she felt powerless to resist. He unlocked Le Shack and propped the door open with a heavy stone and they went inside. She was thrilled at the tiny but fully functional kitchen that smelt faintly of garlic and herbs, with traces of coffee and tobacco mingled in. There was a large urn and a round griddle plate, which she guessed was for cooking crêpes, two gas rings and a worktop into which was set a double sink. Claude set a metal coffee percolator on the gas while he found two tiny cups and saucers and placed them ready on the worktop, against which he then leant and watched as Charlotte took in her surroundings.

"This is so sweet! You've got everything you need in this little kitchen, but I hope you don't mind me saying, it seems an odd place for a French café."

"Ah yes, but that is the attraction for the visitors. It is something quite unique. They love it."

They took their coffees outside to one of the tables as Claude told Charlotte that he had bought the café so he could spend the summers at the beach. In the winter he worked in London as a chef in a West End restaurant. "And the name of my London restaurant is Le Papillon, so, it is, 'ow do you say? a coincidence that you 'ave come to me with that little mark?"

"Where do you live when you're here? Do you stay in one of the guest houses?" Charlotte was surprised at her directness but wanted to find out as much as she could about this enigmatic man who lived a life half in London and half here on the beach.

"Ah no Lottie, I 'ave the 'ouse over there. The Sea 'ouse. I will show you when we leave the beach. Come, let us clear away."

They rinsed the cups in the little shed café and Charlotte felt electric shocks every time they brushed against one another in the tiny space. She picked up her beach bag from the floor and as she stood, found Claude staring hard at her.

"You are so beautiful, little papillon," he said and stroked her face and tiny butterfly birthmark with his fingers. He drew her face up towards his and gently kissed her lips.

Charlotte responded eagerly; she couldn't help herself. The gentle kiss became passionate, as their lips parted and their tongues played together, while Claude caressed Charlotte's bare back and shoulders. She pressed herself against him, feeling his hardness and willing him to unfasten the clasp on her bikini top, such was the longing she felt for this man. She knew she would have given herself completely, but Claude pulled away panting and slammed his hands down on the worktop.

"Mon Dieu. You are exquisite but this is too soon. Forgive me Lottie."

Charlotte suddenly felt mortified; had she been too forward, would he think her easy? She took her bag and started to climb from the beach ashamed of how readily she had been prepared to give herself to Claude. He caught up with her. "Lottie, it is OK, no?

Come, I will show you my 'ouse." She climbed from the beach with him but had already decided that she wouldn't go to his house. She realised, almost too late, that she had her reputation to maintain. They stopped when they reached the Esplanade, and he pointed out a house set above them on the opposite side of the road. It was painted white and had a balcony running the width of the building on the first floor, its wooden slats painted bright green.

"It's lovely. You must have great views from up there."

"Yes, right across to the island, what do you call it, Lundy? Would you like to come and see?"

Charlotte was sorely tempted but remembered her earlier embarrassment. "No thank you. I must be getting back now."

"I 'ope we will meet again very soon, Lottie." And again, he took her hand and brushed his lips across it. "Au revoir."

Charlotte was in turmoil. Who was this man, that could stir her senses and drive her to distraction? This man, who called her a butterfly and used a shortening of her name that no one had done before, and which sounded delightful in his French accent. She didn't know him at all but was all consumed by him. Did he feel the same, or was he playing with her? With his looks and Gallic charm, he could have any girl he chose. Was she just another conquest to be notched up on his bedpost? She thought of what her colleague had said about him being good at bumping into pretty girls. And he hadn't asked her anything about herself; what she did, where she lived. Did he even care. She knew she should be ashamed of what had happened earlier, but she wasn't and knew she would do it, and more, again if she could. She thought of Johnny and knew that he had never moved her in the same way. Despite the chaos in her mind, Charlotte had never felt so alive.

***

The hot, dry weather continued. Temperature records were broken, and the country was threatened with drought conditions.

61

The little resort was thriving, and families lying on the beach were as brown as if they'd spent a fortnight in the Mediterranean. Charlotte now only had a Sunday off work and began to dread Johnny coming. She loved him still, of course she did, in a safe and secure way, but knew her heart belonged to Claude. Johnny knew things had changed between them but didn't want to face it and Charlotte couldn't bring herself to tell Johnny the truth. She avoided Barricane beach when he visited, taking him instead to the dunes above the long sands of the main beach. They made love less frequently than before, Charlotte finding an excuse when she could, and talked less of their future together.

Le Shack was open for business and Claude had never been so busy. With temperatures soaring into the 80's day after day, visitors stayed on the beach until late into the night and the café remained open. The atmosphere was heady and intoxicating; people lazed on the beach, brought wine to drink and bought fine French cuisine from the café. Charlotte could not keep away, and Claude was pleased to see her when she returned. They were more circumspect at first, Claude engrossed in running the café, and Charlotte was happy just to hang around in his company. She started to help clear the tables and then to serve food, often carrying it down to groups on the beach when the tables were full. As the café became busier, Claude relied on her help more and more, until she was working alongside him every evening. They made a stunning couple - Charlotte now tanned to a nut brown, her long hair bleached blond in the sun, making her brown eyes appear even darker, and Claude with his olive colouring, slim muscular body, deep brown eyes and dark shoulder length hair – and were regarded locally as something of a novelty, two of the 'beautiful people', and quite a coup for a small seaside resort in north Devon. When the visitors left the beach and the café closed, they would sit and drink wine into the early hours of the morning, and Charlotte would return to the hotel with only an hour or two for a nap before the breakfast shift.

Charlotte told Claude of her up-bringing in Cornwall and her love of the little part of it in which she had lived. She shed tears as she spoke of her mother – her vibrancy in life, her illness and her death and Claude held her and spoke to her tenderly in his soft French accent and soothed away the pain. Claude spoke about his childhood in the South of France, where he had grown up in the resort of St Maxime on the Mediterranean coast. He talked of living in warmth and sunshine for most of the year, of eating fine cuisine and drinking wine on a terrace shaded by bougainvillea trailing over a stone pergola, the scent of lavender in the warm air, of swimming in a balmy Mediterranean Sea, with no tides and no surf, things that Charlotte had never experienced, and which made Claude seem ever more exotic and alluring. His family had owned a string of hotels along the coast, and he had started training in the kitchens at a young age, under the guidance of his father. He had completed his apprenticeship in a large hotel in Paris and moved to London at a time when the demand for French cuisine was growing. His older sister was already living in the city, married to an English restaurateur, and had persuaded him to bring his talents to the UK. After two years of non-stop work, establishing his reputation in the West End and building up a trustworthy team around him, he took some time out to see more of England. When he arrived on the north coast of Devon he fell in love with the wild and dramatic seas, so different from the flat calm of the Mediterranean; the tall, rugged cliffs and deep wooded combes, and knew he wanted a piece of it. He had bought the Sea House and Le Shack and had an arrangement to work the summers here and the winter months in London.

**

It wasn't long before Mr Bramdean got wind of Charlotte's moon-lighting and called her in to his office. "I'm sorry Charlotte, but you can't work two jobs while you're in my employment. I don't want to lose you, but you must choose whether you want to stay at The Bay Hotel or work at the café on the beach."

"I'm just helping out a friend Mr Bramdean, I'm not being paid to work there."

"Well, more fool you Charlotte. I would suggest that you are being taken advantage of if you are working into the early hours for nothing. Please think about what I've said and let me know by the end of the week what you intend to do. And please don't work at Le Shack during that time as it will mean you are breaking your contract."

"Yes Mr Bramdean, and I'm sorry," said Charlotte, although she didn't feel sorry, more indignant at having her wings clipped just when she felt she was flying high. She loved working at Le Shack; the unconventional and carefree nature of working in a wooden shed right on the beach, the sense of feel-good she imparted to the visitors who came to enjoy the alternative dining experience, and, most of all, being part of Claude's world. But without the hotel job she would have no income and nowhere to live. She needed to know exactly where she stood with Claude - was he using her as cheap labour? How would he react when she told him she couldn't work both jobs? She couldn't bear the thought that he might tell her to stop helping him out, that he was only taking what she was giving freely, and that he had no intention of employing her. Not daring to cross Mr Bramdean, she went later to the beach that evening and arrived just as Claude was about to lock up.

"Ah, there you are Lottie. Where 'ave you been? I was worried and so busy, I needed your 'elp tonight. Shall we take some wine?" Claude sounded irritated.

"You look so tired Claude. You sit and I'll fetch the wine." She brought a bottle and two glasses from the cafè and stood behind Claude massaging his neck as he drank and smoked. She felt him relax as she caressed his head and came round in front of him, planting butterfly kisses on his face until she reached his mouth. He groaned as he opened his mouth to her and they kissed fervently, all Claude's tiredness melting away as his desire grew. He pulled her up the steps to the cafè and they fell inside together, pulling clothes off as they went. Their craving for one another no longer contained, they came together against the counter, the weeks of waiting fuelling their desire. Afterwards they collapsed to the floor on a pile of discarded clothes and lay naked in the little kitchen, hot and breathless from their love making.

"Mon Dieu, I think I must change your name to la petite tigresse, you 'ave sharp talons!"

"You're a bit of a stallion yourself," murmured Charlotte, unwinding in the afterglow. But she knew she must tell Claude of her dilemma with Mr Bramdean. Suddenly her head was filled with apprehension; if Claude agreed to take her on as a paid member of staff, she could leave the hotel but would have to find somewhere else to live; if Claude no longer wanted her on those terms, she would be devastated. All at once things looked tricky. With a feeling of dread, she explained her conversation with Mr Bramdean and the consequences of staying at the hotel or coming to work with Claude full time. Claude's expression clouded for a moment and Charlotte feared the worst, but then he took her in his arms. "But of course, you must come and be with me, be la châtelaine of Le Shack. The clientele adore you, you bring more custom with your beauty and your charm. And you will live with me at the Sea 'ouse. C'est simple."

For a moment Charlotte felt elated, that all her dreams were coming true. "Do you mean it Claude? Are you sure? I won't let you down and I love working with you." But later the enormity of it hit her. What a risk, am I crazy or am I just crazy for Claude? she thought, although she already knew the answer and couldn't bear the thought of losing him. She also knew she couldn't string Johnny along any longer. It would break his heart, but she had to tell him soon.

Charlotte arranged to work her week's notice, finishing after her Saturday shift. She felt a little embarrassed as she said her farewell to Mr Bramdean, almost as if she was letting him down. "I'm sorry to be losing you Charlotte, you were proving to be a great asset to the hotel. I think you could have made a career for yourself here had you chosen to stay. However, I wish you well." He was about to say more but changed his mind. Charlotte felt sure he had been about to add 'and I hope you know what you're doing.'

Again, she pushed down the feelings of doubt that were never far from the surface. "Thank you, Mr Bramdean, I've enjoyed working here very much."

Claude had given her a key to The Sea House and she felt nervous as she took her few belongings there from the hotel. She had never been inside the house and here she was moving in. The finger of doubt prodded her again. She looked around and found the sitting room appointed very much in the French style, with large pieces of heavy furniture in a room which was barely big enough to take them. There were thick dark curtains at the windows and the only splash of colour was in the bright orange rug on the floor. This style was completely alien to Charlotte, who had lived in a house furnished by her mother in light colours influenced by sun and sea, and this sombre mix gave her the feeling of being in a headmaster's study. The room smelt of wood smoke and Gauloises and Charlotte inhaled the rich masculine aroma. The air was stifling but she didn't feel she could throw open the windows to let the sea air in. This, after all, was not her home. She wasn't sure where to put her bag so left it in the hall and went to join Claude at the café.

"Your house is lovely Claude; I've dumped my stuff."

"It is your 'ouse too, Lottie. From now it is our 'ouse, no?"

Charlotte was delighted that Claude seemed so willing to share his home with her, but she still had to face Johnny before she could truly settle into her new life. "Claude, I've agreed to work one last shift tomorrow. They're short staffed at the hotel," she lied. She had arranged to meet Johnny but didn't want Claude to know. She hadn't told him about Johnny and didn't see any point now. She would be breaking up with him tomorrow. When she thought about it, she

66

realised how little she and Claude really knew about one another. She chose to ignore the anxiety gnawing at her insides.

***

"Don't meet me at the hotel tomorrow, Johnny, we'll meet at The Red Barn, then we can have a drink before we go for our walk," Charlotte said over the phone as they made arrangements for what would be their last Sunday together.

"I'll be there, can't wait to see you."

"Me too," replied Charlotte, forcing her voice to sound cheerful.

They met as arranged in the quick-service style café. "It's a strange name, The Red Barn, for a place at the beach," said Johnny.

"They say it was given that nickname by the American troops based here in the war, training for the Normandy landings. Way back then it was the Red Cross Servicemen's Club. It's hard to imagine this lovely beach covered with barbed wire and soldiers with landing craft, preparing for war," replied Charlotte wistfully.

After a cooling drink the couple wandered along the hot sands. Johnny sensed Charlotte's edginess. "What's up, you seem jumpy today? Is everything OK?"

"Not really Johnny. Let's go to our place in the dunes, we need to talk."

"That sounds ominous. What about?"

Charlotte didn't reply, and they scrambled up the steep sandy paths to their hideaway. It was even hotter here, sheltered from the sea breeze, and they flopped down on the rug they had brought.

"Before you say anything Charlotte, I've got something for you," Johnny said, as he handed her a small package. He had a defeated look, something Charlotte had never seen in him before; he was always so strong and unshakeable.

Charlotte took the package with shaking hands. She unwrapped the tissue paper and there inside was a little butterfly pendant carved out of wood on a leather band. "Oh, that's lovely, so intricate. Did you make it?"

"Yes, I carved it for you."

Charlotte felt tears prick her eyes as she blurted out in a rush, "I can't take it Johnny, I've met someone else. I can't be yours anymore." Tears trickled down her face. "I'm so sorry."

Johnny was calm, he placed his head in his hands for a few moments before looking into Charlotte's eyes. "I thought as much, you aren't the same Charlotte that I left behind in Cornwall. I knew something was up. I think I always knew I'd lose you eventually, but it didn't take you long, did it?" He paused then and looked across the beach and way out to the horizon beyond. "Don't worry, I won't make a scene or make things difficult for you. I love you Charlotte and always will. I lost my heart to you when I was a lad of twelve. I swear I will never come back to this place, but will you grant me one thing? Can we lay together one last time?"

Charlotte fell into Johnny's arms, feeling his strength and comfort once again. They made love and afterwards lay together, as Charlotte shed silent tears. Then Johnny got up and walked away without a backward glance, leaving Charlotte with the little carved butterfly in the palm of her hand.

Chapter 7

Sophie – 2015

"Bye Nick, see you next weekend. Text me when you get back; thanks for all your help," I said through the car window, as he prepared to drive off.

"The pleasure's been all mine," he said, grinning. "I'm going back to town for a rest." He gave me one last kiss and was gone. My heart lurched from the kiss, and from a rush of anxiety at being on my own again.

I prayed Nick wouldn't fall asleep at the wheel, as we were both weary and aching after three days of non-stop decorating. We'd settled into a routine and the days had passed in a blur of painting and dog walking until, in the evenings, when we were driven to the kitchen by hunger and exhaustion, we cooked up huge platefuls of pasta, which we washed down with copious amounts of wine, before collapsing in front of the television. At the end of day three the living room was done; walls painted in a creamy yellow colour called 'Sand' (which Nick renamed 'Sludge') with the chimney breast in a contrasting dark blue. The room looked fresh, bright and seaside-y; just the look I was aiming for. The heavily textured dark blue rug, with oatmeal flecks, was back in place and one of my slightly battered brown leather sofas was in position in front of the fire, with the low, chunky wood, coffee table. Nick was to bring the rest of my furniture on his next visit; an eclectic mix of pieces left to me by my grandmother, and two large driftwood table lamps, which I'd bought on a previous visit to the West Country. With striped curtains and cushions in shades of sandy yellows and blues, it should all come together.

The sewing machine was already set up in my work room across the hall on an old oak desk, another piece from grandma, which I'd placed under the window for the best light and views across the bay. I planned to get the soft furnishings finished while Nick wasn't around so I could tick off the living room and start on this one. "So Smudge, what do you think of it so far? Does the accommodation come up to scratch? And how did you find your new master? He's hot, isn't he?" Smudge looked up at me with heart-melting doggy eyes, tail wagging furiously, so I guessed he thought everything was okay.

***

"Hi Anna, come in."

"Mmm, nice smell of fresh paint. You managed to get some decorating done then?"

"Yes, come and have a look. The room's decorated. I've just got to finish the curtains and cushions, and Nick is bringing the rest of my furniture from storage, then we can finish off."

"Wow, that looks great, nice and airy. Love the coastal colours."

We headed along the hallway to the kitchen where I had a cafetiere of coffee brewing. It was the end of another week. I'd completed two more days at Devon Dwellings and everything was going well there. I'd returned from work the previous day to find the house encased in scaffolding and a note through the door from Rob saying they'd be starting work next week. So far, so good, I thought. True to his word up to now.

Anna was a part-time teacher and I'd asked her in for a coffee on her day off, in the hope of learning more about Lottie and what had become of her.

"You know, I've never been further than the front door," she said as we made our way to the back of the house. "When Lottie looked after me it was either in the summerhouse, or she took me to the beach so we could go to the café. '76 was such a hot summer, no-one seemed to be inside at all if they could help it."

I poured coffee and fetched the photo album. "This is the album I found when I moved in. Are these pictures of Lottie?" I said, and I handed the album to Anna.

Anna frowned at the early pictures of the young girls together, unsure of who they were, but as she delved further into the album, she suddenly gave a cry. "Oh my goodness, yes that's her!" She held the album up to examine the photos more closely and ran her fingers over the little pieces of fabric tucked behind them. "You know, I think I remember her wearing those hotpants. I can remember thinking what incredibly long legs she had. And that's Claude. Claude Dupont. Even as a little girl I remember being rather smitten with him and his funny accent." She continued to scrutinise the photos until she came to the one of Lottie and Claude in their wedding gear. "I didn't know they'd got married here. Oh look, here's one with the baby."

"Did you know the baby's name? What happened to it when Lottie, you know, committed suicide?" I hardly dared to ask the next question. "She didn't take the baby with her, did she?"

There was a moment of silence as Anna stared at the photos, lost in thoughts of her early childhood. "Do you know what, Sophie, I have no idea what happened to the baby. It was a boy, the baby was a boy, but I'm not sure I ever knew his name, or if I did, I can't remember it now. I think I only saw him once or twice. I remember my mother brought me to give him a present when he was born, a little blue bear it was. I remember it because, at first, I said I wanted to keep it for myself. I threw a bit of a paddy about it, I think. We didn't come into the house; Lottie brought the baby to the door. It was winter when he was born. By then I'd just started school and I don't remember Lottie babysitting me again after the summer, and then she was gone."

"Do you remember it, when it happened?"

71

"To be honest, not really. This was back in the '70s remember. Things didn't get so hyped up by the media back then, so although it was a big deal for the area at the time, it probably died down pretty quickly after the initial drama. Sadly, people die on the coast fairly regularly in these parts. And I think my parents were careful to shield me from it. I do remember my mum being very upset at the time, but I was definitely kept out of it, and I was only just five so most of it would've gone right over my head." She leafed through the album again. "That must be her sister," she said, as she looked at the photos of the two girls together. "Now I do remember her name because it was such a pretty Cornish name, and I used it for one of my dolls. Verity. I don't think I ever met her, but Charlotte used to talk about her. I don't know who that is," she said looking at the picture of the girls with a slightly older boy. "Perhaps she had a brother too."

"What I can't understand is how and why the album is here at all," I said, perplexed once again by the fact that, with the number of times the house must've changed hands since the '70s, it should still be here.

"Yes, that's really strange," said Anna. We sat together in silence for a minute, staring at the album. "What do you think you'll do with it?"

"I don't know. I was thinking of contacting my solicitor to find out if they could track down any Duponts from previous sales of the house, but that's a bit of a long shot. I bought it from people called Leadbetter, so goodness knows how long ago the Duponts sold it."

"Mmm, don't know. I wasn't aware it had been sold before you bought it. I thought it had remained his and he'd just rented it to various tenants over the years. Must have sold it on the QT or I'm sure the jungle drums would've been beating, as they did when you bought it," Anna said with a smile.

"Guess I'll just hold on to it as part of the history of the house. Sad, though," I said finally. We closed the album and chatted about other things. We arranged for Hannah to come and take Smudge for a walk sometime over the weekend. I thought it would help if my four-legged friend was out of the way when Nick and I were unloading furniture and hanging curtains.

***

It was Saturday, and my 'man with a van' was due mid-afternoon with the rest of my possessions. Once again, my anticipation at seeing Nick put me on edge until he arrived. Smudge sensed my anxiety and was excitable himself. It was a foul day with a near gale force westerly blowing right on to the beach, whipping up the surf. Horizontal rain swept in across the bay in heavy squalls. After a largely dry and settled April, it seemed unfair that the weather should break now, just as the holiday season was getting underway.

No matter the weather, Smudge still needed a walk, so I pulled on waterproofs and set off to the beach. Lundy was invisible today, with such heavy cloud cover, and I thought again of Lottie setting off in a storm towards Morte Point. Did she really mean to end her life or was it just a tragic accident? I wondered if I would ever know.

We had a run on the beach, the weather making Smudge skittish, so he barked at everything and anyone in sight, and chased after seagulls that swooped low across the sands before being carried off on the wind. There weren't many braving the beach, a few other dog walkers, and the die-hard surfers in their hooded wetsuits, bobbing about like seals, waiting for the best waves. By the time we arrived back at the Sea House I was soaked through. I gave the garden a cursory look as we hurried up the steps, aubrietia now cascading over the wall in all its purple glory. I would have to get to grips with the wilderness once Rob and his crew had finished work on the house, but was relieved to have an excuse to put it off a while longer. I had no experience with gardening and was daunted by the amount of work.

Nick arrived pretty much on schedule, and it was like a repeat of moving in day as we humped furniture into the house, although the humping was much harder and slower without Will to lend a hand, and with Smudge getting under our feet. He was so pleased to see Nick, leaping at him madly and threatening to send him hurtling down the steps, but if we shut him in the kitchen, he howled like a banshee. I think he'd missed Nick more than I had.

We decided to dump the furniture and go for a walk during a small weather-window, when the rain seemed to have eased, so Smudge could expend some of his pent-up energy. I was amazed he had any left after our run this morning, but it seemed his exuberance knew no bounds. We headed off towards Morte Point with the idea of doing the circular walk I'd done when I found Smudge. Nick and I tried to walk hand in hand, both desperate for some physical contact, but Smudge was pulling so hard on the lead it was impossible.

"You're a pain Smudge, and I think you're jealous because I want to cosy up to my number one girl," said Nick. As Smudge started jumping at him and barking madly, he added, "It's OK, you're my second favourite." And with these words of reassurance Smudge carried on pulling us along. As we rounded the point, I checked there were no sheep on the headland and let him off the lead for a while, so he could have a good run and we could have a moment's peace.

"It's worse than having a toddler in tow. Oh my life, what's he doing now?" Smudge had charged on ahead and was now making up to someone who stood further along the path, overlooking a deep inlet. We ran to catch up, calling for Smudge, but it seemed he had already befriended the woman who was making a great fuss of him. "I'm so sorry," I said, as we came to the spot where the woman was standing. "He's a bit manic today. I think it's the weather."

"That's OK. He's lovely, and in fact it's quite uncanny but he's almost identical to a dog I once had," said the woman.

My heart dropped as I thought she was about to say that she'd recently lost her dog locally and that Smudge was going to be hers. I tentatively said, "Did you lose him around here?"

"Oh no, I'm only visiting the area. No, this was years ago when we were children, but the likeness is amazing." Smudge was bored with all the talk and had run off again, with Nick in pursuit.

"Enjoy your visit, hope the weather improves for you," I said, as I moved off to chase after them.

"Thanks. Have a good walk," said the woman.

Nick had caught up with Smudge and put him back on the lead, so I slowed my pace and looked back towards the woman. As I did so, I saw her take something from the canvass bag she carried across her shoulder, and lay it on the ground, tucking it in amongst some rocks. She stood for a moment longer and then took off back the way we'd come. As I came up to Nick, the rain started hammering down again. "Sod this!" said Nick. "I think Smudge has had enough exercise for now and I know I have."

We turned and retraced our steps and as we came to where we had encountered the woman, I saw that what she had left in the shelter of the rocks was a bunch of wild flowers, tied with raffia. I bent for a closer look and saw a small label which read 'To my beloved sister Charlotte, another year without you. Be at peace.' The flowers and the label were already getting battered and soggy from the rain, even in their sheltered spot, and it wouldn't be long before they were completely ruined. As I was thinking that thought, I was suddenly hit by another, so hard it made me gasp. I called Nick over. "Nick, look at this. D'you think these are for Lottie? Charlotte/Lottie, same name? Is this the spot where she died? Was that her sister Verity? Where did she go? We must catch up with her!"

Nick bent to take a look. "Hold on Soph, I don't know. It could be, I suppose. But after all this time, is it likely? Bit far-fetched if you ask me."

"Well, who else could Charlotte be? There can't be too many Charlottes who have lost their lives round about here. Come on, we must try and catch up with that woman." I started off at a pace but she had vanished, and as we looked at the many different paths that crisscrossed the headland, realised it was unlikely we'd see her again, especially as the weather was closing in so quickly.

I was restless when we returned home and pulled out the album again to see if I could spot any resemblance between the child in the photos and the woman we'd just seen. I couldn't of course, but if the photos of the young girls were taken in the early '70s and they were about ten at the time, she would be about fifty to fifty-five now. "How old d'you think she was, that woman? Fifty? Sixty?" I asked Nick.

"I've no idea. I wouldn't have said as much as sixty, maybe fifty-five tops. Now are we going to get on with sorting out this furniture, or what?"

"Yes OK. I'm just so annoyed we didn't see her again. I have a strong feeling we missed our one chance of meeting Verity. And that dog thing. It was weird that Smudge was obviously so like her childhood dog. It's as if the spirit of her old dog had haunted Smudge to bring us together. Maybe that's why he was so skittish."

"Hey come on Sophie, don't you think that's a step too far?" said Nick laughing. "Your imagination has kicked into overdrive with this whole Lottie thing. You'll be seeing Charlotte's ghost next!"

I gave him a pouty look. He came over to me, took the album and closed it and pulled me up into his arms. I rested my head against his chest and he gently kissed the top of my head. "Come on now, sulky drawers, let's get the sitting room finished then we can light a fire and get cosy together. With the curtains up we can get up to all sorts; make love in front of the fire if you like."

"Oh alright, come on then." I put thoughts of Lottie and Verity to the back of my mind and concentrated on enjoying the feeling of Nick holding me.

A couple of hours later we declared the sitting room finished. Furniture was in place, curtains hung, cushions scattered, and fire lit. It wasn't cold but was a wet and miserable evening outside and I was itching to try it out for the first time. "To the first completed room in the Sea House, and may I compliment you on your style. I particularly like that sludge colour on the walls," said Nick as he handed me a large glass of wine with a kiss. "Cheers!"

I was pleased with the way it looked and how mine and grandma's bits and pieces sat in harmony together. The fire gave the room a warm glow and we snuggled up together on the sofa. Smudge padded in from the kitchen, took one look at the fire and settled himself down on the rug, sighing contentedly. "So much for making love in front of the fire. I think we've lost our spot," I said, nodding towards Smudge, who couldn't have been any closer to the flames without climbing on to the hearth itself. We lay together and Nick began caressing my neck and shoulders with kisses. I closed my eyes, delighting in his closeness, and felt his arousal.

"Bloody hell, he's a right passion killer," said Nick suddenly. "Can you see him, lying there as innocent as you like, but with one beady eye trained on us. Right, into the kitchen with you, young man." He got up and dragged Smudge out of the sitting room. "Do you want something to eat Soph?" he shouted from the kitchen, and I knew the moment was gone. I wondered, not for the first time, if I was being fair to Nick, insisting we kept our relationship platonic, but he never pushed it and stopped himself before he got carried away. He was, I thought, a perfect gentleman.

Nick rustled up one of his specialities - Chinese chicken fried rice, which we ate with prawn crackers and chilled white wine. We sat across from one another at the kitchen table, keeping a safe distance, both knowing how easy it would be to cross the line.

"Can you get away next weekend Sophie? I'm recording in Bristol at the end of the week and Will's band is playing at the Coulsdon Hall on Saturday night - thought we could go? The BBC is putting me up in a budget hotel Wednesday and Thursday, so I could stay on and we could go on a proper date. I'll even wine and dine you before the gig. You could stay over on Saturday night and come back here Sunday."

"I'd love it. Only problem is Smudge. I wonder if Anna would have him, or Jo. I'll work something out. It would be great to have a change of scene. Have we ever been on a proper date?"

"Depends if you count that comic we saw at the Southwark Play-house, with his catch phrase 'Chuckle, wheeze, roll about.' Do you remember?"

"Oh my days, yes. He was awful!" Nick was right; although we'd hung around together in London, met up at friends for barbeques and sometimes gone for meals after work in a group, we'd not really been out as a couple. I was looking forward to it already.

***

Nick left on Sunday evening. We'd started on the decoration of my work room during the day while Hannah took Smudge for a walk, and I'd checked with Anna whether she would be prepared to have him when I was away. Hannah was delighted at the idea and Anna, too, seemed rather grateful. "We've always refused to let the children have a dog, knowing the novelty would wear off and we'd be left with the responsibility, but this way they can have a taste of what it's like without us having to be lumbered with a pooch once the initial attraction has worn off! You'd be doing us a favour."

If I thought the week would pass slowly while waiting for the big date in Bristol, I needn't have worried. It flew by. Rob and his crew turned up again on Monday. He explained what they'd be doing and said he'd be popping in and out himself to keep an eye on the job. I felt he was a little less friendly than last time, not hanging around to talk. Shame really; he was easy on the eye with his curly strawberry blond hair and brilliant blue eyes.

I spent the next two days working at home, putting together design boards for Jo, which I took into the office on Thursday. "These are great Sophie, thanks. Love the colour combinations on this one and I've got just the owner to show it to. They've got a converted barn they want to rent as a holiday let, but it needs some work first. To be honest they haven't got a clue and are happy for our advice. The light greens and soft yellows will work well in the little kitchen-come-living room and we can bring it all together with that checked fabric for the suite, which picks up all the colours and shades. And I love your ideas for farm related accessories; bits of old farm implements and tools, farmhouse kitchen paraphernalia, animal pictures, great."

I set about firing up the computer. "By the way Sophie," said Jo, from her separate little office across the room, "I may have a contact for you about the mysterious goings on at the Sea House."

I was all ears. "There's this old boy and his son who look after the gardens of some of our properties. They live out at Twitchen, just above Morthoe, and they've been gardening in the area for years. I was speaking to the son, Sam, the other day and asked if they remembered anything about it. Seems they do. I've got to go out there later to drop off some keys. Why don't you come with me? It'll help you get to know the area as well."

I couldn't wait and felt like a detective who'd just been given a new lead. I told Jo about the woman we'd seen on the cliffs at the weekend. I remained convinced that it was Verity and still slightly miffed that she'd gone before I'd realised.

***

"Hello Sam. How's your dad today?" said Jo, as we were shown into the little cottage Sam shared with his father. She had explained on the way over that Sam, now in his fifties, had mild learning difficulties but had a real love and talent for gardening and had worked for many local families all his adult life. Sam's father was in his eighties and had also been a gardener but had given up as he became

79

more and more crippled with arthritis and now only mowed a few lawns for the locals.

"'e be proper," said Sam. "'im be down yonder in the veg patch."

"This is Sophie. She's come to work for me, so I wanted you to meet her."

"Hi Sam," I said, and I held out my hand which he took and briefly shook, as he gave me a nod.

"Here are the keys to Nethercott Farm Cottage so you can get to work on the garden whenever you want, but it needs to be done by the end of next week when we've got guests in," said Jo, handing over a set of keys on a big wooden tractor shaped key ring.

"OK," said Sam. A man of few words, I thought.

"Sam, Sophie has bought the Sea House. Do you remember it? I think you and your dad did the garden there years ago. She wondered if you remembered the Duponts who lived there."

There was a moment's hesitation before Sam answered. "Yes, remember them. Nice lady. She were kind to me. They said 'er died, went off the cliffs, but 'er didn't. I knows 'er didn't." Sam looked at the floor as if he was embarrassed by what he was saying.

"Do you know that for sure Sam," I asked.

"Course I do, I'm not stupid. People says I am, but I ain't. I knows what I saw."

"I don't think you're stupid Sam," I said gently. "What did you see?"

"I saw 'er didn't I? 'Twas after they say 'er went over the cliff. I saw 'er next day. Early mornin', before 'twas light." I wondered how Sam could have seen Lottie if it was dark but I let him continue. "'er came up from down yonder." He pointed in the general direction of Combesgate valley. "'er had a rucksack and a torch. I see'd 'er by the light of 'er torch. I knew t'were 'er." He looked up at me and then down again, blushing before continuing. "She were kind and I learned 'er the names of flowers and plants in 'er garden." Sam looked embarrassed again.

"Did you tell anyone you saw her, after she disappeared?"

"No. No point. No one takes no notice of what I says. No one asked, so I didn't tell."

"But were you not questioned by the police after she went missing, seeing as how you'd been working for her?"

"No. They asked me dad but 'e didn't know nothin'. I didn't tell 'im I seed 'er so 'e didn't know. Police didn't ask me nothin'. Said I was the village idiot and I wouldn't know nothin'. They didn't ask so I didn't tell." He looked down again and I felt he'd said all he was going to.

"I don't think you're an idiot Sam and I wondered if you'd like to work at the Sea House again, for me. The garden is in a bit of a mess and I'd really like you to help me sort it out. Would you be able to fit me in?"

"I'd like that, nice garden. Me and 'er made a nice garden."

"Great. I've got builders in at the moment but once they've finished I'll be in touch and we can arrange for you to start. Is that OK?"

"OK," he said. And for the first time since Jo and I had arrived, he smiled.

Chapter 8

Charlotte – 1976

"Verity, it's Charlotte. Is dad in?"

"Charlotte, about time. Haven't heard from you for ages, I've been worried. I thought you were going to write or ring once a week. You haven't replied to *any* of my letters. Are you at the hotel or in a call box? Shall I ring you back?"

"No I'm not at the hotel. I've got so much to tell you but is dad in?"

"No, he's at a church meeting, why?"

"Because I don't want him coming on the phone and giving me a rocket."

"Why would he do that? He's really pleased you've got a live-in job at the hotel, thinks it will mean you and Johnny won't rush into anything. Didn't you get his letter?"

"Yes, but I haven't written back and thought he might be on the warpath. Anyway, things have changed Verity. I've met someone else, my very own Monsieur Dupont, you know, like in that Sandie Shaw song. Claude Dupont, he's French and he's gorgeous." Charlotte braced herself for Verity's reaction.

There was silence on the other end of the phone, then, "What? Charlotte, what are you talking about? Are you joking? What the hell is going on? What about Johnny?"

"We've finished, Verity. Me and Johnny, we've split up. Once I got here and started living my own life, I realised how sheltered I'd been at home in Cornwall, but now I'm spreading my wings, I don't want to settle down yet."

"Are you crazy? Johnny's the love of your life. Oh Charlotte, what've you done? Poor Johnny, he must be heartbroken. He's so devoted to you."

This time it was Charlotte's turn to be silent. A terrible guilt gripped her heart, but she continued in a more subdued voice, "I know Verity, and I don't feel good about chucking him, but better now than further down the line."

"I just can't believe this. You're so heartless. So, you're going to stay there at the hotel then? Is that where your Monsieur Dupont works?" said Verity, spitting out Claude's name with venom.

"Umm no actually, Claude owns a little café on Barricane Beach and I'm running it with him. It's so fab, you'd love it. It's called Le Shack and Claude cooks incredible French food."

"What, you're working there as well as at the hotel?"

"No, I've left the hotel. I just work with Claude now."

"So where are you living?"

"With Claude. He has a lovely house called the Sea House and it's right above the beach."

"Are you *mad* Charlotte? You've barely been gone two months. How can you possibly know this guy well enough to move in with him? And so much for spreading your wings and not being ready to settle down. What you mean is, you don't want to settle down with Johnny any more, but you're happy to move in with some bloke you met on the beach because he's got a sexy French accent and his name is in some stupid pop song."

"Verity, don't start. I just know, OK? But please don't tell dad, he'll go mad."

"So what am I supposed to do? Pretend you're still at the hotel? What happens if he wants to ring you, or write? He was even talking of coming to visit you when he has some summer leave. Good grief Charlotte, you can't really expect me to keep your dirty little secrets, it's not bloody fair."

"Not for long Verity, I promise, just until I'm really settled with Claude and can prove that it's working out. Look, why don't you come and stay, meet Claude and then you'll understand, see for yourself how lovely he is?"

"And what happens next time I see Johnny? He's bound to come home to Boscastle sometime; what am I supposed to say to him? Honestly Charlotte, you're so bloody selfish, you only ever think of yourself and what's best for you, never mind about anyone else's feelings. I dread to think what mummy would say if she were here to see you now." Verity was sobbing with anger and frustration.

"Verity don't, please. Stop it." Charlotte was crying now. "Don't bring mummy into this because the fact is, she isn't here, and she's never going to be here, so I've got to find my own way now, we both have, and I just know that Claude is my future. Please Verity, please come and see me then you can see for yourself how happy I am. I miss you so much and I can't bear it that we're fighting, please?" For a moment there was silence at the other end of the line, save for an occasional sniff. "Verity, please say something."

"Ok, I'll come for a weekend, but don't expect me to like your new Romeo. I just feel so sorry for Johnny. I'll come in a few weeks. I'll tell dad there's going to be a big beach party or something that you've invited me to, so he won't be tempted to come with me. See, I'm already thinking up lies to save your skin. Once I've been to visit, I want you to promise me that you'll tell dad what you're doing. I can't pretend to him any longer Charlotte, it's not fair."

"I will, I promise. It will be so lovely to see you and I know you'll love it here. I'll give you Claude's 'phone number then you can let me know when you're coming. Oh Verity, it will be so good to see you."

***

Over the coming weeks Charlotte was on an emotional roller coaster. One moment confident and self-assured, convinced that this bohemian way of life with her enigmatic Frenchman, serving exotic food from a shed above the beach, was the life she was destined for; intoxicated by the adulation she and Claude received, two beautiful people living the unconventional dream others could only wish for. But in moments alone, when Charlotte was out of Claude's immediate orbit, away from the adoring public, she worried that she was merely an accessory to Claude's powerful persona, a novelty in his show, like some exotic caged creature in a menagerie. Rattling around in the Sea House alone, her confidence slipped away, and she longed for the security of her childhood home. As the summer sizzled on, Charlotte pushed her negative feelings to a place deep inside and continued to sparkle for the ever-growing number of visitors to Le Shack. It was easier to be uplifted and adored alongside Claude than to acknowledge the doubts and fears that lingered just below the surface, as if in doing so her precarious world would crumble to rubble and ruin.

Charlotte's anxiety grew as the time for Verity's visit drew closer – she was desperate to see her sister but Claude's reaction to her impending arrival had been less than enthusiastic. "Mon dieu! 'Ow could you arrange this without asking me first? You are needed at Le Shack, you know 'ow busy we are," he growled through the haze of a Gauloises, when Charlotte told him Verity would be arriving at the weekend. It felt like a slap in the face, her excitement vanishing in the face of Claude's anger and petulance.

"I'll make it up to you, I promise," she squirmed, hating herself for the way she cow tailed to Claude's demands, while using the one weapon she knew would bring him round. Standing behind him, massaging his stiff shoulders and planting butterfly kisses on his neck it wasn't long before his need for her was stirred and they came together, the argument, at least for now, forgotten.

***

As the sisters hugged on Verity's arrival, Claude looked on with amusement, admiring their familial similarities and individual differences. Charlotte was taller than Verity, the length of her legs accentuated by the very short hotpants she was wearing. Verity was a more petite package, dressed in loon pants and a bikini top. Both girls had smooth brown sun-bronzed skin.

"I am enchanted to meet you Verity," he said, as he took her hand and kissed it. Charlotte felt an irrational stab of jealousy, remembering this was how he had greeted her on their first meeting. She pulled herself together – Claude was French, it was his way.

"How do you do?" said Verity, rather formally, but it wasn't to be long before Claude's charm had cast its spell on her.

Charlotte delighted in showing Verity around the village, pointing out the Woolacombe Bay Hotel where she had briefly worked, before they set off to walk the entire length of the beach to Putsborough Sands. Charlotte peppered Verity with questions about home; she was hungry for knowledge of what she had left behind. Verity spoke of their father and how he seemed resigned to the fact that Charlotte had gone and was now grieving for two people lost to him. She didn't add that it made it difficult for her to spread her wings; that she felt trapped knowing if she also left it would be more than he could bear.

As they drew near to the spot that led to the dunes where Charlotte and Johnny had had their secret place, Charlotte felt a stab of guilt and reached for the little carved butterfly pendant around her neck. She didn't mention Johnny, feeling sure it would lead to recriminations and rebukes, which would spoil her time with Verity. She knew the conversation would go that way before the weekend was over, but she wasn't going to bring it up.

The girls swam in the sea to refresh themselves, then lay on the hot sands to dry off before making their way back to Barricane beach. As they walked down the steps towards Le Shack, Charlotte noticed Claude sitting at one of the café tables with a young couple, a bottle

86

of chilled white wine and three glasses between them. Claude and the woman spoke animatedly as the man looked on. Claude offered them a packet of cigarettes, from which they each took one, and he lit theirs before taking one for himself and lighting up. Claude poured them each a glass of wine and they continued their conversation.

"Who's that?" asked Verity.

"I've no idea," replied Charlotte. "I've never seen them before." She felt a pang of unease.

As they approached the café, Claude stood and waited for them. "Ah Lottie, Verity. Let me introduce you to my sister and 'er 'usband."

The visitors stood and the man immediately thrust out his hand. "How do you do ladies, I'm Tom Leadbetter and this is my wife, Nicole." He spoke with a clipped upper class accent and his smile reached his blue eyes.

Claude continued "Nicole, Tom, this is Lottie and 'er sister Verity. Lottie 'elps me at the café."

Charlotte hoped she didn't look as surprised as she felt; she had no knowledge that Claude's sister and her husband were visiting. "Hello, lovely to meet you," she said, suddenly feeling shy and awkward in front of this sophisticated couple.

"And you Lottie, Verity," Nicole replied in a husky French accent, looking from one sister to the other. She wore a puzzled, or was it a worried, frown for just a moment, before it was replaced with a smile so like Claude's. She had his olive skin colour, deep brown eyes and dark hair which she wore in a stylish bob cut. She was dressed in white Capri pants and a navy and white striped t-shirt, and Charlotte thought she looked very chic. Tom was dressed in cream chinos, a light blue shirt and a navy blazer. The pair looked as if they had just stepped from a luxury yacht.

"Lottie, come. I 'ave prepared moules for us to share. Please 'elp me to serve," said Claude as he moved towards the café.

"Claude, I didn't know your sister was coming. Why didn't you tell me?" Charlotte hissed urgently, as soon as they were inside Le Shack.

"I did not know they were coming. They are only with us for one night and they are staying at the Watersmeet 'otel. They are 'ere to talk about our restaurant in London - they are my business partners. They are not 'appy with me I'm afraid. I am meant to return to London to work for three days every week, but I am insisting that while we 'ave this perfect weather, I must stay at Le Shack. When we 'ave eaten, you and Verity must leave us to talk," and with that he hurried out of the café to serve moules mariniere with French bread.

Charlotte was confused as she tried to process what Claude had said. She was furious that he was treating her differently in front of the visitors; more like the hired help than his lover. And what was it he said about returning to London each week? She was sure he'd told her his arrangement was to run the café all summer and return to Le Papillon at the end of the season. She didn't have time to think it through now, so pasted a smile on her face and joined the party around the table.

Claude and Nicole spoke in French for most of the meal, too quickly for Charlotte to pick out any words that she could understand, and she felt excluded. But Tom was a true English gentleman and made easy small talk, mostly about the exceptional weather that continued to break records across the country. "You must excuse them," he said, nodding towards Claude and Nicole, "they're always like this when they get together. Can't understand a word so just leave them to it."

Charlotte sneaked a look at Claude and Nicole whenever she could, and felt a tense undercurrent between them, their voices often raised and both gesticulating vigorously as they spoke, lighting up one cigarette after another. Verity seemed unaware of anything untoward and was captivated by the evening: the charming beach café, these sophisticated French people, eating moules with her fingers and mopping up the garlicky juices with crusty bread, the chilled dry Sancerre wine (so different from the sweet Libfraumilch with which she was familiar); she soaked up the experience that brought a little bit of France to a north Devon beach.

Eventually, Claude asked Charlotte to leave. "Lottie, Verity, would you please excuse us, we 'ave to talk of business now. Lottie, please take the dishes to Le Shack and then you can go. Merci."

Around the table, everyone noticed Charlotte's expression; she couldn't hide her anger at the way Claude had spoken to her.

Nicole came to the rescue. "No Lottie, you must not clear up after us. We will see to everything. It 'as been enchanting to meet you both. I 'ope we will meet again."

Tom stood up and shook their hands again. "Good evening ladies, it's been a pleasure."

Claude came around behind Charlotte and started shepherding her up the steps as he carried the empty moules pot back to the café. He whispered in her ear, "I will see you later Lottie, but first I must face the music, as you English say. I am not in favour with Nicole and Tom." Charlotte looked daggers at Claude, but he winked back at her and grinned. She tried to be angry; he was playing with her emotions, treating her like the hired hand one minute and a lover the next, but as usual his smiled melted her heart.

Verity came and grabbed Charlotte's arm and started pulling her up the steps. "Come on big sis," she said and started giggling. She had had too much wine and was more than a little unsteady on her feet. Charlotte took her arm and helped her the rest of the way off the beach. She was still smarting when they arrived at the Sea House, but there was no point in discussing the evening with Verity, who was swaying about and giggling at everything she said. "Come on you, time for bed."

***

Charlotte was aware of Claude coming to bed sometime in the early hours and although she was determined to be angry with him, when he started touching her, the evening was forgotten and she was lost in their lovemaking. Later, as she drifted off to sleep with a smile on her face, she decided there would be time to find out about Claude's family disputes tomorrow. However, she wasn't smiling the next morning when she was leaning over the toilet bowl being violently sick. "It must've been a dodgy mussel," she said, when she came downstairs to find Verity having croissants and coffee for breakfast. Claude had already left for Ilfracombe to get the best of the catch landed that morning. "Good grief, I feel rough. Even the smell of the coffee makes we want to gag."

"Will you be OK for our walk today?" said Verity. She was looking forward to their planned trek out to Morte Point and beyond, and seemed none the worse for wear herself, after her over-indulgence the night before. "I really want to do some sketches and take some photos for a painting." Verity's art was becoming locally renowned in north Cornwall, where she exhibited and sold her work in a small gallery in Tintagel. She was excited at the opportunity of adding some north Devon scenes to her collection.

"I'll be fine, the fresh air will do me good. Though I'm not sure how fresh it'll be, it's so hot."

They packed up a picnic of French bread and cheese and a punnet of strawberries, and took a large bottle of orange squash. Verity collected her camera, a sketch book and some pencils and they set off. They walked out to the point, stopping here and there while Verity made rough sketches and took photos of the craggy rock formations, deep gulleys and coves along the way. Progress was slow but Charlotte was happy to lie and wait for Verity on the grassy slopes, now parched and brown. She was still feeling tired and a little weak after her earlier sickness and was relieved to have a break from working flat out every day at Le Shack.

Eventually, they descended to Rockham Bay where they flopped down amongst the rocks. They looked out across the iridescent sea, sparkling like diamonds, as they ate their picnic.

"Are you feeling OK now Charlotte? You're not going to throw up your lunch, are you?"

"No, I feel fine now. Don't tell Claude I was sick though, will you?"

"Why not? I should think he'd want to know if there was a dubious mussel in the batch he cooked up yesterday."

"It happens occasionally, and I don't want to worry him."

Despite their lovemaking last night Charlotte was still feeling peeved at Claude's attitude towards her the previous evening, and she didn't want to give him a reason for avoiding the issue of his family, when she spoke to him later.

"OK, whatever you say. He is lovely Charlotte; I can see what you see in him. He's so charming and well, French. And gorgeous to look at. I still feel so sorry for Johnny though, have you heard from him?"

Charlotte's heart sank. This was the conversation she was most dreading. "No, not since our last meeting when I finished with him. He said he would never come back to this place, gave me this little pendant and left."

Verity peered at the carved wooden butterfly. "It's fab, he's so talented. Poor Johnny, he really loved you, you know. I dread bumping into him in Boscastle."

"I know he did, and in many ways I still love him, but Claude moves me so, Verity, I've never known anything like it."

"Are you sure it's not just lust?" Verity said with a wicked smile.

"Well, a bit of that as well," replied Charlotte grinning, "but we make a great team at Le Shack. It's such a lovely lifestyle, so unconventional, so bohemian, I love it."

"You always were a hippy at heart. So what about dad? What and when are you going to tell him? You did promise you would."

91

"Oh Verity, I don't know. I think it would be best if I come home and tell him, at the end of the summer maybe?"

Verity scooped up a handful of sand, and let it trickle through her fingers. "Look, why don't you write to him? Give me a letter to take back, telling him as much or as little as you like and when you're planning to come home for a visit. See what happens. To be honest, if he thinks you've gone even further off the rails, he probably won't want you home anyway!"

"Oh would you? Take a letter back for me?" Charlotte immediately saw this as a way of not having to face her father yet. She could play things down in a letter, maybe not even mention Claude, say she was sharing a house with a friend; build up the beach café job and how busy she was and that she wouldn't be able to get away until the end of the season, and would then return home for a visit.

"You know I will, and as usual I'll be the one to bring dad down from the ceiling if he goes off on one," Verity said, with a resigned sigh.

"You are the *best* sister!" Charlotte gave Verity a huge hug, relieved that they hadn't fallen out. She was already composing the letter to her father in her head.

*****

Charlotte hadn't told Verity that she'd been sick again, on the day of her departure, and had waved her off with a smile disguising how wretched she felt. After Verity had gone, she climbed the steps to the Sea House and as she closed the door behind her, she leant against it for support, while panic swept over her at the terrifying realisation that she might be pregnant. Her mind raced. She knew she was rather erratic in taking her contraceptive pill and could never quite remember whether, if she missed one, she should take two the next day or not take any more at all, which would bring on a sort of pseudo-period, following which she should wait seven days before starting the next pack of tablets. She had tried both options but wasn't sure if either was correct. She remembered that her last period had been just before she left Cornwall, now nearly eight weeks ago, but she had had a couple of light shows since then, which she assumed meant she was safe.

She felt the panic rise again as she thought the unthinkable. What if she really was pregnant? What would Claude say? Would he still want her? Would he want their child? Oh my life, could it be Johnny's?

Another wave of nausea overcame Charlotte and she rushed for the kitchen sink; she had no time to get upstairs to the bathroom. Afterwards, she sat in the sitting room, glad for once that it was dark and cool. She usually found it hard to settle in this masculine and foreboding space and had asked Claude why it was furnished with such heavy pieces and why he always kept the curtains drawn. He had explained that the furniture was inherited from his grandparents and was typically French in style. As he had nowhere for it in London, he had brought it to the Sea House. In France, he described, the windows have shutters which are kept closed during the day to keep the houses cool. "As you do not 'ave the shutters 'ere in England, we must use the curtains instead." Charlotte hadn't felt it was her place to criticise the furniture or suggest alternatives to the way the room was appointed, and at this moment she was thankful for the cool space.

She recognised, as she sat there in the shady room, just how insecure she was. There was no sense of permanency in her relationship with Claude and while this brought an added dimension of excitement when she was feeling strong and desirable, now that she was scared and anxious it highlighted her vulnerability. And his behaviour towards her when his sister had arrived, and the realisation that he had commitments in London that he was avoiding, did nothing to help her sense of unease. She knew the first thing she must do was to confirm her pregnancy. She rang the doctor for an appointment. Until she knew the outcome, she would say nothing to Claude. She knew it would be difficult to keep it from him; when she wasn't feeling nauseous or being sick, tiredness threatened to overwhelm her.

When Charlotte arrived at Le Shack Claude was all over her. "Ah, ma Cherie, I 'ave you back to myself again, you are all mine. It is always good to see Nicole and Tom, and Verity is enchanting, but I want only you. I 'ave missed you being 'ere beside me," he said, as he brushed his lips across her mouth, around her neck and across her bare shoulders to the line of her bikini top. "We shall close early tonight, I must make love to you, I cannot wait a moment longer."

Charlotte's arousal at Claude's touch had not diminished and she responded eagerly to his kisses, but she was tense and her mind raced at the dread of her likely pregnancy, and she was annoyed at Claude's indifference to Verity leaving, and his lack of concern for the business in London. Her head spun.

He drew away. "What is it Lottie? You are OK, no?" He had sensed something in her mood that was different.

"I'm fine Claude, just a little tired and feeling rather low now that Verity has gone. And I am worried that you are upsetting your family by not returning to your restaurant in London."

His response was stern. "Please, let me be concerned about London. It is not your business. We cannot let this affect us, you agree? We need everything to be perfect for our clientele 'ere, no?" He stroked Charlotte's face and looked at her intently. She looked away, not daring to let him see the anxiety in her eyes. Why did he not share anything about his other life? Did he only want her as a cute, crowd-pleasing skivvy for the café? Or had the visit from Nicole upset him in a way she didn't understand? So much about Claude was unknown. She had so many questions but didn't want to upset him further until her pregnancy was confirmed.

"Claude, forgive me. I am only concerned because I love you." She pulled him to her and smothered him with kisses as she pressed her body to him and moved against him. In the small hours of the morning, as they lay together, Claude drew on his cigarette and exhaled with a satisfied sigh.

"Forgive me, for earlier. I am so in love with you that I do not want to leave you 'ere and return to London –"

"Ssshh Claude," Charlotte interrupted, as she placed a finger over his lips. "It doesn't matter now." She knew she was stalling for time, was putting off challenging Claude about his London life and their future together, but all she was focussed on for now was finding out if she was carrying his child.

***

A week later Charlotte knew for sure she was pregnant. The doctor had confirmed she was about eight weeks into the pregnancy, which meant she had conceived sometime at the end of May or beginning of June. This couldn't have been worse for Charlotte - it meant the baby could be Claude's or Johnny's. Charlotte was distraught at the news and after leaving the doctor, she walked along the beach to the spot where she and Johnny had lain in the dunes and sobbed with despair. She ran her hands over her stomach and thought of the new life growing inside her. "I'm so sorry little one," she whispered. "You don't deserve this, a mummy who can't tell you who your daddy is, a mummy who is such a baby herself, such a stupid irresponsible girl." She stayed in the dunes until she could bear the heat no longer, and when there were no more tears left to cry, she resolved to pull herself together, to grow up and take responsibility for this tiny new person. She told herself that the baby must be Claude's and that he would be thrilled to know he had created a new life, that he was to become a father. She returned to Le Shack in a better frame of mind. She realised that she was also feeling much better, physically, than she had for weeks; less tired and for the last few days had stopped feeling sick.

***

"Claude, stop, please! You're tickling me," Charlotte squealed, as she pulled her legs away from Claude, who was placing tickly kisses along the base of her bare feet. He started tickling her naked body and she squirmed with delight, shrieking with laughter and groaning with pleasure. "No, no stop please! I want to have a serious conversation with you."

"My love, what 'ave we got to discuss that is serious?" He pushed his lips out and pulled his brows down in a mock pout. "Come my little butterfly, we need to know only love and laughter together."

"And we will because I have something amazing to tell you that will seal our love and laughter forever."

"In that case I am, 'ow do you say, all ears."

"Claude, I'm pregnant, we're going to have a baby." There, she'd said it. She waited for a reaction, watched Claude closely as he digested the news. He pulled himself away from her, the smile disappearing from his lips as a dark frown moved over his face. He sat up and pulled the white bed sheet across his naked waist and legs. Charlotte came and knelt behind him, wrapped her arms around his bare chest. "Claude, say something, please." Silence. "Claude, you're frightening me. Please say something."

Claude seemed to shake himself and suddenly the frown was gone. "Mon Dieu, are you sure? Are you completely sure?"

Charlotte's heart sank. This wasn't the reaction she had imagined.

"Yes, of course I'm sure Claude. The doctor has confirmed it."

"And you didn't think to tell me before you saw the doctor?"

"I wanted to be absolutely sure before I told you." Another silence. Charlotte had no idea what Claude was thinking. She waited, her heart beating fast in her chest.

Suddenly he stood up and the sheet slipped away. He lifted her to him, and she tentatively put her arms around his neck and wrapped her legs around his waist. "You are a clever girl Lottie, this is indeed amazing news."

Chapter 9

Sophie – 2015

"Oh my days, I'm nervous," I said out loud, as I took one last look in the rear-view mirror to check my hair and make-up. "For goodness' sake, calm down girl, this is ridiculous." I was so excited about the big date with Nick, and now that I'd arrived in Bristol my guts were in knots. What would the weekend bring? I knew things would be different this time; on neutral ground, no other distractions, not even Smudge who had been safely delivered into Hannah's eager care. We met in the hotel lobby and it was like I was on a first date.

"Are you as nervous as me?" Nick said, as he greeted me with a kiss on each cheek. "Come on, let's take your bag up to the room and then we'll go and get some lunch." I relaxed immediately in Nick's company and laughed that he was as anxious as I was.

"I know, I feel like a teenager. Crazy isn't in?"

As we went into the room, Nick seemed slightly embarrassed. "Look Soph, I've got a family room, you know, so there are two beds….."

I placed a finger on his lips "It's OK Nick, let's just see what happens shall we? We'll probably get completely smashed and end up in a heap on the floor. Then we'll wake up tomorrow morning and realise what an opportunity we missed!"

"Aha Soph, you know me so well. Come on, I'm starving and after lunch I want to show you the sights of this lovely city."

We had a perfect day. It was surprisingly refreshing to be away from home, to have a break with no responsibilities for a couple of days. We ate lunch in a place that served up the most amazing American style burgers, took the river taxi to the SS Great Britain, wandered along the waterfront and then settled into a pub in King Street, reputed to be one of the oldest in the city, to while away the time before going to see Will's band, Benbecula, in concert. Nick told me about his recent radio recording and that he'd been successful in getting the part of Macduff in Macbeth. "The good news is I've got the part; the bad news is I'll be away for at least six weeks touring in Scotland."

"That's great Nick. That you've got the part I mean, not that you'll be away. How will I cope? When do you go?"

"Rehearsals start next week in town, for four weeks, then we take off for bonny Scotland. We're doing the highlands and islands. It'll be quite a grand tour – the Isle of Skye, Harris and Lewis and other wee islands, ending on the Isle of Arran. It's not confirmed yet but something like that anyway."

"Sounds lovely. I've never been north of the border."

"Well why don't you come? You could join me at the end of the tour on Arran and we could have a short break there. I'll be ready for some R&R by then."

"Mmm sounds perfect. Why not? Let's make a plan when you know your itinerary."

The concert was even better than I was expecting. Benbecula was a folk-rock band with an assorted line up of instruments, of which each band member played at least two. Will played fiddle and bass guitar, while others in the group played accordion, concertina, banjo, beatbox and harmonica. The sound was electric and there was plenty of polkaing in the aisles. We joined Will and the other band members for a drink after the gig and were still on a high when we arrived back at the hotel.

"That was fantastic, what a great band," I said, as I flopped into the only comfortable chair in the room. "I'd love to go to one of their ceilidhs. What a buzz."

"Yeah, they're just about the best in my book. Coffee, or something stronger? I've got a bottle of bubbles here." Nick produced a bottle of Prosecco from a coolbag. "Not sure how cold it'll be now but it might beat the complimentary sachet of Nescafe."

"Lovely, yes please," I said, as I heaved myself out of the chair and wandered into the bathroom to fetch the standard issue tooth mugs.

Nick popped the cork and poured us a measure each. I felt my nerves tingle with anticipation as he handed me my glass with a kiss. "Here's to us Sophie, to our weekend." We clunked our plastic glasses together and drank the fizz, neither of us moving apart.

"Cheers, to us," I replied, my voice husky with anticipation, looking straight into Nick's eyes.

We simultaneously put our glasses down and came together. I knew then that this would be the time. We kissed, gently at first, and then with a long-anticipated desire; a need to satisfy the years of waiting for the right moment, for this moment. As clothes were removed, we delighted in what we saw, admiring the treasure that was before us and there for the taking. We fell together on the bed, touching, teasing, gasping and sighing with pure pleasure, coming to the point of no return then holding back, until with unspoken understanding, with perfect rhythm, we reached the summit of our lovemaking. And afterwards Nick brushed me with the gentlest of kisses and said "thank you my love" before lying back and holding me in our totally contented afterglow.

After lying together, each re-living every moment of our first time together, Nick got up and re-filled our glasses. He handed me mine and climbed back into bed. "Bloody fantastic, that's what you are Soph. Everything I could have imagined and more. Can we do it again?"

I nearly spurted bubbly all over the bed, as I burst out laughing. "How long do you need Big Boy? Want to go again already?" We roared with laughter, shaking so much we were in danger of losing the fizz over the edge of the tumblers, and I realised just how much I loved Nick. To be at the height of ecstasy one moment and laughing like a couple of hyenas the next; that's how it should be.

After a few hours' sleep we awoke simultaneously in the early hours, already aroused and wanting. This time our lovemaking was slower and less frantic, savouring every touch, every caress and steadily moving as one to a perfect climax.

"Mmm, I could go on all night," said Nick, as we lay together afterwards.

"We nearly have. It's three a.m."

We snuggled up together and were asleep in seconds.

***

It was difficult leaving Nick on Sunday, after a very late breakfast and check out. Things were different, but in a good way. I knew it would be harder now, each time we had to say goodbye, and already I was feeling the pain of separation, knowing we were unlikely to be together until the end of his Scottish tour.

I was in a detached, dreamy state as I arrived back at the Sea House on a beautifully clear afternoon and, having pondered our relationship all the way down the M5, felt calm and serene knowing Nick was the right man for me.

I unloaded my bag and went to collect Smudge from Hannah's care. "Hi Hannah," I said, as Smudge launched himself at me, nearly knocking me over. "Oh my goodness, I hope he hasn't been this crazy for you all weekend. Hi Anna."

"No, he's been great," said Hannah. "I've really loved looking after him and he didn't drive mum and dad mad, did he mum?"

"No, he's been a joy actually and gave us all an excuse to get out walking. Would you like a coffee Sophie, or something stronger, it is after six after all?"

"Mmm, yes please, could do with a pick me up after that drive. A glass of wine would be good if you've got it."

"Here you are, a nicely chilled white," said Anna, as she handed me a glass.

"Would it be OK if I took Smudge out for one last walk?" asked Hannah, as Anna and I settled down in the garden with our drinks.

"Fine by me, save me having to do it later. Thanks Hannah, you're a star. Oh, here we are, I almost forgot, I got you this in Bristol." I had bought a collection of colourful bangles on a market stall as a thank you for Smudge-sitting.

"Oh wow, thanks Sophie, they're lovely. See you later. Come on Smudge, walkies," and they were gone.

"Well?" said Anna, as soon as we were alone. "How did it go?" She gave me a knowing look. I felt myself colouring slightly as a smile spread across my face. I didn't need to say anything. "Oh I'm so glad Sophie, Nick is lovely, so right for you. Was it an amazing weekend? When can we expect wedding bells?"

"Whoa, hold on!" I laughed. "Yes, it was amazing but we're not rushing up the aisle any time soon. Actually, Nick will be away for a while." I told Anna about his success with getting the Scottish play.

"Well, if you do go and join him at the end of the tour, we'd be more than happy to have Smudge again. Oh, by the way, I took her out for a run first thing this morning, Hannah was still in bed, and as we went past the Sea House a woman was just coming out of your gate. Smudge went absolutely mad, jumping up at her as if she were some long lost friend. I think he must have mistaken her for you. Anyway, I asked if I could help, said who I was and apologised for his rather over-zealous behaviour. She seemed a bit flustered so I thought perhaps she didn't like dogs, and at first she said no thanks, but then asked me to give you her phone number which she scribbled on a scrap of paper. I've got it with Smudge's bowls and stuff."

"What was her name?" I asked, thinking maybe Jo had called round, but then I knew her number so that didn't make sense.

"I don't know, she gave me the piece of paper with her number on,

101

said thank you and then she hurried off along the Esplanade. She didn't write her name because I checked. She seemed in a bit of a hurry."

"What did she look like?" I was intrigued, and my imagination was already starting to run wild.

Anna thought for a moment. "She was a good-looking woman, wavy hair going grey and piled up in a loose sort of bun. She was short, petite. Didn't really notice much else."

I told Anna about the woman Nick and I had met out beyond Morte Point, leaving flowers on the cliff for someone called Charlotte, and how I'd thought it could be Verity.

Anna looked puzzled. "I suppose it could've been her. I'm trying to think if there was any resemblance to how I remember Charlotte, but it was all so long ago and I was so young. And why would she be here now, after all these years? I don't know. You'll have to give her a ring and find out."

"Yes, I rather think I will."

***

It was the middle of the following week before I sat down with the phone to ring the mystery woman. I'd kept putting it off, partly because I'd been busier than expected and partly because I wasn't quite sure about making the call. If it wasn't Verity, I knew I'd be disappointed, and if it was, I didn't know where it might lead.

I'd spent hours on the phone to Nick most evenings and almost as long skyping my parents, while they were at a static step of their world tour in Australia. I'd also been working flat out - four days on the trot for Devon Dwellings. Jo was so taken with my design boards that she'd bandied them about several potential clients, and then asked me to do some variations on my initial themes. "I wish I'd had your design expertise when we first started out. We really had no idea then; it was just a matter of doing what we thought looked all right and hoping for the best. It's so much more sophisticated now." I was surprised to learn that Jo was a farmer's wife. She and her husband had taken on a farm on the edge of Exmoor, on the Devon and Somerset border, in the '90s. They'd suffered badly in the Foot and Mouth epidemic in 2001, just as they were getting established, and had decided to convert two of their barns into holiday cottages to boost their income. Before long Jo had found herself advising others how to do the same and from there, Devon Dwellings was born. Over a decade later, the business specialised in top of the range rural and coastal holiday retreats across north Devon.

At the weekend I'd carried on with decorating the house, walked Smudge on the headland and even spent time sitting on the beach with a book. The little café on Barricane beach was open for the first time in the season so Anna, Mark and I, armed with our own beers, went for a curry, freshly cooked and served to us at a picnic table on the terrace above the beach. This early in the season, it only opened occasionally, if the weather was favourable at the weekends, and it would be some weeks before it opened daily. I felt rather smug at having swapped the city life for this little piece of heaven – an altogether alternative dining experience on a North Devon beach – and considered that Le Shack must have offered much the same uniqueness back in 1976. It's been said that North Devon is the deathbed of ambition, but I believe it's more a matter of realigning one's ambitions to fit this exceptional part of the country.

"Can't wait to bring Nick here. Hope he gets down before the tour or he'll miss the café this summer. Funny to think this belonged to Claude and Charlotte all those years ago."

"Yes," said Anna. "I can still remember the smell of garlic and those really strong-smelling cigarettes Claude smoked. And eating crêpes covered with sugar. I think I probably only came here a handful of times, but it was so different, so ahead of its time for a place like this; the memories are etched on my mind. Of course, after the tragedy it closed down and was abandoned for ages."

"Shame it's not open all year," I pondered.

"You wouldn't say that if you'd spent a winter here," said Mark, laughing. "No fun sitting here in a force ten gale!"

"No of course not, stupid of me." I still had a lot to learn about the local way of life and how it was so aligned with the seasons.

Wednesday was damp and dreary, and my mood was much the same. I was working at home on a design board that I just couldn't get right. I was trying to complete a coastal theme, but inspiration was lacking and it was going nowhere. I took Smudge for a walk and got soaked, which didn't improve my mood. I knew Nick couldn't ring that evening, which added another dampener to my day. I'd been sitting at my work table for most of the afternoon and felt cold, so decided to light a fire, pour myself a glass of wine and make the phone call that I'd been putting off. Once I was connected, after checking I'd dialled the right number, I didn't really know what to say. "Umm, I'm Sophie Chapman, from Woolacombe. You left your number with my neighbour so I'm returning your call. Can I help you at all?"

There was a slight pause and then, "Oh yes, my goodness, thanks for ringing. I didn't really think you would." Then another pause. "I don't really know where to start. I'm Verity Tremayne."

"I knew it!" I said, before I could stop myself. "You're the woman we saw on the cliff a few weeks ago! Sorry, but do you mind me asking, are you the sister of Lottie Dupont?"

"You mean Charlotte Tremayne, yes I am, but how did you know?" Verity's voice had dropped to a near whisper. "Look, I really can't talk now, it's good of you to have called me but it's not a great time."

I wasn't going to let this opportunity slip away. "Oh OK, would you like to meet up somewhere instead? How about the Red Barn?"

"No, I live in Cornwall, just outside Tintagel. I was only visiting when I left my number."

"Oh, well, could I come to you?" I said, not really knowing how far Tintagel was, but aware it was somewhere in north Cornwall. "I could come this Saturday." I was being a bit pushy but was determined to keep hold of this one real link to Lottie.

"I'm afraid I won't be available this weekend, I've got an exhibition in Tintagel."

"What sort of exhibition?" I asked. So forward!

"I'm an artist."

"Well I'd love to see your work, perhaps I could come along?" What was I saying? I knew nothing about Verity or her work! But it could be worth going to the exhibition to get a chance to talk to her.

I heard a man's voice in the background. "Verity, who's that?"

"Hold on a moment," Verity said to me. "It's just someone ringing about the exhibition, Dad," she called to the voice. Then to me she said, "Yes OK, please do come, it's in the Ocean Gallery on Fore Street, you can't miss it, starts at 10.00am. Thanks for ringing. Goodbye," and she hung up.

I was buzzing when I came off the phone. I could hardly believe it really was Verity, Charlotte's sister. I was so excited I didn't give any thought to why, after going to the trouble of leaving her number at the Sea House, she'd seemed in rather a hurry to get off the phone. Poor woman, losing her sister in such tragic circumstances. And then I thought of Sam and what he'd said about seeing Lottie the day after she'd supposedly disappeared off the cliff. I wondered what Verity would make of that piece of news, or did she know already? Hopefully I would find out the answers at the weekend. I really wanted to talk it through with Nick, but he was at some publicity event for Macbeth. Instead, I unearthed the photo album from amongst papers and design boards and looked at the pictures for the umpteenth time. "Maybe I'm nearer to finding out what really happened to you all those years ago," I said to Lottie's photo. "Maybe your sister will have the answers. Time will tell."

***

"Hi Rob," I said, as I climbed the steps up through the garden. "How's it going?" I hadn't seen him for a couple of weeks, but his crew had been busy repairing and re-painting the outside of the house, and it was starting to look as if it had been given a facelift, wrinkles and whiskers replaced with a smooth freshly painted render. "I'm glad I've caught you. I wanted to let you know that my gardener, Sam, will be starting soon. He knows I've got work going on but is so keen to get started that I didn't want to put him off. He's um, a gentle soul, so just thought I'd mention he'll be around so you can let your guys know."

"Shouldn't be a problem if he doesn't mind dodging around the scaffolding. Soon be done, probably about one more week, weather permitting, just got the fascia boards and the balcony to do. Then we can talk about getting the kitchen roof done if you like."

"Great, have you got time for a coffee now? I've had a few more thoughts about the kitchen which I'd like to run past you."

"Yes OK. I'll just have a word with the lads and then I'll come in."

"There you go," I said, as I handed Rob a coffee, and then his mobile rang.

"Sorry, I'd better take this in case it's a client. Hello? Oh, hi dad." Rob's face dropped as he got up and walked through the back door so he could take the call out of earshot. I couldn't catch the conversation, but Rob's voice was getting louder and when he'd hung up, I heard him say to one of his lads, "Bloody hell, what is it with the old man and this place? Now he won't deliver the timbers for the kitchen roof. Darren's off so he can't do it. Suppose I'll have to do it myself."

He came back into the kitchen. "Everything all right?" I asked brightly.

"Yes, just my old man being a grumpy old git. He's always had a thing about the village and not coming here, but he seems to be taking it as a personal insult that I'm working at the Sea House."

"Strange. D'you know why?"

Rob looked down for a moment before saying, "No not really. Anyway, let's talk about your plan for the kitchen."

We discussed the possibility of them doing the most disruptive work while I was away in Scotland, to minimize disruption for me and to give them a free run at the place without me and Smudge getting under their feet. I said I'd let Rob know as soon as I had definite dates and as I watched him go, I had that niggling feeling again that I'd seen him somewhere before.

After seeing Rob off, I wandered over to the old summerhouse. I'd barely glanced inside it since my arrival and decided it was time to give it the once over. I pulled open the doors, which were wooden and warped at the base, with diamond shaped leaded light windows atop. Amazingly, the rusted hooks and catches were still in place and intact so, with a bit of a shove and a kick, I was able to throw the doors wide and secure them against the exterior walls. I stepped into the cobwebby interior and a dank smell of earth and compost, so evocative of garden sheds, rose to tickle my nose. All at once I was transported back to childhood days, pottering along with my grandfather in his shed and garden. I found a muddle of collapsed deckchairs, the canvass faded and worn; and a folding card table, the wooden legs stippled with mildew, the baize mottled with damp, stacked in one corner, and I imagined Charlotte sunning herself in the garden in the once brightly coloured seats. Along one wall stood a tall cupboard which, I found on closer inspection, contained a tangle of antiquated gardening tools propped against the back wall. A vintage lawnmower stood in front of the tools, and I decided this was a job for Sam. I would ask him to sort through everything in here and decide what might be worth keeping. Only then would I decide how I wanted to restore this splendid old garden room. I had plenty of other projects to keep me busy for now. As I turned to leave, I saw something metallic poking out from under the jumble of broken garden furniture. I delved into the moulding pile and heaved out a weather vane in the shape of a mermaid. She was an exquisite wrought iron creature whom, I presumed, had graced the top of the summer house. I dusted her down and knew I had to get her restored and returned to her rightful place.

***

"Guess where I'm going tomorrow? You won't be able to, so I'll tell you. I'm going to meet Verity, you know, Charlotte's sister." The words tumbled out in my excitement to tell Nick about the phone call to Verity and my plan to visit Tintagel.

"My goodness Soph, how come? Your sleuthing is paying off. 'Mystery of the Sea House solved by local super-sleuth Sophie Chapman.' I can see the headlines now."

"Don't be daft, Nick. She found me, remember. I still don't know why she called at the house but hopefully that's one of the things I'll find out tomorrow. Shame you can't come too, I could do with some moral support, I feel a bit nervous to be honest."

"Yeah but she probably does too, and if you turned up with me in tow she might feel outnumbered and run a mile. No way I can get down anyway; rehearsals are non-stop and the director is no respecter of weekends. Blimey I miss you Soph. Keep dreaming of our amazing night together and wondering when we'll get another. How about you come up to town and we'll sneak in a night of unbridled passion together?"

"Mmm, that would be nice," I said, as I felt myself stirring at the sound of Nick's voice and memories of our love making. "I'm getting turned on just thinking about it."

"Me too gorgeous girl. Think we'll just have to save ourselves for a week of rumpy-pumpy amongst the heather, and for now I'll go and take a cold shower."

I was to join Nick on the Isle of Arran off the South West coast of Scotland at the end of his tour, and spend a few days together exploring the island. It was known as 'Scotland in miniature' and was reputed to contain similar features to the whole of the country, condensed into the small island. As I'd never been to Scotland it seemed an ideal place to start. I was longing for Nick now, for his company and his body, and had to keep myself busy to avoid slipping into the doldrums.

***

I set off for Cornwall with a sense of anticipation and a fair amount of unease. I had played the conversation with Verity over in my head, a thousand times. It was an exhilarating drive along the Atlantic Highway. The hedgerows were at their most colourful: the vivid green of beech leaf, freshly unfurled in the Spring sunshine and vibrant in the brilliant light; Devon banks scattered with yellow Primroses, the pinks and blues of Campion and Bluebell, and sprinkled with the delicate white flowers of Greater Stitchwort. In the gardens, as I sped by, Rhododendron and Azalea caught my eye, almost luminous in their intensity as they broke from bud into full flower. Every now and then I caught a glimpse of the sea, sparkling in the distance.

I found the gallery easily, set amongst various gift and tea shops in the centre of Tintagel, most of which boasted a tenuous link to King Arthur. I entered the gallery and was immediately taken by the diversity of the art on display. From vibrant acrylics to subdued water colours; rough pencil sketches to detailed, almost architectural, drawings - it was all there. Several local artists were exhibiting, and I found Verity's offerings towards the back of the gallery. I liked her paintings at once, especially those of harbours and fishing boats, but one that really stood out was a head and shoulders portrait of a girl that had to be Charlotte, painted, I would guess, at about the time of the later photos in the album. It was a watercolour that portrayed a delicate beauty, but also captured a vitality in the eyes and smile. I was intrigued by a tiny, but perfectly shaped, butterfly mark on one of her cheeks. I hadn't noticed it in the photos.

109

I sensed someone behind me and turned around to find Verity staring at the painting over my shoulder. I vaguely recognised her from our brief meeting on the cliffs in the pouring rain, and now that she wasn't wrapped up against the awful weather, I saw before me an attractive woman in, I guessed, her late 50s. Her shoulder length, wavy, greying hair was tied back in a casual way and kept in place with a pretty scarf. She was dressed in a loose-fitting blouse over smart straight legged jeans and I could see she had a lovely figure. She wore little make up and her naturally healthy complexion suggested she spent plenty of time outdoors. We simultaneously reached out to shake hands and when she smiled, it reached her gentle brown eyes.

"Hi, I'm Sophie," I said.

"Hi Sophie, good to meet you. I'm Verity."

Chapter 10

Charlotte - 1976

The summer drew on and a scorching August followed a sweltering July. The country was in the grip of a record-breaking heatwave and the government had appointed a Minister for Drought. Signs warning 'You are now entering a drought area' were erected and slogans told people to 'Save water, bath with a friend'. Standpipes were set up in towns and villages across Devon and Charlotte worried how they would keep a sufficient supply for Le Shack. "Ah, laissez-les boire du vin," was Claude's response - let them drink wine instead. The heat was so intense, the air itself seemed to simmer. Shimmering mirages could be seen hovering above baking hot pavements. The beaches were packed with holiday makers, basking in the blazing sun or sheltering under parasols, and the golden sands were hot to the touch in the blistering heat.

With the new life growing inside her, Charlotte felt an unexpected confidence and sense of calm. The morning sickness of a few weeks ago had passed and with it, the mood swings and crippling anxiety. Despite the soaring temperatures, her energy was returning, and she looked radiant, her hair shining and her skin glowing. "This is what we call blooming," she explained to Claude.

"Blooming? Ah, like a flower. S'épanouir comme une fleur."

"Oh Claude, why does everything sound so much more romantic in French?" Charlotte sighed, as she wrapped her arms around him.

But it was Claude whose emotions were now in turmoil. The carefree charming Frenchman was less carefree, less charming, and plunged into black moods in an instant, sullen and brooding, or flew into a rage at the slightest thing. At first, Charlotte was frightened by Claude's temper but her indignation at his unjustified behaviour soon overtook her fear, so she stood her ground and gave as good as she got. Some of the shouting matches that ensued were epic, but each one left Charlotte feeling stronger and Claude in no doubt that she possessed a spirit to be reckoned with.

When Claude's sister, Nicole, telephoned, which she did with increasing frequency, conversations between her and Claude were heated, leaving him distressed and uneasy. He would pace up and down the hall muttering to himself or leave the house, slamming the door behind him, to sit outside Le Shack, smoking his beloved Gauloises. Charlotte had rarely spoken to Nicole herself; Claude was always quick to answer the 'phone, but when she did, Nicole was polite but cool and immediately asked to speak with Claude. Charlotte wondered if Nicole thought of her as the hired help with extra on the side, and if this was what the disagreements were about. After one particularly stormy row with Nicole, Claude stormed off as usual, but this time Charlotte followed him. When she found him at Le Shack she sat quietly beside him, as he stared out across a moonlit sea. Eventually he spoke.

"When I found Le Shack, we agreed I would open it only for the weekends, Friday to Sunday, and would return to Le Papillon on a Monday, to work there Tuesday to Thursday. This I did last summer and all was well but this year, this summer, 'as been so incredible and then you arrived in my life and I could not go back. My assistant chef, Francine, is running the restaurant but she is un'appy and wants me to return. I must go, of course, but will not do so until the end of the summer. This is what is upsetting me, Cherie. Francine is very angry, but I can't bear to leave you just yet."

Charlotte's stomach plummeted. She knew, of course she did, that Claude had another restaurant in London that would need his attention, but she had buried her head in the sand and not allowed herself to think beyond the heady days of sunshine and love. Just like Claude, she couldn't bear to think of them being apart. "Claude, we will deal with it when it happens, let's enjoy what's left of the summer." She snuggled into his embrace, started caressing his body and blanked out thoughts of anything beyond the endless summer days.

As the weather continued to sizzle, Claude was flat out at Le Shack, as the visitors came in their hoards to enjoy the sun, sand, sea and his magnificent food. The couple had little time to dwell on what was ahead. Charlotte spent less time there, Claude insisting that she took things easier, and when not working, she spent time in the garden and cleared out the charming hexagonal summer house, which sat to one side of the plot. She found two old directors' chairs and a battered wooden table under an old tarpaulin. Once the dust and dead spiders were swept away, she covered the chairs with brightly coloured rugs and the table with a chequered cloth.

Charlotte was visited regularly by Grace, the local district midwife, who was caring for her during her pregnancy and delivery. She and her husband Reg, and young daughter Anna, lived in a house at the top of the lane that ran steeply uphill beside the Sea House. "I'm so sorry I'm late," said Grace, panting, after running up the steps to the front door. "I had to wait until Reg got home before I could leave Anna. My mother usually has her but she's ill. Anyway, how are you, Charlotte?" After doing the usual baby checks, Grace seemed rushed and flustered, and in a hurry to leave.

"Is everything alright?" asked Charlotte. "You don't seem your usual calm self."

"I'm fine. It's just that I'm not sure what I'm going to do with Anna over the next few weeks while mum's laid up. Reg can't have her every time I'm on duty."

"Can I help at all?" asked Charlotte. "I'd love to look after Anna and I'm sure I could juggle my work at Le Shack to fit. I did a spot of nannying back in Cornwall so you wouldn't need to worry."

"That's kind of you to offer, but I think it may be seen as unprofessional, with me being your midwife." After a moment's thought,

Grace continued. "Oh, what the hell. It would only be the odd day and only for a couple of weeks. Are you sure you don't mind?"

"Of course not, I'd love to have her. And it will give me a change of company."

Anna was an enchanting child, with a sunny nature and infectious giggle. They set up camp in the summer house; fetched a mat for the floor and painted pictures for the walls. When it was too hot inside, they moved the table and chairs to the wooden decking outside and played tea parties with Anna's dolls and teddy bears. She loved to visit Le Shack, where Claude showed her how to make crêpes, which they carried back to the garden to enjoy in the cool shade.

Anna was fascinated by a mermaid weathervane on top of the summer house roof, and Charlotte invented a tale about how she came to be perched there, blown up from the sea in a raging storm and stranded, waiting for her merman hero to rescue her. He was waiting for a wave, big enough to carry him out of the sea and over the cliffs to the summer house. Until then, she waited. Anna was agog at the story, and every time she came would check if the mermaid was still there.

After a couple of weeks Charlotte's babysitting duties were over, and she was filled with a longing to start work on the garden, remembering how Lizzie had transformed the land at Trethevy into a beautiful space. Claude insisted she hire a gardener to help, and she was given the name of a young lad named Sam, who worked with his father. They came together to look at the garden and Charlotte took to Sam immediately. He was a gentle soul of few words and, while his father was protective, she sensed that he would like Sam to become more independent, so she asked if he could take on the project of re-modelling the garden with her. Sam was delighted, and it was agreed that he would start when the weather became cooler. "Tisn't no point doin' nothing now. Ground 'tis baked 'ard like concrete. Us'll wait 'til us've 'ad some rain."

The summer wore on, and Charlotte was increasingly aware that she would soon have to tell Verity and her father about the pregnancy. She was putting it off for as long as possible and had been given a few weeks' grace, while Verity was busy working at a gallery and their father was away at a retreat. She decided she would wait until the end of the season when Claude returned to London. She knew it had to be done but was terrified of their reaction.

And then, over the August bank holiday weekend, the weather broke. Suddenly the heatwave ended with a massive thunderstorm, and the long hot summer started to fade. Claude became increasingly anxious, but at the same time, more affectionate, more demonstrative, seeking Charlotte out for reassurance, as if he was suddenly insecure in their relationship. One evening, as they were closing the café, Claude took Charlotte's hands. "Lottie, I want you to be my wife. I must return to London soon, and I want us to be married before I go."

"What?" replied Charlotte, laughing. She sat on his knee and smothered him with gentle kisses. "Don't be silly. We can't arrange a wedding just like that. There's all sorts of legal stuff to do."

"Then we shall 'ave our own wedding on the beach. We shall 'ave a party at Le Shack." He was laughing now, and returning Charlotte's kisses. "It is a splendid idea, no?"

"It's a wonderful idea Claude, but who are we going to invite? We only know a handful of people."

"Then we shall 'ave our own party. Just the two of us. Our own wedding and our own party. C'est bon, non? You shall 'ave a new dress and I shall wear my tuxedo." They were both giggling at Claude's crazy plan, as he carried her upstairs.

And so, one Monday early in the day before they opened the café, they dressed in their finery - Claude in his white tuxedo and Charlotte in a white Indian cotton dress with a flowing skirt and sleeveless bodiced top, with blue cornflowers woven into her hair. Soon her body would change shape dramatically, but for now she still had her figure and felt beautiful and feminine in her dress, the bodice accentuating the curves of her already swelling breasts. They stood in the shallow waves breaking on the shore and exchanged words of love and promises of being together forever, and Claude placed a silver ring on the third finger of Charlotte's left hand. A small group of café regulars gathered and watched the proceedings with amusement, and someone snapped the happy couple with an instamatic camera. A party atmosphere developed. Le Shack was opened, a cassette recorder was fetched, and people danced on the beach and smooched to the ballads of James Taylor, as the celebrations continued. Claude cooked up a huge pan of chicken and chorizo paella and the smell of smoky spicy meat and garlic wafted across the beach into the late summer breeze. More people joined the party and corks popped as bottles of champagne were passed around and poured into plastic picnic mugs, thermos flask tops and even hastily rinsed out sandcastle buckets, so that everyone could join in a toast to the bride and groom.

It was a perfect day and one that Charlotte felt she would remember forever. She tucked the couple of instant photos away, in the small wooden box with her earrings and bangles, and the little wooden butterfly pendant that Johnny had given her the last time they were together. As she spotted it, she felt a sharp pang in her heart, but quickly brushed it away. She was not going to allow guilt and regret to surface on this idyllic of days.

***

Over the next few weeks there was an almost imperceptible shift in the angle of the sun, the quality of the light, the length of the days, as one of the longest, hottest summers on record was finally coming to an end. Always intuitive to the changing seasons, Charlotte felt, as she usually did at this time of year, a sense of melancholy, as the summer started slipping away.

Phone calls for Claude came almost daily from Nicole, and conversations became more and more heated. Charlotte had little idea what they were talking about, but she heard the name Francine crop up with increasing regularity. She watched as Claude became more and more sullen and moody and then the day came, as Charlotte knew it would, when he announced that Le Shack must close; that it was time for him to return to London. "I must go, I can delay no longer. I will return to you every Sunday - I will drive 'ere as soon as we finish service on Saturday night, then we can spend Sunday and Monday together, but I will 'ave to leave again early on Tuesdays. You must wait for me to join you in bed in the early hours of Sunday," he said, a smile forming on his lips as he imagined climbing in beside Charlotte, waking her gently with kisses and loving her. "You will stay and look after our 'ouse, create a beautiful garden with Sam and keep our baby safely growing inside you."

Charlotte was surprised at how calm she felt; that she could accept Claude's departure so easily. She would miss him dreadfully, miss the buzz and busy-ness of Le Shack, but felt secure now that she was, at least in name, Claude's wife, Lottie Dupont, and was safe at the Sea House where their baby would be born.

And then the day came when the café was cleaned out and closed up. Weather fronts streamed in from the Atlantic, bringing wind and rain and big seas. Such a contrast to the weeks of dry searing heat. As Claude and Charlotte worked together packing up the kitchen paraphernalia, they talked about the wonderful summer they had spent together. "Do you remember when we made love on the floor?" said Charlotte, with a wicked grin.

"Ah oui, 'ow could I forget, and I would do it again if you were not pregnant," Claude responded, as he put down the stack of pots and pans he was holding. He gently pinned Charlotte against the worktop and started kissing her mouth and neck. She pulled away, still grinning.

"Claude, I'm pregnant, not ill. Let's do it again," she said with a giggle. She shut the door against the stiff breeze and laid some beach towels on the floor. Suddenly they were in an embrace more passionate than they had known for many weeks and then they were naked on the floor, Charlotte astride Claude, their bodies moving together in harmony.

***

It wasn't as much of a wrench as Charlotte had feared, when Claude finally left. He went early in the morning and left her in bed with a gentle kiss, promising he would return at the weekend. She got up soon afterwards and wandered around the house, connecting with the place in a way she hadn't when Claude was there. She sat in the front room window and watched as dawn broke over the sea and felt a great sense of peace in the empty house. Even the heavy dark furnishings no longer bothered her, and she started planning how to brighten up the room.

The first week flew by. Claude had left several tasks for Charlotte, to complete shutting up Le Shack for the winter – a few more utensils to be brought up to the house, calls to local trades to remove the large Calor gas cylinders to safe storage, and securely shutter up the shed against the winter weather. Charlotte thrived on being in charge and prided herself on being an equal partner in the business.

She didn't give the other part of Claude's life, the life he led in London, much thought at all and accepted without question the apparent problems with his assistant chef, Francine, and the resulting rows with his sister. She didn't stop to think for a moment why he hadn't asked her to return to London with him.

Claude had asked Charlotte to bank the takings of the last few weeks, but to make sure she kept some cash back for herself. "You must be sure to keep some of the money 'ere for your own use when I am in London, so you are not short," he said. She put £50 in an old stone jar in the kitchen and then, with a slight pang of guilt, tucked away another £100 in the chest where she had carefully stored her wedding dress. 'For a rainy day' she told herself, but thought she would use the money for baby equipment and to pay Sam for work in the garden.

***

It was time to tell Verity and their father about the baby and Charlotte arranged to return to Trethevy for an overnight stay. She was dreading her father's reaction but as luck would have it, when she rang to fix the date, he was away in Penzance on an auditing job. It was due to finish on Friday, but he was staying on to visit his sister in Helston and wouldn't be home until Sunday.

"I was thinking of coming on Friday but must come home on Saturday, to be here when Claude returns from London," Charlotte said, relief mixing with guilt, knowing she could visit without facing her father.

"How convenient," said Verity, with an edge in her voice. "You know, one day Charlotte, you will have to face up to him. You did promise me you would do it in September and, oh look, here we are and you're avoiding him again."

"And I will, but I have some momentous news I want to share with you first. Look, I've got to go now," she said quickly, not wanting to get into it over the phone. "I'll see you on Friday, bye."

"Charlotte there's something –" said Verity, but Charlotte had hung up. "Damn," she muttered, as she replaced the receiver. She had wanted to tell Charlotte that Johnny was coming home at the weekend and they'd arranged to meet for a drink after Verity finished work. She really didn't want to cancel; Johnny was such a good friend and she had promised herself that she would never let him down in the way Charlotte had. Oh well, we'll have to play it by ear, she thought. I'm not going to tiptoe around Charlotte forever.

Charlotte left early on Friday and, after stopping in Barnstaple to do the banking, set off along the North Devon and Cornwall coast

119

road, with the roof down on the Triumph and the wind in her hair. She had plenty of time, knowing that Verity was working all day, and as she passed through Bude and drove down Penally Hill into Boscastle, her heart soared with love for this small corner of Cornwall and memories engulfed her. She drove on to Trethevy and parked the car. She climbed out and took in the view across the fields to the rocky cliffs and headlands – her childhood playground. Her heart was racing as she took the path into St Nectan's Glen and along the wooded river valley. The summer canopy had lost its vibrancy, the leaves a duller green, and some had started curling and drying. Charlotte sighed; the seasons were turning.

As she approached the top of the glen, she ran down the rocky steps to the place where her stone still lay. She grabbed it and held it closely to her chest, as she felt the peace of the place wrap itself around her. She studied the stone and found that the letters of her mother's name were still clearly inscribed. She was alone as she stood beneath the waterfall in the cold clear water and felt her mother's presence once again. "Oh mummy, it's been so long. How could I ever have left this place? But I have found a new life, a new love and now we are having a baby. How I wish you were here to share it with us. You would adore Claude." But as she said his name, all she could think of was Johnny and how much her mother had loved him. 'Like the son I never had,' she used to tease him. Sadness overwhelmed Charlotte and she sat on the rocks and wept for her mother, for her childhood home, for her childhood itself, and for Johnny. And as she sat there, she felt the tiniest flutter inside her.

Eventually, she replaced the stone and meandered, like the river, slowly back through the glen, trying hard to convince herself that the new life she had made with Claude was her future now, a future in a beautiful house in North Devon, with an exquisite French husband and a precious baby growing inside her.

Next, she went to The Mill House, the house that had been her home since she was ten. She felt slightly afraid as she let herself in - supposing her father was there after all? But he wasn't, and she wandered around, waiting to be enveloped in that comforting feeling of coming home, but instead she felt like an intruder, as if she no longer belonged. She stopped in the kitchen beside the big green Aga and imagined the family sitting round the huge pine table in the middle of the room. Still the heart of the house and such a warm place, but Charlotte felt a shiver run down her spine as she stood there with her memories. She recalled the last few weeks living there and the rows between her and her father, and she couldn't bear to stay indoors a moment longer. She walked down to the path that ran along the coast into Tintagel. She would walk into the town and meet Verity at the gallery, and they could return to the house together in her car.

As she clambered down into Rocky Valley she felt like she knew every stone and boulder in the place and later, as she dropped into Bossiney, she was transported back to picnics on the beach, swimming in the sea with their dog Jasper, rock pooling and shrimping with Lizzie while Verity sat sketching, horsing around with Johnny and his brothers. These were the things that made a perfect summer, she thought, and promised the little life inside her that theirs would be just so.

By the time Charlotte had climbed the steep hill into Tintagel she was hot and puffing. She collapsed on a bench that sat on a grassy bank on the edge of the little town to get her breath and cool down. She could see the Copper Kettle, the little tea shop where she had worked earlier in the year – it already seemed like a lifetime ago. Further along the main street she saw the gift shops she knew so well and the Old Post Office, one of Tintagel's famous landmarks. And then, to her surprise and horror, she saw Verity and Johnny on the corner of the street that led to the gallery. They were talking for a moment and then they hugged and kissed, and Johnny walked away. Charlotte's heart raced and she shrank back against the bench, but she needn't have worried about being seen, Johnny walked away in the opposite direction, his head down and shoulders rounded.

Charlotte felt a wave of jealously – was that just a friendly hug or a more meaningful embrace? And what did it matter to her anyway, Johnny wasn't hers any longer. But she was surprised just how much it did matter.

She waited for another few minutes before making her way to the gallery. Verity looked up as she heard the door open. "Charlotte, my gosh, how fab, you're here already," and the sisters hugged one another tightly. "I've missed you so much, it's so good to see you."

"You too. It's so good to be home," said Charlotte and she felt tears welling up again.

"Come on, I'll lock up and we can go and have a drink. Shall we go down to Trebarwith? Where's your car?"

"I left it at home and walked over. You can drive." As they made their way to Verity's car, and along the steep narrow lanes to the pub overlooking Trebarwith Strand, they talked non-stop, desperate to catch up with what had been happening in the weeks since they were last together in North Devon.

Once they were settled in the pub with their drinks, Verity finally asked the question that Charlotte was dreading. "So, what's this momentous news then?"

"Oh Verity, I almost don't know how to tell you. I'm pregnant," she said, and burst into tears. Verity sat open mouthed for a moment, before gathering Charlotte into her arms. "I'm sorry Verity, it's just such a relief to tell you," sobbed Charlotte.

"It's OK, it's OK," said Verity, as she held her sister and rubbed her back. "It's OK." As the sobs subsided, Charlotte told Verity how the sickness that had started when she was staying, continued.

"And we thought it was a dodgy mussel!" said Verity.

"I went to the doctor after a bit, and it was confirmed."

"So how far gone are you?" asked Verity.

Charlotte felt herself colour slightly. "Well, about twelve or thirteen weeks now. The doctor wasn't sure, but it must be because the first time Claude and I, well you know, did anything, was the beginning of June. Anyway, I'm booked in for one of those new scans - they've just started doing them at the hospital in Barnstaple - and then I'll know for sure and I'll actually be able to see the baby inside me. Isn't that amazing?"

"What, you mean you're not sure?" asked Verity.

"Well no, not to the day but it must be about right." Charlotte could sense what Verity was thinking.

"But Charlotte, if you're a week or so out, couldn't it be Johnny's?" Charlotte didn't reply. "Oh no!" continued Verity, "you're not sure, are you? It could be Claude's or Johnny's, couldn't it?" Charlotte started crying again. "Does Claude know?"

Charlotte sniffed away the tears. "Of course he knows. Knows I'm pregnant and is really pleased."

"But I'm guessing he doesn't know he might not be the father?"

"No, of course not. I'm not likely to tell him that, am I? But I'm sure it's Claude's. It must be. Anyway, it's mine, and that's all that matters to me. Claude and I have a great future and now we have a baby on the way too." Charlotte told Verity about how she had taken Claude's name, about their 'wedding' on the beach, and that now she would be known as Lottie Dupont. She sniffed again and stuck out her chin defiantly.

As Charlotte calmed down, having at last shared the news with her sister, Verity's mind was spinning, trying to take it all in. What would happen if the baby wasn't Claude's? What sort of a future would Charlotte and the baby have then? And what on earth was their father going to say? How were they even going to tell him?

"I'm going to leave him a letter," Charlotte said, when Verity asked the question. "I'll stay tonight and go back to the Sea House tomorrow, leaving him a note. I'm sorry Verity but I can't face him, not when I know how he'll react. And please don't tell me off. I know I've already burnt my bridges where dad is concerned. Maybe one day, when the baby is born and he sees that I am a happily married woman with a child, he may see things from my point of view. But now I just couldn't cope with more anger and rejection from him." A tear trickled down Charlotte's cheek.

Verity could see just how vulnerable Charlotte was, so didn't argue. She knew, once again, she would be the one to console and comfort their father and she feared that this would ruin any chance of a reconciliation between him and Charlotte. She sighed heavily, and the two girls gazed out of the window over the rocks, as the early evening sun cast a golden glow across the sea, both lost in their own thoughts.

"So, have you seen Johnny?" Charlotte asked eventually, not letting on that she had seen him and Verity hugging earlier.

"Yes, he's down this weekend as a matter of fact. We were due to go for a drink tonight but I put him off, he didn't want to see you Charlotte."

"I can understand that, I know I must have let him down." A wave of sadness came over her as she thought about the good times with Johnny, here in North Cornwall. "Do you see much of him?" She knew she was fishing for information, fearing that he might have turned to Verity after losing her.

"Let him down? That's an understatement! You broke his heart Charlotte, and it's still broken. Yes, we usually go out when he comes down but all he ever talks about is you." Verity's tone was steely, and she gave her sister a hard look.

Charlotte felt a strange mix of jealousy and relief. Jealousy that Johnny should spend time with Verity but relief that he still carried a torch for her. She knew both feelings were unjustified after the way she'd treated him, but she couldn't shake them off.

The rest of the evening with Verity was strained and the natural chatter between sisters was replaced with an awkwardness, as both struggled to find anything to say to one another. Eventually, after a half-hearted attempt at a bar meal of chicken in the basket, they drove home to The Mill House in silence.

"Look Charlotte," Verity said, as they sat across from one another at the kitchen table, "I don't want things to be bad between us. I'm so shocked to hear about the baby and I don't like the way you're planning to tell dad, but I want you to know that I'm here for you, whatever happens. I'm so worried about how you'll cope up there in North Devon with no family around. If only mummy was alive, she'd know what to do, how to support you. I'm scared for you Charlotte." The girls held hands across the table and cried silent tears.

"I'll be OK Verity, honestly I will," she said, but fear gripped her heart.

Charlotte left the next morning, after a restless night in her childhood bedroom. She was dismayed that she hadn't felt a sense of security and belonging at being home. Instead, she was weighed down with hopelessness and knew she had to leave this part of her life behind for good and concentrate on building her future with Claude. She only hoped the bond with Verity wasn't broken beyond repair; they'd always been so close, especially after their mother died, but everything was strained and difficult now, and as Verity had started a Foundation course at Falmouth School of Art, Charlotte knew it would be weeks before she would see her again.

She left a note for her father, pre-empting his anger and disappointment by saying she didn't expect anything from him but hoped they might be reconciled one day. She felt devoid of feeling towards him, as if she were writing to a stranger.

Charlotte had wanted to visit her mother's shrine in the glen once more before leaving, but it was raining hard, so she left Trethevy with a heart as heavy as the miserable weather.

Chapter 11

Sophie – 2015

"It's good to sit down for a while. Thanks for the coffee, Sophie." Verity and I were sitting in The Copper Kettle, a touristy tea shop, while she took a break from the exhibition. "I've got about half an hour before I need to get back." Verity paused and looked at her watch for a moment before continuing. "So, you probably want to know why I called at the Sea House and left my number?"

I was intrigued, on the edge of my seat and desperate to dive in with all the questions buzzing round in my head. Instead, I said as calmly as I could, "Well I'm guessing it has something to do with your sister Charlotte?"

"Where do I start?" said Verity with a heavy sigh. "Have you by any chance come across an old photo album in the house?"

I kicked myself for not bringing the album with me. "Yes, I found it when I moved in. Did it belong to Charlotte?"

Verity looked slightly embarrassed. "No, it's mine. I put it together years ago and then on some stupid impulse, left it at the house. Oh Lordy, this won't be making any sense, let me re-wind a bit."

I could see Verity was struggling and tried not to fidget while she gathered her thoughts. "Some months after Charlotte disappeared, you know about that I suppose?" I nodded, determined not to interrupt now Verity had started. "Well, sometime later, when all the hue and cry had died down and it was presumed she had drowned, I went to the house to collect her belongings. It had been shut up after the events of Charlotte's disappearance and I believe Claude Dupont never returned to live there, but I was given access by the police, solicitors and such, so that Charlotte's things could be returned to

126

her family. There wasn't all that much, some of her clothes and painting gear, and I brought it back to Trethevy - that's where I live, just along the coast - and some years later, put a few of her old photos in an album. Before I got rid of her clothes, I took little pieces from the outfits she was wearing in the photos and tucked them in beside the pictures. I knew I couldn't keep the clothes but wanted something tangible, something more than just the fading images, to remember her by." She stopped for a moment and looked steadily at me, as if to be sure I was grasping what she was saying. I gave an encouraging nod and she continued. "Years ago, I made a promise to myself that I would visit Morte Point once a year and lay flowers on the cliffs."

I couldn't help myself. "Yes!" I interrupted, "I saw you there the other week. It was my crazy dog that came and jumped all over you. But what brought you back later to leave your phone number?"

"Of course!" replied Verity, recognition dawning. "I thought you looked vaguely familiar, though we looked like a couple of drowned rats that day! What a coincidence that it should be you living in the Sea House." She paused for a moment, then, "Let me continue - when I was there last year I saw that the house was for sale. On impulse I arranged for a viewing and took the album with me and left it there. I don't know why really. Maybe it was to return a part of Charlotte to the place where she had been so happy in that summer of '76. Or maybe I was hoping it would be found and questions asked. You see, I never believed, and still don't, that Charlotte drowned. Anyway, this year, I noticed the house had sold, so knocked at the door, but no one was in. To be honest, I'd regretted leaving the album and hoped I may be able to get it back, so I left my number with your neighbour. And here we are."

I was about to launch in with the first of the questions I was itching to ask, when her mobile rang. "Sorry, I'll have to get this, it's the gallery." She got up and popped outside to take the call. "Sorry," she said again when she returned, "they want me back at the gallery now. Some American art dealers have arrived earlier than expected." She started collecting up her bag.

"Can I just ask you one thing before you go? What happened to the baby?" As soon as I'd uttered the words, I could feel myself colouring. How insensitive was that? She must think I'm such a busy body!

Puzzlement, then surprise passed across Verity's face and I thought I may have blown it. But after a moment's pause, she answered. "You know about Bobby? Of course you do, he was in one of the photos. He was with me when Charlotte disappeared." She gave a sort of half smile, a distant look in her eyes. "It was a horrendous time, but Bobby was such a blessing out of something so awful. Look I'm so sorry we haven't had longer to talk. Why don't you come back with me to the gallery, have a look round and when I've finished smooth talking the Americans, we can arrange another meeting?"

"Great!" I said, as I followed her out of the tea shop and back through the town. The place was buzzing when we arrived, and Verity was quickly swallowed up in the crowd. I wandered around the little gallery again, but this time paid more attention to the works of art and found not only paintings, but also sculptures, pottery and jewellery. This exhibition was a real showcase of local craft.

Eventually Verity reappeared. "Sorry Sophie. We're far busier than I ever imagined we would be. I won't be able to give you any more time today. Come into my office and I'll give you a card with my contact details and we can arrange another time to talk, if you want to, that is?"

"Definitely," I replied. "I'm so interested in Charlotte's story. But I don't want you to think I'm butting into something that's none of my business. It's just that when I found the album and started hearing local stories about the Sea House's history, it kind of took hold of me." As I walked into Verity's small office, I was faced with a number of exquisite watercolours and pastels displayed on the wall behind her desk. "Why aren't these in the exhibition?" I exclaimed. "They're lovely."

Verity followed my gaze. "These aren't for sale, I'm afraid. They were all done by Charlotte."

"Charlotte? My goodness, what talent. Two of you in one family, such accomplished artists!"

"When I found these, I had no idea that Charlotte painted. When we were young, I was taught by our mother who had her own studio attached to the house. Charlotte showed no interest at all and was happier out on the cliffs or at the beach, swimming and surfing with friends. She was far more exuberant than me, always on the go, flitting from one thing to another. I think she must have done these while she was pregnant, judging by the autumnal shades and the angle of the light. She spent many weeks alone during her pregnancy. I found them in amongst her possessions when I cleared the house."

I was about to ask why she had been alone during her pregnancy and why Claude hadn't wanted the pictures, all of which were of the area around the Sea House – the garden, the summerhouse, Barricane Beach, and the little wooden café - when someone poked their head into the office and asked for Verity. "Sorry Verity," I said. "I can see how much in demand you are. I'll get out of your hair. It's great to have met you and let me know when we can meet again." I handed her a note with my numbers and email address.

"Thanks Sophie," Verity replied, as she started ushering me back through the gallery to the door. "I'll be in touch very soon."

"Bye and good luck with the rest of the exhibition."

***

A few weeks later Verity was coming to The Sea House. We'd been in touch by email and 'phone and I'd spent many hours thinking about how it must have been for Verity, left with Charlotte's baby at such a young age and losing her sister in such dreadful circumstances. I couldn't begin to imagine how hard it must have been for her. There were so many unanswered questions, but I was wary of moving too fast; I didn't want to jeopardise the trust that was building between us. During one of our recent 'phone conversations I'd mentioned Sam. I was amazed that Verity wasn't aware of Sam but then, as Sam had said, he wasn't questioned at the time of the investigation, so there was no reason she would've known about him. Her shock at hearing what Sam had told me, that he'd seen Charlotte the day after her supposed disappearance, was tempered with caution – she'd had her hopes raised and dashed so many times since Charlotte's disappearance, especially in the early days. "Every time there was some significant item, or sadly, body, washed up around the coast, for months after she disappeared, I was contacted. Each time I was filled with a dreadful expectation that this time I would know for sure, only to be kind of morbidly disappointed time and again when it wasn't her. After a while I became scared to hope and it was easier just to resign myself to never knowing."

Sam had agreed to meet Verity and I'd invited her to stay at the Sea House, but she had only a day to spare for her visit. The American art dealers who attended her exhibition had invited her to present her work in New York. This was a huge career break for her and one she wasn't going to pass up. "I can't believe it's taken until I'm in my fifties. Tintagel to New York, who'd have thought it! What an opportunity!" she said, when she told me about her success. "It all seems to have come at once. An unbelievably successful exhibition at my own gallery and now the chance to show my work in the States. And only a few weeks in between to get everything shipped across the Atlantic."

I'd arranged for us to visit Sam, so Verity could hear first-hand what he'd told me about seeing Charlotte. Sam was a shy man and could be anxious and awkward around people he didn't know, so I hadn't wanted to pressure him into meeting Verity, but with some gentle prompting about how Charlotte might have liked him to meet Verity, he agreed that we could call and see him.

Sam had started work on the Sea House garden as soon as the scaffolding at the front of the house had been removed. He had pruned the Escallonia and Hebe which ran along the top of the garden wall and tamed the Tamarisk that formed the boundary between the side of the garden and the lane that ran up to Anna and Mark's house. The house was beginning to look well cared for now and had lost its air of neglect. Scaffolding had been moved to the back of the house ready for the next phase – the re-design of the kitchen roof. I couldn't wait for this stage to be completed and for the dark kitchen to be transformed into a light and airy space.

Nick was due to be home when Verity visited, having managed to get a weekend off before he left for Scotland, and I was glad that he too would be able to meet her. It was the beginning of June and Woolacombe was having a bit of a breather between the end of half term and the start of the summer holiday madness. After a full-on week, when every parking space was occupied right along the Esplanade, it was as if the little resort was relaxing for a few weeks; weeks when the locals could enjoy the beaches before they were once again taken over by the masses.

Nick was fairly pre-occupied with all things Macbeth when he arrived, but after a good long walk on the beach with Smudge and a pint in the garden in the warm early summer sunshine, he was restored to his usual self and I could sense him relax and unwind. "This place is good for the soul Soph. I love it. Beats London any day. Sam's doing a great job on the garden." He leaned back on the rickety bench and closed his eyes, his face turned to the sun.

I had been fretting that there may be an awkwardness between us after our time together in Bristol, but I needn't have worried. We came together as we always did, only now there was an added contentment between us, and a growing frisson of excitement as we awaited our first night truly together in the Sea House. Nick dumped his bag in my bedroom on his arrival, with no prompting from me, and it was the most natural thing in the world to go up to bed together at the end of the day. Our lovemaking was both passionate and gentle, moving and sensuous and afterwards we fitted together perfectly as Nick spooned in behind me and we fell asleep.

We slept well and were woken by Smudge whining to go out. "I'll go," said Nick. "Tea for the lovely lady?" and I watched with approval, as he slipped his naked body into a pair of boxers before heading downstairs.

"So what time is Verity coming?" he asked, as we supped our tea snuggled up together.

"She said she'd be here about 11.00. We'll have coffee and then pop over to see Sam. Then I thought we could either have some lunch here or go to the Red Barn. I'm not sure how Verity will feel about being in the house."

"Good point," said Nick, taking my mug and putting it next to his on the bedside table. "And talking of good points," he grinned, "I've got one here that it would be a shame to waste," and we tumbled together again and made sweet love once more.

Nick and I were so wrapped up in each other, having been apart for a few weeks and anticipating another spell of enforced separation, that I almost wished Verity wasn't coming to interrupt our precious time together. But when she did arrive, I could see how anxious she was and realised what a huge a step this was for her. My irritation vanished and I felt a sense of protectiveness towards her. After all these years, Verity was possibly going to hear what she'd always believed; that Charlotte hadn't drowned but had chosen to leave her life here, and her precious baby, without telling anyone, not even her sister, what had driven her to it. I couldn't begin to imagine the emotions this must be stirring in Verity. I only hoped Sam's story hadn't changed since the first time we'd met. We were soon to find out.

After introducing Nick and calming Smudge down – he was all over Verity like a rash – we moved into the sitting room and Nick disappeared to make some coffee.

"Are you OK with being in the house? I wasn't sure how you'd feel about it," I said, as Verity's eyes wandered around the room.

"Nor was I," she answered. "To be honest, my mind's been in overdrive since you told me about Sam, and I nearly didn't come. I'm not sure I need all this just before my trip to New York, but then I didn't want to spend the whole trip thinking about it so thought I'd better get it over with before I go." She gave a slightly wobbly smile then looked about some more. "You've made it look lovely. So light and airy and you've got a great artistic flair with the design." Coming from Verity this was a great compliment. "When Charlotte lived here the living rooms were dark and furnished with heavy French furniture, Claude's. Not really Charlotte's taste at all, but she'd have loved this."

Nick returned with the coffee and chatted easily to Verity about art in general and her impending visit to New York. He was so good at putting people at ease and I could see Verity relaxing a little as she talked about her passion for painting, her career so far and her long-awaited big break.

Despite the little I knew of Verity, I was beginning to like her enormously. Although she was nearer my mother's age than mine, there seemed to be an innocence underlying the maturity of her years, as if in the middle of her childhood she'd been forced to grow up very quickly and the child, not yet fully developed, had been lost under the layers of responsibility imposed upon her.

"I think it's time we were going if you're OK Verity," I said, as she finished her coffee.

"Yes of course," she replied, getting to her feet.

"I'll rustle up some lunch while you're out," said Nick, as he started collecting up the coffee cups.

Verity and I drove the short distance to Twitchen in silence. I could sense the tension returning and thought it best to leave her to her own thoughts. As we pulled up outside the cottage Sam shared with his elderly father, Verity looked at me with a worried expression.

"You know this could be huge Sophie. If he tells me that he really saw Charlotte, what then? What on earth do I do next?" I was at a loss to know how to reply, but was saved from having to do so as the cottage door was opened by Sam.

"Hello Sam, how are you?" I said, as we approached the cottage, "This is Verity."

"Hello Sam, it's very good of you to see me."

Sam beckoned us into the little cottage and once inside, Verity and I sat side by side on an old, worn sofa to one side of a large inglenook fireplace, while Sam took his place in an equally shabby armchair on the other.

"How's your dad doing?" I asked to break the ice; Sam was looking embarrassed and awkward.

He looked up at me for a moment before answering. "'im's alright. He's over me auntie Vi's." There was a pause as Sam looked fleetingly at Verity before looking away shyly. "You don't look like 'er," he said quietly.

"No I don't Sam, you're right," she replied gently, "and it was a long time ago that you saw Charlotte, I believe. Can you tell me about the last time you saw her?"

Another pause, as Sam pulled nervously at a loose strand of wool on the cuff of his jumper. "It's like I already told 'er," he said, nodding towards me. "'Twas early morning, proper dimpsey. I saw 'er by 'er torch light; 'twas day after 'er s'posed to be drowned. I knows what day 'twas 'cos next day 'twas 'er birthday and I was going to take 'er some flowers, and 'er were going to make me a cup of tea, with 'er and the baby, but 'er 'ad gone so I couldn't." While he was talking, he continued to worry at the thread and as he finished, he looked at Verity and blushed before looking away.

"How kind Sam, she would've loved flowers. You're absolutely right, she disappeared the day before her birthday."

"I know that," said Sam, "but them what came thought I were stupid so they didn't ask me nothing. And I didn't tell 'em." He stopped for a moment before adding, "I wish 'er didn't go. 'Er were kind." As Sam looked down at his hands again, I noticed Verity wipe away a tear from her eyes.

"Yes, she was kind Sam, and I wish she hadn't gone too. Is there anything else you can tell us?"

Sam shook his head without looking up. "Well thank you, Sam. It's been good to meet you and thank you for telling me what you know."

Verity looked at me and as we were about to make a move, Sam stood up and, wringing his hands together, he said, "There is something," and he pulled a dog-eared, dirty old envelope from his pocket. "'Er sent me this," and he handed the envelope to me. I looked at it for a moment before passing it to Verity. Her hands were shaking as she took it from me.

"What's this?" She removed a folded piece of paper, out of which slipped a small carved wooden butterfly. "Oh my life," said Verity, tears trickling down her face.

"Are you OK?" I asked, feeling panicky, as things seemed to be moving to a different level. Without replying, Verity unfolded the piece of paper and started reading.

Dear Sam.

I am so sorry I wasn't able to have tea with you on my last birthday, but I am sending you this gift on this, my next birthday. I know how you always liked it. C.

"Oh my days," said Verity, as she started examining the envelope. "Look, you can just make out a postmark, it says 1978. Johnny made her the butterfly; she wore it all the time on a leather string around her neck." She started turning the little wooden butterfly over and over in her hands. "Oh Sophie, this proves she didn't drown. Oh Sam, did you not tell the police when this arrived? They could've re-opened the case and started looking for her."

Sam was becoming agitated and was pacing the room while continuing to wring his hands.

"It's OK Sam. Verity isn't cross with you. She's just shocked to see this and what it means," I said, hoping to calm Sam down.

"Oh Sam, I'm sorry," said Verity. "No, I'm not cross, just surprised and upset as Sophie says. Can you tell me what you did when you received this?"

"I didn't do nothing. 'Er sent it to me and 'tis mine. T'in't no one else's."

A thought struck me. "Sam, did you read the letter?"

Sam blushed bright red and looked away, almost as if he was ashamed, and I realised that he probably couldn't read much more than his own name.

"I read the envelope. Got my name on." he said indignantly.

"Yes, you're right Sam," said Verity. "It has got your name on it and it is very much yours, and I'm so glad you kept it all these years. Thank you for showing it to me." She looked wistfully at the carving before placing it back in the envelope with the note, and handing it back to Sam. She wiped away her tears with the back of her hand. Sam took the envelope and stuffed it quickly back in his trouser pocket as if he thought we might try to take it from him. "Sam, we're going now. Thank you for talking to us and showing us the butterfly. It was very kind of you. I hope we haven't upset you by coming," Verity said kindly to Sam.

He shrugged and said, "No," and he seemed calmer now that he had the envelope safely back in his possession, then he turned to me. "I'll be down to do mowing in the week."

I was surprised at the sudden change of subject, but then I saw that Sam's emotions were very much of the moment and he appeared to have moved on already from the drama of a few moments ago. Maybe that was another reason why he hadn't said anything when he'd seen Charlotte leaving in the early hours all those years ago.

He would only have been about sixteen at the time and perhaps he just couldn't understand the implications. One thing was apparent, however, and that was that he had connected with, and remembered, the kindness shown to him by Charlotte. I reflected that he probably hadn't been shown a great deal of it in his life.

Verity and I were both in a state of shock as we drove back to the Sea House. Neither of us spoke and Verity had her head turned away from me, staring out of the window. When I had parked up neither of us moved for a moment, then Verity turned to me and pulled a tissue from her pocket to wipe her damp eyes. "I take it you didn't know about the butterfly?" she asked.

"I had no idea. He didn't mention it when he told me he'd seen Charlotte. I'm sorry it's been so upsetting for you."

"It's OK. You weren't to know. But it changes everything. It's the first proof I have that Charlotte didn't drown. My goodness, it has so many implications. I will have to think very carefully about what I do next; it could affect so many people." It was as if Verity was talking to herself now, engrossed in her own thoughts about Sam's revelations and the possible consequences.

I was feeling more than a little awkward at having brought all this about. Although I was desperate to quiz her more to satisfy my own curiosity – who was Johnny for a start? – I had to bite my tongue and leave her to deal with this in her own way. I hardly knew the woman and it wasn't my place to interfere more than I had already. After a minute or two I suggested we go into the house for some lunch.

"Yes, of course. Sorry Sophie, this is just such a shock. I need some time to process it. Thank you for taking me to meet Sam. I really appreciate it. What a sweet guy he is."

We went into the house and Nick called from the kitchen that he had prepared a prawn and avocado salad for lunch. I showed Verity into the sitting room and went to fetch her a drink of water, and quickly gave Nick the bare bones of our visit to Sam. He took the glass of water from me and went through to Verity. I could hear him

137

talking softly to her. A few moments later they appeared together in the kitchen, and we took our places around the table.

I didn't think for a minute that Verity would feel like eating, and wasn't sure I did, but when Nick fetched freshly baked baguettes from the oven, my mouth started watering and Verity commented how hungry she was. We ate in silence for a while, punctuated with satisfied mouth-filled grunts and comments about how good the lunch was.

"That was delicious, thanks Nick," said Verity, as she finished her meal. "You've got a good one here Sophie, worth holding on to!"

"I have to agree with you there Verity," I replied, smiling at Nick.

"Please ladies, you're making me blush!" said Nick, feigning a dramatic swoon.

Becoming more serious, Verity thanked me again for taking her to meet Sam. "I just can't believe none of this was discovered at the time of Charlotte's disappearance. We can't blame Sam, of course, he wouldn't have known any better, but if only I'd known this forty years ago, I could've tried to find Charlotte. I feel so bad that I didn't try harder to find out what had really happened to her."

"Maybe Verity," Nick said gently, "Charlotte didn't want to be found."

Verity was silent for a moment before replying, "No, you're right. I guess she didn't want to be found or she would've come home. It's just so hard to believe that she would do that to us, to her family, to her baby. Up until now, although I've often had those thoughts, they've always been tempered with the official line that she drowned, but now that I know she didn't, it beggars belief that she could just walk out on us all." Verity sighed. "Although maybe not. After all, that's more or less what she did when she left Cornwall in the first place."

Nick and I didn't comment. I thought about fetching the photo album but didn't feel this was the right moment. Again, Nick gently interjected. "So what do you think you might do now?"

"Oh Lord, I've no idea. One thing I do know though, is that I mustn't do anything rash. Charlotte's been gone for nigh on forty years so a few more weeks pondering what I do next, if anything, can't hurt." Verity gave a wry smile. "That would infuriate Charlotte. She always thought I was too sensible, too cautious. She was so impetuous where I was, still am, far more careful in my approach to everything. I need to think about everyone else this will impact, our father, Johnny, Bobby. And isn't it typical that this trip to the States comes up right now. It's all I need."

I was about to ask who Johnny was when there was a knock at the back door, and Anna arrived.

"Hi!" she said, then stopped. She looked from me to Nick to Verity and picked up on the somewhat melancholy vibe in the room. "Oh, sorry. Didn't realise you had company. I'll call back, it was just about the dog sitting dates when you're in Scotland."

"Don't mind me," said Verity, gracious as ever.

"Anna, this is Verity Tremayne, Charlotte's sister. Verity, Anna. She lives in the house behind us and you left your number with her the other week, when I was away."

Anna's look of surprise was priceless. "Oh goodness, you are Charlotte's sister! Sophie was right. I named one of my dolls after you!"

Chapter 12

Charlotte – 1976

Charlotte awoke, as she did every morning, with a knot in the pit of her stomach. It was November and Claude hadn't been home in six weeks. After leaving for London in September, he had only returned once. She was dismayed when Claude didn't return after his first week away, but he had been so apologetic and sounded so dejected on the 'phone that she forgave him immediately. His husky French accent and words of love had melted her heart in a moment. "Forgive me, Cherie, it is so busy 'ere getting everything 'ship-shape' as you say, but I will return next week and make love to you again, just like in the summer." Early the following Sunday morning, Charlotte woke with a start at the sound of the key turning in the lock, and then Claude was on the bed beside her, brushing her face with the gentlest of kisses. "Lottie, my darling, are you awake? Mon Dieu, it is so good to see you." Charlotte raised herself up and responded eagerly to his kisses, drinking in his masculine scent and the hint of Galouises. Within seconds he was in bed beside her and they came together urgently, their time apart making them hungry for love.

But the weekend wasn't quite the perfect idyll Charlotte had imagined it would be. Although Claude was attentive and caring, their lovemaking sweet and gentle, and they wandered hand in hand along the beach in the early autumn sunshine, discussing names for the baby which had become known as 'Le Bump', Charlotte sensed a deep underlying tension in Claude. There were moments when, unaware she was watching him, his expression was dark and brooding, as he stood at the long windows staring out across the sea. At times he was jumpy, unable to relax and became snappy and impatient. Charlotte had been so excited to show him how she had cheered up his stuffy sitting room with brightly coloured rugs on the floor, throws on the sofas and tie backs on the curtains, but his reaction seemed cool and disinterested. Maybe she had overstepped the mark by changing his masculine space into something more vibrant, but when she asked his opinion about other plans she had, she found his indifference exasperating. Determined not to spoil their time together, she swallowed the angry words of frustration at his disinterest and decided if Claude wasn't bothered to have any input to her plans, she would get on with them anyway. All too soon the weekend was over, and Claude left in the early hours of Tuesday to return to Le Papillon.

***

Over the next few weeks, Charlotte was surprised at how she coped with so much time on her own. It wasn't many months ago she would have hated her own company but now, as she approached the third trimester of her pregnancy, she was content in her own space, building a safe cocoon around her and her precious baby. She walked on the beach every day, whatever the weather. The days were shortening, the sun low in the sky, and in the mornings reflected off Lundy, making the island appear to stand high in the bay. Charlotte loved these days; she wrapped herself up in Claude's old duffle coat that stretched over 'Le Bump' with the toggles straining, put on her wellies and tramped across the sands, lost in her thoughts. She bought herself a sketch book, some pencils and a palette of watercolours and tucked herself in the dunes or in amongst the rocks at Putsborough Sands, to draw and paint the ever-changing sea- and landscapes before her. Painting had always been a pastime Verity and their mother shared together, of which she wasn't a part, but now she found a talent of her own and began to understand the pleasure from putting pencil and brush, to paper. She spent hours in the summer house, which had become something of a studio, refining and finishing her paintings, while listening to an old Bush radio tuned to Radio 1 and the latest hits. On stormy days she lit the paraffin heater and wrapped herself in a big woollen rug, cradling her tummy and listening to the weather howling around her.

In the evenings she cosied down in front of the fire, sometimes watching a bit of television, but more often reading and sketching. One evening, while searching through the drawers of the heavy wooden desk in Claude's study for a pencil sharpener, she came across a large official looking envelope addressed to a Mr and Mrs Leadbetter. For a moment Charlotte was puzzled and then remembered that this was the surname of Tom and Nicole, Claude's sister and her husband. She assumed it must be papers concerning the restaurant and, feeling a little guilty and rather nosey, decided to take a peep. A solicitor's letter, paperclipped to a wad of papers, explained that they were enclosing the deeds of The Sea House, on completion of the purchase. Charlotte glanced at the date on the letter, 28th March 1975, and looked again at the addressees - very clearly Tom and Nicole, not Claude. 'So does this mean he doesn't own the Sea House?' she asked herself, unease starting to gnaw at her insides. Her feeling of security and sense of belonging to the place started to slip away. She studied the documents for a while longer but couldn't make out the legal jargon, so replaced the envelope and its contents in the drawer. Charlotte felt unsettled and uncomfortable for the rest of the evening and decided she would ask Claude about the tenure of the property when he was next home. 'No point in worrying about it now,' she told herself determinedly, while doubt prodded like an accusing finger.

***

As arranged in the summer, Sam started work in the garden at the beginning of autumn. After his initial shyness, he relaxed around Charlotte and they worked companionably together to transform the garden. Sam planted Escallonia and Hebe along the top of the retaining wall which, he said, would grow to form a hedge able to withstand the strong winds from the sea. Charlotte marvelled at his knowledge of plants and his obvious love for the garden. He planted Daffodil and Crocus bulbs under the hedging and little Grape Hyacinth in the bed at the top of the steps. He proudly told Charlotte the names of the plants as he put them in place and although she already knew most of them, learnt from her mother in the garden at Trethevy, she enjoyed seeing Sam's pleasure and pride in his work. When Charlotte needed a break, they drank tea together on the bench set against the house, Sam watching as Charlotte made sketches of the garden, or when a strong wind blew in from the west, retreated to the summer house to shelter from the weather. Sam was a young man of few words but was comfortable in Charlotte's company.

"Ow's baby?" he asked every time he came. "'Im's growing, 'tis bigger this time," he commented as 'Le Bump' grew. One day he noticed the little carved butterfly that Charlotte still wore on a cord around her neck. "'Tis proper, looks like the butterflies what land on the flowers in the summer. Where d'you get it to?"

Charlotte fondled the carving and felt a pang as she thought of when Johnny had given her the pendant. "It was made for me by a very good friend," she replied. Sam stared at the butterfly for a moment longer. "'Tis proper," he said again, as Charlotte felt the baby move inside her.

***

A pattern started to emerge over the coming weeks. Claude called Charlotte on a Wednesday, late afternoon, full of how much he missed her, enquiring how 'Le Bump' was growing and asking what their plans were for the weekend. But these calls were invariably followed by one late on a Friday when Claude said he was unable to come home due to the demands of the restaurant. He was busy introducing 'Nouvelle Cuisine' and hoped to gain a Michelin Star, he said, and couldn't get away. Charlotte felt a mixture of pride at Claude's ambition for Le Papillon and frustration that it seemed to be more important than she was. She started to dread the phone ringing on a Friday night, and plunged into moods of gloom and dejection, but as the weeks went by her despondency turned to anger at his continued absence. Her mood became more defiant, and when Claude called late one Friday in November to say, yet again, that he wouldn't be coming home, Charlotte decided that, if he wouldn't come to her, she would go to London to see him.

Having made the decision, Charlotte's mood lifted, and her excitement grew as she planned to surprise Claude at the restaurant. In her mind, she saw the amazement and joy on his face at her arrival, his wonder at her changing shape, nights of tender lovemaking and afterwards, Claude lighting up a Gauloises and caressing her with words of love in his sensual French accent.

***

Charlotte felt a mixture of dread and anticipation as she boarded the London train in Exeter. She could hardly believe that at twenty, she had never been to the capital and reflected on how sheltered her life in Cornwall had been. As the Intercity 125 sped at an alarming rate towards London, she studied the A-Z she'd bought at the news stand on the platform and found Gambon Street, where Le Papillon was located, right in the heart of the West End. She planned to take a taxi from Paddington to Trafalgar Square and walk from there, arriving during Claude's break between lunch and evening service.

Charlotte disembarked at Paddington with her heart pounding, her senses assaulted by the sights and sounds of the London station. She stood and looked at the masses of people moving with purpose along the platform, not quite knowing what to do next. A few people were meeting and greeting one another, but most were intent on their own mission to get from A to B, with a practised oblivion to everyone around them. She felt inexperienced and naïve, watching the city sophisticates in their tailored suits and chic outfits, striding confidently on their way. She was thankful she'd put her hair up, applied some make up and treated herself to a smart new maternity coat for the trip, but still felt something of a country bumpkin amongst these cosmopolitan people.

As she left the platform and headed out of the station to find a taxi, she realised it wasn't all glamour and smart suits. On the streets around the station were people from every walk of life, in all sorts of attire. An old lady pushed a wobbly shopping bag on wheels in front of her. Her hair was grey, greasy and straggly, her coat worn and dirty and she wore scruffy, threadbare slippers on her feet. No one seemed to notice her as they hurried by. Snippets of the Ralph McTell song ran through Charlotte's mind as she watched the woman shuffle on her way.

Where in North Devon they were still in the soft and floaty world of cheesecloth and flares, here the harsher, more brutal, punk fashions were in full swing. Charlotte tried not to stare as a group of lads passed by with attitude, chains and oversized safety pins dangling from their jeans, faces adorned with piercings and kohl. She found it intimidating and was glad to reach a taxi rank and grab a black cab.

"Trafalgar Square please," she said more confidently than she felt, as she climbed aboard.

"First time in London is it love?" asked the cabbie.

"How did you know?" replied Charlotte, surprised.

"Tell 'em a mile off love, it's that 'rabbit in the 'eadlights' look," he said, but he was smiling kindly and Charlotte relaxed a little.

"I've come to surprise my husband," she said.

"Blimey, some surprise 'e's gonna get!" he said, as he nodded to Charlotte's bump in the rear view mirror.

Charlotte laughed. "Funny," she said, and found herself explaining. "Obviously he knows about the baby, but he hasn't been able to get home to Devon for weeks; he's proprietor and head chef at Le Papillon in the West End, d'you know it? So I thought I'd surprise him and visit before I get too huge to move."

"Le Papillon, in Gambon Street? Yeah, I can take you right there if you like."

"Oh, its OK thanks. I'll walk from Trafalgar Square. I want to see some of the sights while I'm here."

"Tell you what, consider it done love," and he took Charlotte by way of Buckingham Palace, the Houses of Parliament, Big Ben, White-hall and Marble Arch, to the famous square and Nelson's column. She felt like a little girl at Christmas, unwrapping her presents with wonder as she watched all the city's landmarks go by. When they reached their destination, she realised she'd been staring with her mouth wide open in amazement.

"Right love, you wanna 'ead up Charing Cross Road, over there," the Cabbie said, pointing across the square.

"Thank you so much for showing me the sights," said Charlotte, and gave a generous tip.

"Pleasure love, all part of the service," he said, and in a moment he was gone, swallowed up in the traffic, merging with the other black cabs fighting their way around the square and off along the Strand.

Charlotte stood in the square and stared up at Nelson, who appeared smaller than she had imagined, perched high on top of the column. She was amazed at the plethora of nationalities milling around the monument and its fountains, the assortment of languages being spoken. She had never seen such a mix of different peoples and started to feel small, insignificant and rather vulnerable. Before panic threatened to take hold, she headed in the direction the cabbie had pointed and set off along Charing Cross Road towards Shaftes-bury Avenue. As she reached Cambridge Circus, she saw the impos-ing Palace Theatre where the rock opera 'Jesus Christ Superstar' was showing. Words of the Mary Magdalene song 'I don't know how to love him' wafted into her thoughts, and then out again, as she looked at her A-Z to get her bearings. She found her way to West Street and passed St Martin's Theatre, where the great Agatha Christie show 'The Mousetrap' was still running after twenty-four years, making it the longest running show of all time. Jesus Christ Superstar is in its infancy, she thought, as she muddled her way through the maze of streets that make up the West End of London.

And suddenly, she was there, standing on the corner of Gambon Street and she could see a hanging sign with a purple butterfly logo and Le Papillon printed in black, just a short distance along the road. Her heart was in her mouth as she approached the restaurant, and she was about to enter, when a group of people tumbled out full of bonhomie, laughing and talking loudly. Charlotte shrank back, suddenly feeling unsure of herself, and her confidence began to ebb away. She started walking back along the street, away from the revellers. Gambon Street was one of those narrow roads in the West End, with an even narrower way, more of an alley, running behind it and as Charlotte reached the corner, she saw that the back entrance to the restaurant was visible a short way down the alley, which was littered with boxes of rubbish and dustbins. She decided it might be better to surprise Claude in the kitchen rather than embarrass him in the restaurant and started along the narrow lane, when the door to the back entrance opened and two people in chef's whites burst out, laughing and horse-playing together. Charlotte's heart lurched and she was about to call Claude's name, when she saw him grab the other person in a tight embrace and start kissing her ravenously, to which she enthusiastically responded. Charlotte cowered behind an industrial sized dustbin, not quite believing what she was seeing, hating it but not able to look away. The kitchen door opened again and another man emerged and deftly assembled a roll-up. He leaned against the wall and watched as Claude and the woman continued their embrace, still laughing and teasing one another. Smiling, he said, "Bleeding 'ell chef, can't you wait 'til you're upstairs, and in 'er condition too?"

Claude and the woman pulled apart and both said something to the man in French, which Charlotte couldn't catch. They were all laughing now, and Charlotte watched in horror, as Claude took the woman by the hand and led her towards a metal stairway that climbed to a small balcony and door above the restaurant kitchen. As the woman turned, Charlotte saw that she was heavily pregnant, her bump showing clearly under her straining whites. On the balcony Claude leaned over and said in English to roll-up man, "Eh Billy, make sure you get my pots cleaned and gleaming for evening service, comprendre?"

"Yes Boss," replied Billy, saluting to Claude and drawing on his cigarette.

"Francine, attends-moi!" said Claude, as he followed the woman in through the door before it slammed shut behind him.

Charlotte was frozen to the spot. She watched Billy take a last drag before stubbing out his cigarette and returning to the kitchen. She slumped down on the dirty pavement beside the dustbin, her legs giving way beneath her. She had no idea how long she was there, numb with shock, but eventually the emotional dam burst and sobs racked her body. She scrambled to her feet and blindly stumbled away from the alley. She didn't know or care where she was heading, what she looked like, what people thought of her, she just wanted to be anywhere but there. She weaved her way in and out of the busy little streets with no idea where she was going. All she could see was the image of Claude and Francine laughing together, kissing and embracing, and as the tableau played over and over in her mind it became distorted, so that they were laughing at her, mocking her as she hid behind the oversized dustbin in the dirty alley. She was in a living nightmare and stumbled on until she came to the Strand, where the traffic and noise almost overwhelmed her. It was late in the afternoon and the light was fading, as the London rush hour built to its peak. Charlotte felt close to panic, propelled along with the flow of people moving towards Charing Cross station, and she forced herself to concentrate on getting her bearings before she found herself hopelessly lost. And then she saw Trafalgar Square up ahead and relief swept over her. She struggled through the throngs of people, no longer the wandering tourists taking in the sights with snapping cameras, but hundreds of workers purposefully making their way home, with no awareness of a distressed pregnant woman in their midst. Charlotte dodged out of the flow and perched beside one of the huge lions, not caring that her smart new coat was getting crumpled and damp as a cold drizzle started to fall.

Charlotte was almost overcome with panic. She was shaking from shock and cold. It was nearly dark now and the lights, noise and bustle of the city threatened to engulf her. Just as she was about to become overwhelmed by fear, the baby gave an almighty kick. Charlotte automatically put a hand to her swollen belly; her instinct as a mother took over and a fury towards Claude fuelled a determination to protect her baby and get herself and unborn child out of London. With an unexpected resolve, Charlotte hauled herself to her feet and pushed and shoved her way through the crowds until she was on the pavement, hailing cabs with the rest of them, as if she'd been doing it all her life. Eventually she was back at Paddington, sitting in a station café, munching hungrily through a sandwich with a steaming mug of tea. She would not allow herself to think about Claude and Francine; she would have plenty of time to process it when she was home. She drained her tea and boarded the Penzance train. It was packed, but someone offered a seat which she gratefully accepted and within minutes of leaving the station, she had fallen into an exhausted sleep.

****

Back in Woolacombe, the nightmare of London plagued Charlotte's every thought. She raged at Claude for his deceit and treachery. How could she have been so utterly stupid to be taken in by him? She cried for the long hot summer of love, now lost forever;

how reckless and irresponsible she'd been, how vain to think she had won Claude's heart. Why had he even shown an interest in her? Did he love her? Did it mean anything to him? Her head spun with questions which had no answers. Why did he lead her on if he had Francine in London? What was Francine to Claude? Obviously more than just his assistant chef. The not knowing was torture. But worst of all was the shame and mortification she felt at having thrown herself at Claude; the humiliation made her physically recoil. And now she was in an impossible situation, one she could never share with anyone; pregnant by a man who had another woman, another pregnant woman. Her wild thoughts shifted to Johnny and his devotion to her: for the cruel and easy way she had thrown his love away for the charms of a disarming Frenchman; to the pain she had caused her father and the way in which she had used Verity, and a huge burden of guilt settled in her heart.

Charlotte became obsessed by the relationship between Claude and Francine. What was their connection? Were they married? Was Claude the father of her baby? She raged with jealousy at Francine. Why was Claude with her and not here in Devon? How long had they been together? What greater hold did she have over Claude? Charlotte convinced herself that Francine must be better than her in every way: prettier, more sophisticated, smarter and a better lover. She hated her with a passion and had to find out for sure what their relationship was, before she went mad. With her heart in her mouth, she dialled the number of the restaurant. It was late afternoon and she guessed that lunchtime service would be over and Claude would be taking a break, no doubt in the arms of Francine, before starting on the evening menu.

"Hello. Le Papillon. Can I help you?"

"Good afternoon," said Charlotte, in her best telephone voice. "I wonder if you can clarify something for me. I have an order for a delivery of flowers for Francine at Le Papillon, but I can't make out the surname. Can you confirm if it is Francine Dupont, wife of Monsieur Dupont, the proprietor?"

"Of course. I'm not aware that Monsieur Dupont has ordered any flowers but yes, his wife is indeed Francine Dupont."

"Thank you for clarifying."

"You're welcome. Goodbye."

Charlotte replaced the receiver with trembling hands. So it was true. "You bastard!" she screamed, and her heart froze.

The weather matched Charlotte's mood. Rain battered against the windows and the wind howled for days on end. The soaring temperatures and water shortages of the summer were a distant memory. Even the Minister for Drought, created in the heatwave, had been given a new title of Minister for Floods.

Charlotte continued to walk each day, while the wind and rain swept across the beach and whipped the sea into a frenzy; huge rolling waves crashing to the shore. In despair, she ranted at the God that her father so devotedly worshipped, one moment blaming Him for taking her mother from her, and the next, pleading forgiveness for having messed up her short life so spectacularly. Almost before the words were uttered, they were torn away by the fierce wind, the force of the Almighty Himself.

Her paintings became darker, reflecting her mood and the wild winter weather. The summerhouse was her refuge where she created her artwork, warmed by an old paraffin heater, with candles and a hurricane lamp for light. Some of her paintings were so dark that, once completed, she didn't wish to look at them and placed them in a leather portfolio, which she kept on top of a cupboard along one section of the hexagonal wall.

Sam continued to come faithfully each week to tend the garden, until the weather became too inclement, and they agreed to call it a day until the spring. Sam looked so dejected that Charlotte invited him back in February. "Come for tea on my birthday Sam. We can sit in the summerhouse and make plans for the garden. Here, I've written the date down for you," and she handed him a slip of paper, which he folded and put in his pocket.

"That'll be proper," he said, giving Charlotte one of his rare shy smiles. "I be looking forward to it. Bump'll be proper big."

"It will indeed Sam. I'm sure I will hardly be able to move at all by then," and as Sam turned back to give her a wave, Charlotte gave thanks for Sam's uncomplicated friendship.

Charlotte's tummy (she could no longer bear to refer to it as 'Le Bump') continued to grow, and amid all her misery, so did the love she felt for the little person inside her. More and more she found herself wondering whether it could be Johnny's and daydreamed of an emotional reunion, as she handed him his new-born baby. She forced herself to ignore that hope, knowing she could never go back there, to that strong and faithful man who had given himself completely to loving her and whose love she had squandered so easily.

The weeks passed by, and Claude continued with the sham that he would return each week, followed by excuses as to why he couldn't. Charlotte was incensed at how stupid he must think her to believe his lies, but went along with his game, feeling a perverse sense of power at knowing the untruths before he uttered them. She played the part of the pleading wife when he let her down week after week, laying it on so thick she could almost feel him squirm at the other end of the 'phone, as he fumbled about for another plausible reason for not returning. As Claude's guilt grew, so did the size of the cheque he sent and which Charlotte cashed each week. Once she had bought what she needed and added to the growing collection of paraphernalia for the baby, Charlotte stashed away anything that was left in the chest with her wedding dress. Keeping a hidden and growing amount of cash gave her some small sense of security, in her otherwise desperately insecure existence.

Chapter 13

Sophie - 2015

I was missing Nick madly – he'd been on tour for four weeks – but, as usual, time flew by here in North Devon. My feet hadn't touched the ground. I'd grappled with running Devon Dwellings for a fortnight while Jo was on holiday, while delving into the world of project management as the kitchen refurb got underway. Deliveries of building materials arrived at an alarming rate in oversized Ikea-like bags, while scaffolders dumped poles, planks and ladders all over the lawn. Sam came regularly, and diligently trimmed hedges and cleared overgrown flowerbeds of weeds and grasses, tutting frequently at the imposition of the construction gang tramping all over his territory. After a couple of near misses with the builders, I saw Rob and Sam sitting together on the old bench and hoped Sam wasn't being given a hard time. He was a special person, and I didn't want him to be put off coming to tend the garden by a gang of burly builders. I think Smudge had the best time, darting between an endless stream of willing humans, ready with a friendly ear fondle or a tasty tidbit.

Nick and I managed chats or texts most days, depending on our schedules and Nick's access to a signal. The Scottish play seemed to be going down well with the inhabitants of the Highlands and Islands and Nick raved about the beauty of the West of Scotland. I was desperate to join him for a week of R and R on Arran.

Verity's foray to New York had been a huge success and she was due to return there within the month, to set up and sign contracts. Since her trip to the Sea House and meeting Sam, we had kept in touch and arranged for another visit, this time to meet Anna's mother, Grace, the district midwife who attended Charlotte during her pregnancy. Verity was still undecided about how to move things forward in the search for Charlotte but was desperate to meet as many people as possible who knew her.

"This feels a bit like déjà vu," I said, as we headed to the kitchen for a coffee. "Another meeting with someone from Charlotte's past." I cleared a space at the table, which was covered with boxes of kitchenalia, packed up ready for the onslaught of the builders. "Sorry about the state of the place. Rob, my builder, starts work as soon as I take off for Arran."

"I can't quite believe it myself," said Verity. "It seems incredible now, that I didn't meet these people at the time of Charlotte's disappearance, but it was all so different then. I was so young myself, so naïve, and struggling to cope with Bobby, my own grief and a grieving and angry father. It was all such a blur. Looking back, I don't know how I did it, or why I didn't ask more questions, make more fuss. I remember meeting with the police and coming here with them and dad; he was in pieces, but I didn't really get involved in the investigation and was more intent on collecting baby equipment and stuff for Bobby. I never saw Claude again. I know he was questioned, but he'd been in London on the day of her disappearance and had a watertight alibi. Because of the articles of clothing that were washed up a few days later, it was assumed she'd taken her own life. Back in the 70's they didn't have the resources or technology they do now and the whole thing was out of the news quite quickly; no social media sensationalising the story in those days.

"I know the case was kept open locally, but as a body wasn't found it was eventually closed or became one of those cold cases, I'm not really sure. It will be interesting to hear what Grace knows, how involved she was at the time, but I don't remember her name coming up. I don't even remember Charlotte mentioning her during her pregnancy. In the last couple of months, whenever we spoke, it was always about how wonderful Claude was, what a success he was in

London, what fab times they had at the weekends, and I was pretty wrapped up with the start of my studies in Falmouth and so pleased that at last I had my own opportunity. Of course, all that changed when I took on Bobby......." Verity's voice trailed off. "Sorry, I'm rambling on," she said at last. "Such mixed feelings. I wouldn't have missed bringing up Bobby for the world, but I had to give up so much of myself to do it."

"Did you ever get the chance to complete your degree or is it natural talent that's earned you your success?"

"I was lucky. I was able to defer my studies until Bobby started school. Then Johnny and I shared his up-bringing. He went to school in Barnstaple where Johnny was based and came home to Trethevy at weekends and during the holidays. Amazingly, it worked well and yes, it meant I was able to finish my degree."

"So what does Bobby do?" I asked, but before Verity could answer, the doorbell rang and Smudge was barking madly and racing up the hall to the door.

"Calm down, you mad dog. Hi Anna," I said, as I opened the door and grabbed Smudge's collar.

"Are you ready?" Anna asked. "The car's just over the road."

I dumped Smudge in the kitchen with a chew and we piled into Anna's estate for the drive to her mother's bungalow in Braunton.

"It's so good of you to have arranged this meeting, Anna," Verity said.

"No problem," replied Anna. "I was so amazed to meet you, the real Verity, and when Sophie explained how you'd met Sam and that you wanted to talk to anyone who knew Charlotte, I asked mum, and she was more than happy to meet you."

***

"Charlotte was a lovely girl and one of those whom pregnancy really suits. She sailed through it and as we know, the birth was easy, labour coming on so suddenly and baby born within a couple

155

of hours. It took us all by surprise with no time to get to hospital," explained Grace, Anna's mother, a lively seventy-year-old woman who had devoted her working life to bringing babies into the world.

"Can I ask about how you found her emotionally during the last few months of her pregnancy?" asked Verity. "Did she seem happy?"

A frown settled on Grace's brow. "To be honest, she was difficult to read. She appeared calm and content on the surface, but I often wondered if she was being completely open and honest with me. On the occasions when I attempted to delve a bit deeper, she brushed me off with a show of flippancy, making light of my concerns. I have always berated myself for not pressing her further, given what happened."

"What concerns did you have?"

Grace took her time before answering. "I don't know. I just felt there were things she had on her mind that she didn't tell me. I don't want to be rude, but she was always talking about Claude and what they were planning at the weekends, but I never saw him come home. When she spoke of what they had done, I think she was lying to me. We lived in the house behind the Sea House, where Anna lives now, and I'm sure we would've seen him some weekends, but we never did. I was concerned that there was something wrong, but she also talked of seeing you a lot, so I felt she at least had some family contact."

"But I didn't see her at all in the last eight weeks of her pregnancy," replied Verity. "I was studying in Falmouth."

"Not even at Christmas?" asked Grace. "She made a big thing of setting off to Cornwall for Christmas."

"No, Claude was coming home for Christmas," replied Verity.

"Oh no, she was definitely going to ….." Grace stopped. She didn't want to cause unnecessary upset and maybe her memory was not quite as sharp as it used to be. "Well, maybe I got that wrong. But she was definitely away over Christmas. The house was closed up. Perhaps she went to London."

156

"Not that it really makes any difference now," said Verity. But it puzzled and upset her, that Charlotte had seemingly fabricated more lies. And Verity felt a pang of pity that Charlotte had spent those weeks alone, including that Christmas in 1976. She gave a heavy sigh and moved on. "So, can I ask what happened when Bobby was born? Obviously I know Charlotte's account but I would like your perspective, if that's OK?"

"Well, as you know the baby came very quickly and, according to our dates, about two to three weeks early. But given that Charlotte was never sure of her dates, and given the size of the baby, I think he was at full term." Grace stopped for a moment before continuing. "And of course, when little Bobby arrived with a mop of red hair, I couldn't hide my surprise. I had met Claude several times, and I've delivered a lot of babies, and I knew he wasn't the father of this one!"

Anna brought mugs of tea for us all so there was a moment's kerfuffle while they were handed round and we all settled down again. Grace continued. "I visited every day until the health visitor took over, and in that time, she told me that Johnny was the father, and that Claude knew and they had come to some arrangement. She appeared to be doing so well in every way, physically and emotionally, that I didn't have any reason to doubt her. I have to say, Charlotte was very good at pulling the wool. I think she even fooled herself at times." Grace stopped. "Sorry if that sounds harsh, but I've beaten myself up over the years about whether I should have spotted that something was wrong, whether I missed anything ….."

"Please don't apologise," said Verity. "I agree, she was good at make believe. She had such a stubborn streak, and she could never back down and admit if she'd got it wrong. As you may know, I came to see her and Bobby a couple of days after he was born. She was an emotional wreck to be honest, and swore me to secrecy about Bobby's father. I was only eighteen and hadn't got a clue about what she should do. She told me she would sort everything out with Claude but asked me not to tell anyone until she had spoken to him.

She reckoned she had a couple of weeks before anyone was expecting her to have the baby and that gave her time. It was a nightmare for me, to be honest. I couldn't tell Johnny, I hadn't even told him that she was pregnant, and I certainly couldn't say anything to our father, so I kept her secret until the day she left Bobby with me, on the pretence that she was going to have it out with Claude when he came home that weekend. I never saw her again."

"You poor young thing. It must've been hell for you. It would've been after Charlotte had left Bobby with you that we saw her, and what we thought was Bobby in the baby sling, heading off to Morte Point. We'd been walking the dog, but the weather turned, so we were making our way back when we passed Charlotte. She stopped briefly and we advised her not to go on, but she said she was trying to get Bobby off to sleep. I couldn't see him as he was so well swaddled, but of course he wasn't there." She paused. "If only we'd insisted that she come back with us. The weather was awful, why on earth did we just walk away....."

Verity's head was bowed. It was difficult for her to hear this even now, but she didn't want Grace to be burdened with it all over again. "Please Grace, you didn't know what Charlotte was intending any more than I did. Don't beat yourself up about it now. Back then, I remember the police saying something about some locals seeing her on the cliffs. That must've been you. Was that the last you saw of her?"

Grace replied softly, "Yes it was. I called at the house the next day but there was no reply. Her car was in the garage so I thought she couldn't be far away. I tried again a couple more times and then raised the alarm. I guess you know the rest."

You could've heard a pin drop. We all sat in silence while we digested the conversation. Verity asked if Grace had learnt any more during the police investigation. "Not really," she replied. "I can remember being so relieved when they told me Bobby was with you. They questioned some locals and of course, Sam's dad. He and

Sam were Charlotte's gardeners, but they didn't bother with Sam. He was only about sixteen and, dare I say it, wasn't considered bright enough to provide any reliable information. If only they knew what he's told you. Anyway, when the clothing was washed up, they quickly assumed she'd gone over the cliff and once the search had drawn a blank, it all went quiet. We didn't see Claude again."

***

We drove back to the Sea House in silence, immersed in our own thoughts. "Thanks so much Anna, it was good to talk to Grace, another connection to Charlotte," said Verity, as we climbed out of the car.

"I'm glad it went OK. To be honest, it's the first time I've really heard about mum's involvement. Back in the day I was only five and we weren't exposed to media in the way children are now, and mum didn't talk about it, professional confidentiality and all that. But I do have happy memories of Charlotte looking after me during that summer. She was like a fairy princess to me."

"Thanks Anna, that's good to hear. No doubt I'll see you again." She smiled and waved as Anna turned into the lane leading to Tamarisk.

***

"Verity, will you have a cuppa before you head off?" I said, as we climbed the steps to the front door. As we sat at the kitchen table, Smudge fussing about between us ready for some company and hoping for a walk, Verity's mobile rang.

"Oh God! Oh no! Yes OK. I'm in North Devon but can be there in a couple of hours. Yes, tell him I'm on my way. Thanks Alice. Bye." Verity looked at me with panic in her eyes. "Oh God, it's dad. They think he's had a stroke. He's been taken to Treliske Hospital. I'll have to go straight there."

"Oh no. I'm so sorry. Are you OK? Is there anything I can do?" I said, feeling helpless.

159

I shepherded Verity to her car, advising her to take it easy and drive carefully.

"Thanks Sophie. I'll be in touch," and she was gone.

*****

My head was spinning and I offered up a prayer for Verity's dad, as I took Smudge for his long-awaited walk. Summer was in full swing and dog walking restrictions were in place, so we trudged along to the southern end of the beach where dogs are allowed all season. I mulled over the day's events and tried to figure out why Claude hadn't come home in the weeks leading up to the baby's birth, if what Grace had said was correct. Had things gone wrong with Claude before she gave birth to the baby? Was it simply that he was flat out in his London restaurant? Or was there some other reason? I felt so sorry for Verity and tried to put myself in her shoes. How brave she'd been all those years ago, left with a tiny baby. I doubt I'd have managed. And now she had an ailing father to cope with, just as her career was taking off. I felt angry at the injustices of life - how some people seemed to be sent so many trials, while others breezed through with barely a backward glance.

I took my frustrations out on entertaining Smudge, flinging a ball into the sea and dodging the spray as he emerged, shaking himself violently. I tired of the game before he did but kept it up as we made our way back along the beach. The day was cool and cloudy, the sea flat, and the holiday makers braving the beach were sheltered behind windbreaks, but many had already left for the day. Only the ubiquitous surfers were out in the bay awaiting the elusive waves. Despite the walk, by the time I reached home, I was feeling irritable and unsettled. It didn't help that I'd missed a call from Nick and his phone went to voicemail when I tried to call him back. The kitchen was a half packed up mess and those childhood insecurities of being on the move again threatened to re-surface. I dithered about for a while, attempting to bring some order to the packing chaos but gave up after a while, poured a glass of wine and took it with me for a soak in the bath.

Chapter 14

Charlotte – 1977

Charlotte cradled her new-born baby and wept silent tears. Alone at last with her tiny child, she let them fall unchecked as she rocked him in her arms, overwhelmed with love for the new life in her arms, and dread at what lay ahead.

A few hours earlier she had been in the throes of labour. The contractions had been strong and regular from the off and by the time she'd called Grace, the baby was coming and nothing was going to stop it. Grace arrived with less than fifteen minutes to spare and when Charlotte was handed a baby boy with a mop of red hair, she knew at once it was Johnny's. Grace hadn't hidden her surprise at the baby's colouring and Charlotte had confided in her; she guessed Grace probably already knew more about the whirlwind summer romance than she let on – this was a small community, and Charlotte and Claude's alternative lifestyle would have been irresistible gossip material. Charlotte was so convincing about how Claude was willing to take the baby on as his own, and that they would live between Woolacombe and London, that Grace was persuaded all would be well.

Now alone with her beautiful baby, Johnny's baby, she had no idea what she should do. The only thing she was sure of was that Claude would be home for the planned delivery date in two weeks, and by then she had to have a solution. But for tonight, she let her emotions go and held her tiny baby, her tiny piece of Johnny, tightly to herself.

Verity came a couple of days later, full of surprise at the baby's early entry into the world and excitement at becoming an auntie. The sisters hugged tightly and for a moment Charlotte naively imagined all would be well, but Verity took one look at the baby and exclaimed, "Good grief Charlotte, he's the spitting image of Johnny! So, you were pregnant before you even met Claude. Oh my Lord, what's he going to say?"

"And congratulations would be nice. And by the way, his name is Bobby."

"Well, sorry if I've not quite caught up with you Charlotte. I mean, how long have you known? And what the hell are you going to do? What's Claude going to say? And what about dad? I just can't believe it."

The girls faced each other off, as baby Bobby slept soundly in his crib, the tender moment of Verity's glimpse at her tiny nephew, lost in anger and confusion.

"It'll be all right Verity. I'll make it right for Bobby. He's the most important person now. Just promise me you won't tell anyone yet. You haven't told dad, have you? Please, just wait until I've told Claude before you tell him Bobby's arrived. Ask him if I can come and visit with the baby in a few weeks. Maybe when he sees him, he'll let me move back home?"

"So, you're planning to tell Claude and then run back home? And what happens if dad won't have you? Are you hoping Johnny'll just welcome you back with open arms? You've got a nerve Charlotte."

"Stop it, stop it, stop it!" Charlotte shouted through hot angry tears. "I don't know, but have you got a better idea? Ask Claude to bring up the baby as his own? I can't see that happening, can you?" But what Charlotte couldn't bring herself to tell Verity was that Claude was expecting another baby with his wife in London, one that was his own flesh and blood.

Bobby stirred in his crib and Charlotte handed him to Verity. She gazed at his tiny form in wonder and her heart melted, her anger dissolved. "Whatever happens, Charlotte, we will make sure this little fellow is loved and cared for by his family. I'll speak to dad and see if he'll come round."

"I'm so sorry Charlotte." Verity was sobbing down the phone. "Dad won't have you back with the baby. We've had the most awful row about it, he's so upset with you. He says you've made your bed and you've got to lie in it."

Charlotte felt the blood drain from her face and sat down before she collapsed. She could feel the panic rising as she saw her hopes of a reconciliation, and a return to Trethevy, dissolving in her tears. In her alarm, adrenaline pumping, she thought quickly.

"Listen Verity, Claude's coming home at the weekend, for the so say birth of his baby." She heard the bitterness in her voice as an image of a heavily pregnant Francine flashed before her. "I'll tell him about Bobby and then I'll make a plan. But I don't want Bobby to be here when Claude is home, so can I leave him with you overnight? I'll drive down to Falmouth on Saturday before Claude gets here, then pick him up again on Sunday." Verity was silent for so long at the other end of the 'phone, Charlotte was afraid she'd hung up. "Verity? Are you there?"

"You know I'll help you out Charlotte. What else can I do? Honestly, this is just impossible."

"I know Verity, but it will be OK in the end. I promise." But her father's rejection settled like a cold, hard stone in her heart.

***

Charlotte moved around the house like an automaton, her senses numb, as she planned her way out. Just as she'd walked away from her life in Trethevy she would leave her life in Woolacombe. It was the only way. She tended to Bobby's needs and put on a brave face for the health visitor, acted the capable new mother so as not to raise any concerns, and was praised that Bobby was thriving. If only the health visitor knew the hell Charlotte was living through and how wretched she felt but, despite her breaking heart, she showered the little man with the love and care he needed.

Charlotte had resumed her daily walks, with Bobby snuggled into a papoose next to her warm body, but now her outings took her out towards Morte Point where she surveyed the rocks, noting where she could safely climb down as close as possible to the sea, and where the cliffs were at their steepest and most vertical. As she walked, she planned.

While Bobby slept in his cot next to Charlotte's bed, she sat at the Olivetti typewriter in Claude's study and typed him a letter. She used a sheet of carbon paper between two pieces of 'Sea House' letter-headed paper, to ensure she had two copies. All the anger and hate she felt towards Claude spilled onto the pages of the letter. With a clinical precision, she folded and placed the letters in envelopes, one addressed to Claude and one to Francine, at Le Papillon.

***

Friday dawned fine. Charlotte was woken early by a hungry Bobby and as she nursed him, sitting by the window, the dawn broke, a vivid pink sky reflected across the sea. The beauty of it still took her breath away and it was at times like this, when nature was putting on one of its greatest displays, that Charlotte understood her father's faith. Surely it was only some higher power that could orchestrate such splendour. How she wished for those carefree childhood days, when life was simple, and she felt secure in the love of a caring and faithful family. Her parents had very different ways of expressing their beliefs but there was no question that for each of them, their faith was genuine and deeply felt. And then Lizzie became ill. That was when it all started to unravel for Charlotte, when her world fell apart and the great Almighty did nothing. While Lizzie and Gerald maintained their faith, Charlotte's childhood acceptance of a Christian way of life was shattered, and prayer was replaced by anger towards the God that so cruelly took her mother.

"Well, it's no use asking you for help is it? You didn't help then so why would you help me now?"

165

Bobby gave a small cry and Charlotte realised she'd spoken aloud and heard the anger in her voice. Once again, she smothered her feelings and disconnected with her emotions; it was the only way she could cope.

****

Charlotte walked down to the post office with Bobby snuggled to her in his sling.

"Mornin' maid. Red sky in the mornin', shepherd's warnin'," said the friendly postmaster, as Charlotte purchased stamps. "In for some rough weather over the next few days, so they say. How's baby doin'?"

"Fine thanks," replied Charlotte. "He's really good." She smiled and left; she wasn't in the mood for small talk. She paused in front of the post box and hesitated, before pushing the letter addressed to Claude into the slot. As she heard it land with a thud in the bottom of the box, she knew there was no going back. She was about to do the same with the letter to Francine, but something stopped her. She didn't know why, maybe it was some kindred sentiment from one mother to another, but when it came to it, she couldn't inflict such a cruel blow on the other woman. Let it be enough that Claude should suffer. When she returned to the Sea House, she went to the summer house and tucked Francine's letter in her portfolio, with her dark and melancholy paintings.

The day remained fair but cold, so Charlotte sat in an old rocking chair, cradling Bobby in her arms as she swayed to and fro, hunkered down under a thick blanket. She wanted to hold him and feel his little body close to her. Despite her anger at God, she prayed fervently that, whatever happened, He would take care of Bobby and not punish him for the waywardness of his mother.

That evening Bobby settled well and as he slept soundly, Charlotte collected some of his things ready for the trip to Falmouth. She was careful not to pack too much but made sure she didn't leave out the little teddy bear Anna and Grace had delivered the day before. Charlotte smiled as she remembered the delight on Anna's face at the sight of Bobby. "He's so tiny," she'd said in wonder and gasped as he wrapped his tiny fingers tightly around one of hers. "Look mummy. He's holding my hand!"

"The teddy bear is lovely, thank you so much. Has he got a name?" Charlotte asked Anna.

"Oh yes," she answered assuredly, "he's called Jeremy Bear."

"That's a great name. I'm sure Bobby will love him, and Jeremy Bear will live at the end of his cot until he's old enough to play with him."

"Can I give him a kiss?" Anna asked as they were leaving.

"Yes of course," and Anna placed a gentle kiss on his tiny cheek. "Can I come and see him again soon?"

Charlotte baulked at the question but didn't miss a beat. "Of course you can. Bobby will love to see you."

Charlotte gave Bobby his last feed and settled him in his cot. She sat on the edge of her bed watching him sleep peacefully, and cried until there were no tears left, then fell into bed exhausted.

***

"How many clothes d'you think he's going to need? He's only here until tomorrow," said Verity, as she took the holdall from Charlotte.

"I know, but just in case he's sick or has a massive poo. Believe me, he can get through a good few Babygros in a day. And I've written down how much formula to use for each feed, and you will remember to sterilize his bottles properly won't you? And he likes to be put up on your shoulder to wind him, or you can lay him across your lap but don't –"

"Charlotte, calm down. I'm sure I'll cope. Remember when I used to stay over and help with the twins? Neither of them came to any harm in my care."

167

Verity had spent one summer holiday helping a local mum with her new-born twins thinking she might want to train as a nanny, but her talent and love for art had trumped child minding.

"Are you OK Charlotte, you seem really jumpy? Don't worry about Bobby, I'll love having him. You go and sort things out with Claude. I just hope to goodness you can work something out. Surely he can't just throw you out of the Sea House? Not with a baby in tow."

"I don't know Verity. Why would he let me stay when it's not his baby, we're not officially married, it's not my house ….." her voice trailed off and the tears started again. "Look, I'm just going to go." She stroked Bobby's head as Verity held him. "Be a good baby for Aunty Verity. God bless you both." She hugged them both together and left.

How she managed the drive back to Woolacombe, she had no idea. The stormy weather had already arrived in Cornwall and with rain pelting the windscreen and tears obscuring her vision, it was a miracle she didn't drive into a ditch.

Charlotte parked her car in the garage, but as she let herself into the house, her resolve almost left her and the temptation to get back in the car and return to Bobby was overwhelming. She forced herself to shut out her feelings and focus on what had to be done. She packed a rucksack with a few clothes, newly bought, and stuffed the cash she had been saving in amongst the garments. She put a couple of photos of Bobby in an interior zipped pocket. Nothing else. There would be no need for anything else. She took another old rucksack and crammed one of Claude's thick winter jumpers inside with a pair of her jeans and a blouse. Her nerves were jangling like bottles on a wire, and she wasn't sure she could go through with it. But what choice did she have? There was no other way out.

Charlotte paced the floor, running over her plan again and again. She kept an eye out for Grace and her husband Reg, knowing they would soon set off with their dog for his late afternoon walk. At last she saw them and was relieved to see Anna wasn't with them. In her turmoil, Charlotte had the clarity of mind to remember that Anna often spent Saturday afternoons at a friend's house and supposed, thankfully, that's where she was.

She gave them about a ten-minute start, then placed the old rucksack on her front, and put on Claude's old duffle coat, which easily fitted over the bump of the bag. She popped on her woolly bobble hat and set off towards Morte Point, following in Grace and Reg's steps. The wind had worked itself into a frenzy and was howling about her as she strode off across the grassy headland towards the point, repeating over and over to herself, "This has to work. Forgive me Bobby."

Adrenaline was coursing through Charlotte's body as she saw Grace and Reg striding towards her, their dog pulling at the lead. As they drew level, the wind buffeting them so they could barely stay upright, Grace shouted above the roar of the gale, "Charlotte, what on earth are you doing out here? We've turned back, it's too wild out there," nodding towards the point.

Charlotte wrapped her arms around the bump in her coat and was careful to keep a few paces away "I'm trying to get Bobby off to sleep, he's not settling. A walk in the sling always works. I won't be long, it's crazy out here."

"Well, you mind how you go my dear," said Reg, "And don't venture right out to the point or you'll get blown over."

"Are you sure you're OK, Charlotte?" asked Grace, moving closer.

"Yes fine, really. Got to keep moving or he'll start again. I think he's nearly off." And Charlotte started walking, turning to wave as the couple watched her go. 'Go on, go home,' she said to herself, and when she looked back a moment later, they were continuing on their way towards the shelter of the lane.

Charlotte continued walking until she was sure Grace and Reg had dropped into the lane that ran between Woolacombe and Mortehoe and were safely out of sight. She forced herself to keep going as far out to the point as she could manage, in the strengthening gale. The

169

sea held no fear for Charlotte, and as she stood at the very pinnacle of the Morte Point rocks looking down at the raging waters of the tidal race, whipped up like a cauldron of boiling water, she felt a magnetic power pulling her towards the tempest below.

Chapter 15

Sophie - 2015

I breathed a huge sigh of relief, amazed I'd made it this far. Take off was, as always, panic inducing – I wasn't keen on flying – but now that we were airborne, my body relaxed for the first time that day. It had been manic, tying up the loose ends before leaving home. I'd spent most of the journey up the M5 mentally ticking my 'to do' list, to check I hadn't forgotten anything. Why did I do that? There was nothing I could do about it now so why stress about it? But I always did. Smudge had been safely delivered into Anna's care, much to Hannah's delight. She'd promised two walks a day and Anna had raised her eyebrows at me and mouthed 'Let's see', but I knew I needn't worry about Smudge's welfare while I was away. The whole family loved him and enjoyed having a dog they could borrow for a few days.

I'd left the kitchen refurb in the hands of Rob Penrose and his gang, and Sam had promised he'd keep an eye on them. I hoped they wouldn't come to blows over Sam's freshly tended beds and newly mown grass. During the early summer weeks, Rob and Sam had taken to spending regular breaks chatting together on the rickety old bench, so I felt confident Rob would look out for him if tempers got frayed. We had planned that Sam would start sorting out the summer house while I was away, and he arrived on the day of my departure to make a start before I'd even left. It nearly caused me to miss my flight; he'd come running over just as I was about to heave my case into the car.

"Ere, come and see this?"

"I haven't really got time, Sam, I've got to be off or I'll be late. Anything you're not sure of, just leave in a pile and we'll go through it when I get back."

"No, you'm need to come now. Cupboard's fallen."

'Bloody hell,' I thought, but what I said was, "OK, but it'll have to be quick."

The large wooden cupboard that spread along one side of the summer house and which I had assumed was fixed to the wall, wasn't. Sam had somehow got one of the garden tools caught when trying to remove it from the tangle of equipment propped against the back of the cupboard, and it had unbalanced the piece of furniture. It had toppled over until it knocked into the opposite wall and come to rest at a precarious angle. But this didn't seem to be bothering Sam. It was what had fallen from on top that had caused his agitation.

"What's this?" I enquired. I lifted an old leather portfolio from where it had landed, half propped up against the cupboard, and put it on the floor where I could open it, all the while thinking this was really bad timing.

Behind me, Sam said, "Them be Charlotte's, 'er did 'em," as I unzipped the case and exposed a pile of artwork. I gasped at the dark beauty of the pictures; never before had I seen such moodiness captured in paintings of sea and sky.

"These are amazing," I said, as much to myself as to Sam. "Look, Sam, I haven't got time to look at these now. Can you take the case into the house for me and put it in the sitting room? I'll look at them when I'm back. I really must go or I'll miss my flight."

Sam started gathering up the pictures as I got to my feet. "'Er did these before baby was born," he said, and then, "'Ere, what's this?" and he pulled an envelope out from amongst the artwork and handed it to me.

I shoved the envelope into my bag as I fussed about trying to find my car keys. "Where the hell have I put them?" I said, starting to get in a flap. I hated being late.

"Them's in the car, sticking out the lock," Sam replied, and he ambled over to my car and lifted my case into the boot.

"Thanks Sam. Look after those paintings for me and we'll go through them together when I'm back."

"Bye" he said and walked back toward the summer house.

***

As I'd hurried into the airport, I noticed two missed calls from Verity and three from Nick. I figured that Nick was making sure I was on track, but was more worried by Verity's calls and hoped her father hadn't taken a turn for the worse. His stroke had been serious, but the medics were hopeful he would improve over time with rehabilitation, and she was in the throes of arranging care before he could be discharged from hospital. Now that we were cruising at some ridiculous height of about 30,000 feet - how does it stay up there? - I listened to her voicemail.

'Sophie? I can't remember when you're leaving for Arran but I need to ask you something. Don't say anything about Charlotte to...' And the message had ended.

Damn, I thought, and called up the second voicemail.

'Sorry Sophie, in a signal blackspot here. I've been speaking to Johnny and he told me Bobby is ....'

"Bloody hell," I muttered, and replayed the messages as if they might be more complete on a second hearing. They weren't of course and I puzzled over them until the stewardess arrived offering refreshment.

Once I, and the couple next to me, had been served with drinks, I listened to the first of Nick's messages. He must've called while I was scrabbling about in the summer house with Sam.

'Soph, I've only got a moment before we do director's notes, but can you bring the photo album with you? I'll explain when I see you. Can't wait gorgeous girl. Bye'

'What?' and 'Damn!' I thought simultaneously. I tapped the phone to listen to the other two messages but he hadn't left another one, there were just two missed calls. 'Damn it! Must've got fed up with me not picking up.'

I stuffed the phone back in my bag and as I did so, found the crumpled envelope from the summerhouse. The paper was yellowed with age and mottled with damp, and the name and address were rendered illegible by dark smudges, as if paint from the pictures in the portfolio had leeched into the envelope. I turned it over a couple of times before deciding, guiltily, to open it. Inside was a letter.

Claude, I read, my hands trembling.

This will be a surprise, I've not written to you before have I? I wonder, will you manage to spirit this away before Francine sees it?

Oh yes, I know all about your wife and the baby you are expecting together. I guess you thought you'd be able to keep me safely tucked away in Devon, your very own mistress. But Claude, I will not be your dirty little secret.

When, week after week, you didn't come home, I came to London to surprise you. Well, I certainly got a surprise – you and Francine together, and her with a bump bigger than mine. So, here's one for you. The baby I was expecting isn't yours. My baby, who is already born, is that of a man worth a thousand of you, someone who loved me faithfully but whose love I carelessly threw away for a summer romance with a charming Frenchman. What a fool I was. Just like the summer that is over and lost in time, I've lost that true and constant love forever.

You might think you've been 'let off the hook', as we say. I've confessed, so now you owe me nothing. You can destroy my letter, Francine will never know and all will be well in your world. But why should I make it easy for you? I have kept a second copy of this letter and will one day send it to Francine;

you won't know when. She will know you for the two-timing, smooth-talking cheat that you are. It could be tomorrow, it could be in a year when you think you've got away with it, so be careful Claude, you will be found out one day.....

You won't see me again.

Charlotte

Head spinning, I carefully folded the delicate paper and placed the letter back in the envelope, having re-read it at least three times. I glanced at the couple next to me, feeling sure I must have been gasping and harrumphing out loud as I read, but they were absorbed in books and plugged into headphones, and didn't appear to have been disturbed by any exclamations from my direction. The letter explained so much. What a desperate situation Charlotte found herself in – Claude, the so say love of her life, with an expectant wife in London, while she struggled through her pregnancy alone in Devon. 'What an absolute bastard' I ranted in my head, remembering my last boyfriend's two-timing activities. I was amazed at how angry I felt on Charlotte's behalf. I was desperate to talk to Verity about the letter. She would have no idea of this twist in the sorry tale of Charlotte's last months in Devon. I pondered this latest revelation as the plane continued its trajectory towards Scotland, and wondered why this copy of the letter was tucked in amongst Charlotte's paintings. Had she not sent it to Claude? Or was this the copy she intended to send to Francine? I studied the envelope again, willing the writing to become legible but it didn't and as the captain announced that we would soon be beginning our descent into Prestwick, I frustratedly stuffed the letter into my bag.

***

The Isle of Arran was growing in stature as the Caledonian Macbride ferry chugged across the Firth of Clyde towards the island. The landing at Prestwick had been smooth and I'd offered up a silent prayer of thanks at being safely back on terra ferma – I smiled as I remembered a Michael Flanders and Donald Swann soliloquy on an ancient album Grandma owned, in which the gents reflected 'If God had intended us to fly he would never have given us the railways.' I was with them on that.

I'd navigated the airport and the car hire desk, and managed the journey from Prestwick to the small port of Ardrossen without incident, and was now on the top deck of the ferry with the sun on my face and the wind in my hair, watching as the island approached. My excitement at seeing Nick after so many weeks apart was off the scale. After the final performance of The Scottish Play (I daren't even *think* the play's name on Scottish soil!), we had a delicious week ahead of us to delight in one another and this charming Scottish island. Thoughts of Charlotte and her letter faded as I was taken in by the emerging scenery - the tiny Holy Isle sitting just off Lamlash Bay, which, I had read in my guide to the island, has an ancient spiritual heritage dating back to the 6th century, now a centre for world peace and health; and Goat Fell, the highest point on the island, rising behind the little town of Brodick, both coming into clearer focus as we neared our destination and prepared to dock.

***

The first twenty-four hours on Arran was a bit of a blur. Falling into Nick's arms at the ferry terminal was the best thing ever - a mixture of relief, comfort, excitement and awakening to be back in the embrace of the man I loved. I couldn't stop touching him and as he took over the driving, I gazed dreamily at him while resting my hand on his leg. He must've said at least twenty times in the first hour "My days, Sophie, it is so good to see you," and I was in no doubt that he'd missed me as much as I had him. Not that we had far to drive. The play was being staged in Brodick town hall, which stood at the far end of the town that ran along the shoreline from the ferry terminal. We hastily dumped my bags in our rather meagre

B&B ("Sorry it's not the Ritz Soph, but I've found a great little place along the coast where we're moving on to tomorrow," apologised Nick) and grabbed a bite to eat ("We'll get a slap-up meal tomorrow when all this is over,") before heading over to the hall.

The play was excellent and well received by Arran's residents. I don't think I'd ever seen such a rudimentary set – a few scaffolding poles put together to represent locations from Dunisnane Hill to Birnam Wood; some strategically placed old wooden tea chests which depicted everything from the witches' cauldron to a banqueting table – but it worked and, as Nick explained, it was easy to build, strike and transport, as they moved from venue to venue. "And believe me, Soph, some of the venues have been a wee bit tiny, so we needed a set that would fit in anywhere." Nick shone, obviously, in his role as Macduff, and I felt a surge of pride as he took his bow along with the rest of the cast at the close of the performance.

Once the applause faded and the hall emptied, the crew and cast wasted no time in striking the set, the promise of the last night party driving them on through the exhaustion of a gruelling six-week tour. The party lived up to expectations, Nick having regaled me on previous occasions with tales of legendary wrap parties in the world of theatre. The cast were a great bunch and welcomed me with open arms into the fold with "Ah, you're the lovely Sophie, we've heard so much about you" comments, while Nick looked on with a twinkle in his eye and cheesy grin across his lovely face. We arrived back at our B&B totally pooped, but not so spent that we didn't fall together on the bed, sating our desire for one another, built over the weeks spent apart. The squeaky bed and overwhelming tiredness prevented us from a whole night of passion, and we soon collapsed into a contented sleep, closely wrapped together.

It wasn't until we were sitting over a cup of coffee at breakfast the next morning, having chewed over the unlikely success of The Play being performed in Scotland by an entirely English cast, that the subject of Charlotte came up again. I suddenly remembered Nick's request to bring the photo album and asked him what it was all about.

"Oh yeah, I'd completely forgotten about that. You're such a distraction, Sophie Chapman." He paused, as if unsure whether to go on. "It seems a bit stupid now but the other day, a few of us drove to Blackwaterfoot. We had the morning off the day after we arrived, so decided to drive right round the island. I was sussing out possible places for us to stay so we went to the hotel there, the Kinloch. We had a drink, obviously, and - this sounds ridiculous now - the woman who served us had a butterfly shaped birthmark on her face and kind of looked like Verity."

"What?" I exclaimed, my pulse quickening. "Are you sure?"

"Well, no, of course I'm not sure. In fact, it sounds absurd now, but the resemblance to Verity ..... and that birthmark ..... oh I don't know. Perhaps I imagined it all."

"Well, we've got to go back there and check her out. I mean, say she came to Arran after leaving Devon and settled here? I suppose it's possible. I wonder if there is some family connection here that nobody considered at the time. How far is it to Blackwhatsitfoot?"

"Steady on Soph. I may just have imagined the whole thing. I mean, it's pretty unlikely really, isn't it?"

I felt my sudden enthusiasm for this new theory ebbing away at Nick's words. "Yes, it is, I guess. Still, wouldn't hurt to call in there again while we're here. You didn't book us in there then?"

"No, because I found this intimate little hotel just along the coast at Sannox, right on the shore - well actually, just about everywhere is right on the shore, there's only one main road around the island and it hugs the coast most of the way – and it looks across the Firth of Clyde. Talking of which, we ought to be making a move, come on."

"Wait a minute, I've got something to show you," and I retrieved the letter that I'd put carefully in a zipped pocket in my bag, to save it from getting more crumpled than it already was.

Nick's eyes widened as he read the words that Charlotte had written to Claude. "Wow. That's pretty tough. No wonder she was in a state. Perhaps she felt the only way out was to disappear. And she made sure she exposed Claude's game along the way."

"Yes, but why did she keep this copy of the letter? Maybe she never sent it, either to Claude or to Francine. Or maybe she sent one and then decided not to send the second. I've tried to read the name and address but it's too faded. The letter is definitely a copy, you know, the sort you get when you put a piece of carbon paper between two sheets of writing paper. Imagine doing it like that, lining up all the sheets of paper, using Tippex to correct mistakes. No laptops back then." I told Nick where the letter had been found, in amongst the moody paintings that came crashing down with the cupboard in the summerhouse.

"Lucky for Sam he didn't get squashed," said Nick vaguely, as he pondered this new nugget of information.

"Oh, and another thing. Verity left me a bit of a cryptic message yesterday which kept cutting out. Something about Johnny," and I pulled my mobile out from the bottom of my bag, but it had run out of battery. "Damn, needs charging."

"Johnny? Wasn't he the baby's father?" said Nick, "Hmm, in the words of Alice, 'curiouser and curiouser'. Maybe we should just take a trip back to the Kinloch Hotel before we leave the island, but I'm not even going to think about it for a few days, this is *our* time and we're going to concentrate on nobody but us for a change."

I melted at Nick's words, chucked my dead mobile back in my bag and all things Charlotte faded to the back of my mind.

***

The next few days were a pure delight. The little hotel at Sannox was charming, the food delectable and the setting sublime. For the first twenty-four hours we didn't venture further than the village, ambling hand in hand, sitting on benches dotted along the waterfront, watching seals sprawled on the rocks strewn along the seashore and the birdlife on the water, or in the hotel garden where we talked about our future together, vaguely making plans. After our evening meal and a wee dram or two in the bar, we retired early and made up for the last six weeks apart. As the days drew blissfully on and our energy levels increased, we decided on a lose itinerary of things we wanted to do while on the island. The summer weather was set fine and cool for the next couple of days, so we took the little boat across to Holy Isle and explored the place which was bought by a community of Buddhists and is now a designated sacred site. We climbed Goat Fell, which rises to some 874 metres and was no walk in the park – a long climb through woodland skirting the Brodick Castle estate then on up across open moorland, ending with a steep scramble over boulders to reach the summit - but worth it: the reward at the top, far reaching views of the island and, looking north, the Mull of Kintyre and mainland Scotland beyond.

"This is spectacular Nick. I couldn't wish to be anywhere else in the world right now, or with anyone else," and I snuggled into Nick, as we soaked up the breath-taking landscape before us.

"Stunning, isn't it? Almost as stunning as you and made totally perfect because we're here together." He turned me round to face him and held my face in his hands, as he kissed me gently. Then after a few moments, "Right, time to start the long trek back down." I groaned, as I thought how stiff I would be tomorrow. "You know Soph, some people come over on the ferry in the morning, whiz up and down Goat Fell and catch the ferry back in the evening. No time for dawdling then, eh?"

As the week wore on, the weather deteriorated, so we visited the whisky distillery at Lochranza, the most northern village on the island. It was a damp, drizzly day and we decided to continue on and drive the road that circumnavigates the island. "Fancy checking out the Kinloch Hotel at Blackwaterfoot?" asked Nick.

"Thought you'd never ask." I'd been hoping we would eventually visit the hotel; my curiosity had started building and now that we'd settled into being together again, I felt ready to pick up the thread of the Charlotte saga.

It was mid-afternoon, and we settled ourselves in the lounge for afternoon tea. "How very civilized. I could get used to this," said Nick, cucumber sandwich in hand as we gazed out across the slate grey sea, while seals lolled on the rocks right in front of us on the shore, unperturbed by the steadily falling rain.

I watched eagerly as the waitress approached, but she was a young girl, not Charlotte. The place was fairly busy, and my gaze swept the room to take in the other hotel staff going about their business. None of them resembled Charlotte.

After a while, I was getting fidgety. "Hmm, so she's obviously not here. Should we ask someone d'you think?"

"Yes, I suppose we could," and Nick ambled over to the bar to engage the young girl in conversation. "Could you tell me, does anyone called Charlotte Dupont work here?" he asked.

The girl thought for a moment. "No, I don't think so," she replied with a Scottish lilt. "But I'm fairly new here, so I'll go and check with the manager in a wee minute. He's in his office. Who shall I say is asking?"

"Ah, she won't know me but you could just say, umm, I'm looking her up for a friend. My name is Nick. Thanks."

"Well?" I said eagerly. "Does she work here?"

"The girl doesn't know anyone called Charlotte Dupont, but she's going to check with the manager. She's quite new."

"OK," I said, glancing over to where the girl was now serving an elderly couple. "No, wait a minute. She might not be using Dupont. What was her maiden name? It was Tre- something. A Cornish name. Damn it, I can't remember." And I started running through a whole host of names beginning with Tre-.

"Well, let's just see if there's a Charlotte, that would be a start." We sat in silence, Nick watching me as I kept looking over towards the bar, willing the girl to come back with some news. "Relax Soph, we're not in any hurry." And then I had a light bulb moment.

"Hang on, I've got Verity's card in my purse. She gave it to me at the gallery," and I yanked my purse out of my bag and retrieved the business card. "Tremayne. Of course. Charlotte Tremayne. What an idiot forgetting I had the card."

And with that the young bar girl – Flora, I noted from her name badge - came over shaking her head. "I'm sorry, I've checked and –"

"No, sorry," I interrupted. "We got the surname wrong. It's not Dupont, it's Tremayne. Charlotte Tremayne."

The girl frowned for a moment and then, "D'you mean Ruth Tremayne? Ruthie? Oh aye, I know Ruthie. She'll be in later, helps out in the bar during the summer. But, Charlotte? I didn't know –"

"Of course," I interrupted again. "She uses her middle name, has done for years. Silly of me to forget." I wasn't going to let this opportunity slip away and I glanced at Nick who was watching, open mouthed, as I slid so easily into this fabrication. "We'll just have a drink and wait for her to come in, if that's OK, Flora? What time did you say she starts?"

As Flora went off to get us some drinks and we settled in to wait for Charlotte to arrive (it *had* to be her), Nick chuckled away to himself.

"What?" I asked, feigning innocence.

"You deserve an Oscar for that performance, gorgeous girl. I'd better watch out; I could have competition! 'She uses her middle name, has done for years. Silly of me …'" Nick mimicked.

"Well, I had to say something, and you never know, it might be her middle name. Why else would she use it?" and we sat speculating about whether this person was indeed Charlotte and what on earth we were going to say to her if it was.

After about an hour, just as I was thinking I couldn't stand the suspense any longer and wondering if the whole thing might not be such a good idea, Flora appeared in the entrance of the lounge, with a woman by her side, and pointed at us. My heart was in my mouth, my stomach churning, as the woman approached. "Hello, I'm Ruth Tremayne, can I help you?"

Chapter 16

Sophie and Charlotte - 2015

"Sophie Chapman," I said, as I stuck out my hand, "and this is Nick Brewer. We're here from Devon. That is, I'm from Devon and Nick is from London."

Ruth said nothing for a moment, just gave a slight nod. Then, "I knew someone would come eventually. I'm just amazed it's taken so long. I take it you're police or missing persons or something?"

"Good heavens no!" I said. "We're just, that is, oh my days where do I start?" I was turning red and looked imploringly at Nick, while a sinking feeling settled in my stomach. What the hell were we doing?

As usual, Nick came to the rescue. "No, we're not here in any official capacity at all, so if you want us to push off, please just say so. It's just that when I was in here the other day - you may remember a group of us from the cast of Macbeth, sorry The Scottish Play – I thought I recognised you and wanted to check. If you'd like us to go ….?"

While Nick was speaking, I studied Ruth's face and was fascinated by the tiny but perfectly formed butterfly birthmark, so clear on her cheek. We waited while she sized us up, these two random people who had just catapulted into her life. I watched, her head bowed, hands wringing, as she seemingly wrestled with the choice before her – did she engage with us, or did she walk away? I realised I was holding my breath.

"No, it's time," she said eventually, looking from one to the other of us, clearly putting the ball back in our court to continue the conversation.

"Thank you," said Nick. "Can I just check, are you Charlotte Tremayne?"

A slight pause as she looked between us again, a puzzled frown forming. "Yes I am, though I haven't used that name for years. Charlotte Ruth Tremayne. But who are you?"

It was my turn now. I took my cue from Nick and attempted to appear composed, to keep a lid on my growing excitement – were we really about to hear what happened all those years ago?

"Charlotte, can I call you that? I bought the Sea House in Woolacombe earlier this year and I became aware of your story from an old photo album left at the house."

Charlotte's eyes opened wide in surprise, but when she spoke it was with an air of resignation. "The Sea House. That place." She didn't appear to be about to say anything more, so I continued.

"Then, purely by coincidence, Nick was touring with Mac... - The Scottish Play, and saw you the other day. He thought he saw a likeness to one of the photos in the album and recognised the little butterfly mark. I came to join him at the end of the tour for a short holiday and we wanted to check if you really are Charlotte."

"And now you know that I am, what now? And, if you don't mind me saying, what is it to you anyway?" she asked. She was playing things close to her chest and didn't seem in a hurry to give anything away. I was at a loss as to what to say, but Nick took over.

"We don't want to disrupt your life in any way, but we have met your sister, Verity, and, well she has never given up hope of finding you again ..."

Charlotte gasped and her cool demeanour crumbled.

"Verity?" she whispered. "My God, how do you know Verity?" Charlotte looked around the lounge, which was busy with evening guests, her head bobbing like a startled bird. "Please, come with me, let's find somewhere more private," and she led the way out of the lounge and into a sort of ante-room across from reception. As we re-settled ourselves, I noticed Charlotte grip the arms of the chair, her face now etched with anxiety and pain.

And so I started my story. I told it as kindly as I could - of finding the photo album when I moved in and seeing Verity laying flowers on the cliffs. Now the tears came and Charlotte wept for her long-lost sister, moved to know that she had come every year and never given up hope. When I asked if she was OK for me to continue, Charlotte merely nodded. I told how I had learnt that it was Verity who had left the album in the house, and I described the photos and the pieces of fabric tucked alongside them. Charlotte wept more tears, but insisted I carry on. "I want to know it all, don't leave anything out to save my feelings, please."

So I continued, gently I hoped, and told of meeting Sam and how he had seen Charlotte leaving by torch light, how he still had the letter and butterfly pendant which he had treasured, but never shared with anyone. "He never said anything about seeing you go because at the time he was considered too simple to have any infor-mation or an opinion. And the same when the pendant arrived."

"Dear Sam," Charlotte said. "I was convinced after I sent the letter, that someone would come. Maybe I even hoped they would. But as time went on, I knew my atonement wasn't done."

"Your atonement?" I asked astonished. "What d'you mean? What amends do you have to make? After the way you were treated?" I felt an anger rising inside me on Charlotte's behalf, and she recoiled at the change in my tone.

Nick put his hand on my arm. "Why don't you continue, Sophie, and then if Charlotte wishes to share her side of things, she can?"

"Yes, sorry. Where was I?" I told her how I'd taken Verity to meet Sam and then Grace, to hear about Charlotte's last few months of pregnancy. And then I ran out of steam. I couldn't bring myself to tell her how Verity had described being left to care for Bobby, how difficult it had been for her, and the agony of Charlotte never returning. "Well, that's about it really. Verity is due back from an exhibition in New York and she was going to decide her next steps in trying to find you on her return." I didn't mention Bobby, too scared of how Charlotte might react to the mention of his name. I didn't know what else to say, so just shrugged.

For a moment, when I mentioned the New York exhibition, Charlotte's expression cleared and she gave a weak smile, but then it clouded again and she asked hesitatingly, "What about Bobby? You must know about Bobby. Have you met him?" She looked longingly between Nick and me as her hand clutched at her heart.

"I'm sorry, Charlotte, I don't really know much about Bobby. Only what Verity has told me about his early life; that she shared his up-bringing with Johnny."

"Johnny." Charlotte almost moaned his name and her whole body started shaking as she sobbed. "Bobby. My baby. Our baby," she wailed.

I looked at Nick, scared now that we had opened too many old wounds. But Nick took hold of Charlotte's hands and let her cry. Eventually, the sobs subsided, and she sat in a stunned silence.

We must have stayed there, all of us silent, for a full five minutes. Eventually, Nick whispered to me that he was going to get some drinks and reappeared a few minutes later with a tray of tea and coffee. His return seemed to startle Charlotte out of her trance.

"I'm so sorry Charlotte, we never meant to cause you so much pain," I said tentatively. "Please tell us to go if you would like."

Charlotte replied emphatically, "No, stay please. There is so much more I want to know. Just give me a minute." Another silence and then, quite unexpectedly, she started to tell her story. "I've kept all this hidden for so many years but now it's time. Where shall I start? So you know I left Bobby with Verity. And you know about me meeting Grace and Reg out on Morte Point the evening I disappeared?" Nick and I nodded. Charlotte looked down at her hands in which she was wringing a tear dampened handkerchief and continued. "It was all part of my plan to convince everyone that I'd taken my own life. I had timed my walk, knowing I would meet them out on the point. I wrapped a big jumper of Claude's ..." here she paused and looked anxiously at us. We both nodded again, to reassure her that we knew of Claude "... around some pieces of my own clothing and stuffed them into a rucksack, to resemble a baby in a sling type bump. I stopped to speak to them, and they told me to turn back due to the changing weather. My plan had worked, they were witnesses to me being out on the cliffs and I was sure they assumed Bobby was wrapped inside my dufflecoat. When they were out of sight, I took the clothes from under my coat, wrapped them around a massive stone, and flung them over the cliff. Then I returned to the Sea House. The weather was so wild that night. I sat in the house in the dark, all night. I couldn't sleep. I was terrified that Claude would return unexpectedly, before I'd got away. Before it was light, I left by the path through Coombesgate valley. Sam must've seen me up at Twitchen. I walked for about five miles towards Barnstaple and was going to risk getting the early morning bus, when a VW camper van came along. It was a group of German girls and they stopped to ask if I was OK. The weather was still awful, and I was drenched." Charlotte smiled reflectively. "I remember their names – Helga, Heidi and Hannah – and they'd been working over here for the summer and had stayed on to tour the West Country before returning to Germany. Anyway, I took my chance and hitched a lift with them as far as Bristol. Once there, I caught the first train going north. It took me to Glasgow. I spent the night in a B&B and while there, heard the proprietors talking about how some of the island ferries had been cancelled because of the bad weather the previous day. It was then that I heard the name Arran and decided that's where I would go. And I've been here ever since." Charlotte stopped. She looked exhausted and her deep brown eyes, red rimmed from crying, were full of sorrow.

Nick took the opportunity to sort out drinks and we took a moment to draw breath. I saw then that the beauty of Charlotte's youth had mellowed into an attractive resemblance to Verity and, like her, Charlotte wore her long, greying hair tied up off her face with a brightly coloured scarf.

There followed a moment of awkwardness when none of us seemed to know how to continue, until Charlotte spoke. "So, what next?"

"I think it's your call Charlotte. You may still wish us to walk away, to leave you to your life here," Nick replied. I could've kicked him. I knew I couldn't just walk away, not having come this far. I found myself crossing my fingers around my coffee cup.

Charlotte took a moment while she sipped at her tea, then sat up straight, taking on a determined, almost defiant, attitude. "No, it's time to face up to what I did all those years ago, time to face the music and try to build bridges, if it's not too late. In the early 1990's when the Buddhist retreat was being developed on Holy Isle, in Lamlash Bay, I spent a whole summer there working on the project. It was a very healing time for me, and I made a promise then that I would stay here for as long as it took for someone or something to make me return. It seems you are the 'someone.'"

I suddenly gave a great sneeze and fumbled in my handbag for a tissue. I knew I had a handy pack somewhere. I unzipped the side pocket and dug in there. I didn't find any tissues but I gasped, as my hand closed on the letter from the summerhouse. "Oh," I said. I blushed, as if I'd been caught red-handed clutching a guilty secret. Nick and Charlotte looked at me, questioningly, and I decided I may as well go for it.

I handed the letter to Charlotte and told her how I'd found it just before I'd left for Scotland. I waited for her to explain its contents. As she took the old dog eared enveloped in shaking hands, I feared it may be too much. She took a while studying the letter, turning it over in her hands, reading and re-reading it. "This is a copy of the letter I sent to Claude, it was meant for Francine. In the end I couldn't bring myself to send it. It wasn't her fault that Claude had two-timed her and led a double life with me in Devon while she slaved away at his restaurant in London, all through that long hot summer. I knew Claude's copy would make him squirm, never knowing if I'd send Francine a copy, and that was enough ……. My goodness, it all seems so futile now. At the time, I think I must've been a little crazy. I sent the letter to Claude, to arrive after I'd left. You see, Bobby came early and Claude wasn't expected home for a couple of weeks, in time for the arrival of 'our' baby". She raised her hands making quotation marks with her fingers. "I was terrified he would come home unexpectedly, though I don't know why, he hadn't been home for weeks. If he'd seen Bobby, he'd have known at once that he wasn't the father. Bobby was born with a shock of red hair – he was undeniably Johnny's baby. I left Bobby with Verity before I ran away because I was such a coward and she was so strong, so sensible, I knew he'd be safe with her."

Charlotte bowed her head and examined her hands as they lay in her lap. I sensed she had run out of steam. Nick seemed to get the same feeling. "Charlotte, shall we stop there? You look exhausted and it's getting late." She looked up at Nick, weeping silent tears. Nick continued gently. "We'll be leaving in a couple of days. Why don't we leave you with Verity's contact details and then you can decide on your next steps?"

I started fumbling in my bag for my mobile, to find Verity's number, but realised I'd left it on charge back at the hotel. Instead, I fished her card out of my purse and, after scribbling my mobile number on the back, placed it on the table in front of Charlotte. She took the card and clutched it to herself, as if grasping at a lifeline that threatened to be lost to her forever.

"Yes, yes," she said through her tears, "thank you."

We left her then, hoping she'd be OK, and drove the coastal road back to our hotel in stunned silence. By the time we arrived, we'd missed the evening meal but ordered a sandwich, which we ate in the bar with a fortifying dram.

"You know Nick, I thought I'd feel elated at finding Charlotte, but I actually feel quite low, almost like it's a bit of an anti-climax. Does that sound awful?"

"I know what you mean Soph, but it's hardly surprising. We've been through the mill with Charlotte tonight. Imagine what it must've been like for her."

"Oh, I know. It's like we've done our bit and now we've got to sit back and let things take their course. It's out of our control, whatever happens next." I stifled an enormous yawn.

"Yep, you're right. Come on sleepyhead, don't know about you but I'm ready for bed."

We clambered up to our room and I retrieved my now fully charged mobile from the dressing table, as Nick headed into the bathroom. I glanced at the screen and saw the voicemail symbol was showing. I flopped down in a chair and listened, hardly believing what I was hearing.

"My goodness, Nick. You've got to listen to this," I said, as he emerged from the bathroom, toothbrush in hand. I handed him the phone.

'Sophie, it's Verity. Sorry about the garbled messages the other day. You must be on Arran by now so hope you and Nick are having a great time. What I was trying to say was that I'd been speaking to Johnny about you and what I'd learnt from Sam and Grace about Charlotte's disappearance. You won't believe this, but he told me that Bobby has been working at the Sea House. You probably know him as Rob. I got in a panic in case you'd talked to him about Charlotte and the history of the house, hence my earlier messages. You see, Johnny is Johnny Penrose of the builders you're using and Bobby, Rob, is Johnny and Charlotte's son. He knows very little about Charlotte's disappearance. We never really told him but realise we need to set things straight with him now. Should've done it years ago but it never seemed the right time. Anyway, just wanted you to know and will speak to you on your* *return. Hope all that makes sense. Bye for now.'*

Nick handed me the 'phone. "Well, that really is the final piece of the jigsaw, eh Soph?"

Epilogue

2016

"Wakey wakey gorgeous girl. Happy anniversary." Nick placed a cup of tea on my bedside table and a kiss on my lips.

"Mmm, thanks Nick," I replied sleepily, before a rush of excitement jolted me wide awake. I scrambled out from under the duvet and propped myself up against a wedge of pillows. "What's the weather like?"

"I'll show you." Nick drew back the curtains and flooded the room with light. "Set fair I'd say maid," he said in his best Devonian. "'Tiz proper." He opened the full-length window and stepped onto the balcony.

The weather really mattered today. I so wanted everything to be perfect. It was a year since I'd moved to the Sea House and we'd invited Charlotte, Verity, Rob and Johnny to visit. It wasn't a conscious decision, at first, to tie their visit in with my moving-in anniversary, but it had proved to be the best date for everyone, and I liked the significance of it - the day when I first found the photo album and it had all begun.

It was to be the first time we'd seen Charlotte since our fateful meeting on Arran, and the first time we were to meet Johnny. So much had happened in those intervening eight months. Verity had made a number of trips to Arran. She had spent some weeks there and in that healing place, over time, their relationship had been restored and Charlotte had decided to come home. "It was no easy feat," Verity told me, when we'd spoken just before Charlotte had returned. "I had to get care in for Dad, cover at the gallery, put a hold on a follow up trip to New York," she'd laughed. "Charlotte's timing always was rubbish!" But I could hear the joy and lightness in her voice, she sounded like the young Verity may have done when she and Charlotte were teenagers, before the events of the summer of 1976, when Charlotte's life had spiralled out of control.

I hadn't seen Rob since we'd returned from Arran. The main work on the kitchen roof had been completed in the time we were away, and the project was left in the capable hands of Lewis, another of Penrose and Son's gang, to finish off. I guessed Rob had some pretty heavy stuff to deal with and wasn't surprised by the change of project manager, but was secretly disappointed not to see him again and learn his side of the story - how on earth do you begin to cope with discovering the mother you believed had died shortly after your birth, was alive and well and coming home?

Once Charlotte had returned to the West Country, Verity and I had kept in touch by email. I wasn't sure what my role was, if indeed I had a role, now that Charlotte was home, and I was ready to back out gracefully (although I was desperate to know how things would pan out for everyone). But Verity seemed eager to stay in touch and had kept me informed. The reconciliation between Charlotte and her father had, said Verity, been almost too much to bear, and she feared it may trigger another stroke, but it seemed to have had the opposite effect and had given him a new lease of life. Charlotte had moved back to The Mill House and taken on the role of caring for him, which, Verity reported, she did with a tenderness and dedication she wouldn't have believed possible.

This had enabled Verity to concentrate, at last, on the gallery and the New York clients and both were thriving. The frequency with which she mentioned Joe, her Stateside associate, in her emails led me to believe that a more than professional relationship was developing.

Verity made little mention of Johnny and I didn't want to pry, so let my over fertile imagination conjure up a romantic reunion between the star-crossed lovers of 1976. I had to stop my mind running away with itself: the reality would likely be very different.

And then, in an email towards the end of winter, Verity had written that Charlotte, Johnny and Rob would like to visit the Sea House.

'They want to lay some ghosts and I think it would be good for them all and help the healing process. I've told them what you've done to the house and of course Rob knows what his guys have been up to with the renovation but hasn't seen the finished result. Would you mind very much if we came one day?' she wrote.

Mind? I was beside myself with excitement. At last I would get to meet Johnny and see them all together. Would it be too much to hope that a visit to my lovely home would be the catalyst to heal any lasting wounds? To Verity, I replied that it would be an honour for me to have them visit and soon we had a date arranged – exactly one year to the day I moved in.

***

"Calm down for goodness' sake Soph, you're worse than a cat on a hot tin roof and you're making Smudge skittish. I don't know which one of you is more wound up. Everything is fine and they'll love it. Trust me, I'm an actor."

"I know, but I just feel so responsible. What if it isn't working out and all we've done is make matters worse?" I was so anxious, my nerves jangling, and I had been flitting around the place, plumping cushions to within an inch of their lives, wiping down surfaces so they gleamed, picking imaginary flecks of dust from the floor and making regular checks on the contents of the oven and fridge to check the food and drink was ready and in the correct place. I had horrors that the lasagne would be cooling in the fridge and the lemon torte melting to a sludge in the Aga.

Nick took me by the shoulders and made me stop and look him in the eyes. "Sophie. Stop. Everything is looking lovely, including you. This isn't a photoshoot for 'House and Garden'. These are four people coming to visit for lunch. How they feel about being here isn't your responsibility."

"I know, but I just want it to be right," I replied, as my eyes started scanning the kitchen worktops over Nick's shoulder. And then there was a knock at the door. "Oh my days, they're here."

"Well you'd better go and let them in then," said Nick gently, and he gave me a peck on the cheek, turned me around and gave me a tap on my bum as I headed off along the hall.

Verity entered first, with a huge hug and an enormous bunch of flowers. "It's so good to see you again," she said, "and thanks so much for having us." The others followed, and I shepherded them into the lounge, where hugs were exchanged all round. Johnny was introduced and I was intrigued to meet this man who had, apparently, carried Charlotte in his heart across the years. He was a fine looking man, with a fit physique, greying auburn hair and twinkling blue eyes. I had a sudden random thought that it must be a West Country trait, twinkling eyes. It was then that I realised why I had so often been niggled by the feeling that I'd seen Rob somewhere before. He was very like Johnny, and Johnny was still easily recognisable from the photo album. I smiled to myself at that little twist, and looked over at Nick who was just releasing his hand from Johnny's firm grip. Far from being uptight in any way, Johnny appeared completely at ease. He stood close to Charlotte and occasionally one arm moved to hover protectively just behind her back.

After initial introductions, there was a slightly awkward pause and in the blink of an eye Nick took charge. "Well, now that we've done the introductions, how do you want to do this? We're happy to go with what you want. Would you like us to leave you to have a look round? There are also some of your things here Charlotte – the photo album and some of your paintings – which we've put in the study. First things first though, who'd like a coffee? Or something stronger?"

I could've hugged Nick and marvelled again at his knack for making people feel at ease. I decided I'd leave him to it and went off to brew the coffee. My nerves were still clanging like a bell, and I took a few deep breaths to calm myself, and did a quick check on the lasagne while the kettle boiled.

I returned with a tray of drinks and was met by a scene that could've come straight out of an Agatha Christie mystery. Any minute now, I thought, Inspector Poirot would turn up. Charlotte was wandering around examining every inch of the place, while Rob stared at the view from the window, hands held behind his back. Nick and Johnny were in quiet conversation and Verity was admiring the watercolour above the fireplace.

"You've done it up so beautifully," said Charlotte. "It's strange being here but I'm glad I've come. I was haunted by memories of this dark and foreboding house, full of secrets and painful memories. When I learnt that Bobby, sorry Rob," – she looked fondly at her son – "was working here and he told me of the transformation to the place, I just had to see it and lay those ghosts. Thank you so much for letting me come, it's another step in the healing process for me." She took my hands in hers. "Actually, I have so much to thank you for. You've given me a second chance to live the life I wanted, with the people who are so dear to me. If you hadn't found me on Arran, none of this would be happening." She looked over at Johnny. It was as if he sensed her gaze and as he caught her look, they smiled, almost shyly at one another, before he resumed his conversation with Nick. Charlotte caught my look. I must've had 'So?' written all over my face.

She smiled at me, "Oh Sophie, it's still early days but we're all getting through it together and the bond between us seems to get stronger all the time. I just thank God that I've been given this second chance."

We wandered into the study, across the hall, and Verity joined us. We looked at the photo album and Charlotte was moved to tears to see how her sister had lovingly tried to keep her memory alive with the pictures and pieces of fabric. She stroked the little bootie between her fingers then took Verity in her arms, and the two women hugged fondly.

"Goodness knows why I ever left it here at the house," said Verity. "But *He* obviously had a plan, because look where it led." The two women suddenly dissolved into laughter and giggled wickedly together at a memory, something of which I was not a part. "Sorry Sophie," Verity explained. "Our grandfather, he was a minister, was always saying that 'God has a plan for us'. He used to say it was like a road map and we had to choose which path to take. We used to think it was really funny and would get the OS map and try to find the path we were supposed to take." Verity became more serious. "Maybe he was right after all …."

Charlotte moved to look at the paintings, which had spent all those years in the summer house. Some were rather the worse for wear, having suffered from the damp, but others were intact. They were dark and moody, mostly seascapes, and no doubt reflected Charlotte's state of mind at the time. As she quietly leafed through them, Johnny came and stood beside her, and again he rested his arm gently across her back. She looked at him over her shoulder and pain was etched in her face. Verity and I left them to it; this was something for them to share alone.

Rob had kept slightly apart from the gathered group and taken the opportunity to admire the finished result of the kitchen works. The light now streamed in through three skylights, making it bright and airy, and the use of wooden beams, which echoed the shade of beechwood worktops, gave the room a warm glow. I wasn't sure how to start a conversation with Rob and focussed on discussing the build.

After a successful lunch where we had all gathered round the kitchen table and devoured the lasagne - piping hot - accompanied by a fresh green salad, followed by the lemon torte - nicely chilled

– Nick brewed more coffee. Charlotte and Johnny took their coffee mugs and went to have a look round the garden and summerhouse. Rob excused himself, saying he had to pop out but would be back shortly. Verity stayed at the kitchen table, while Nick and I cleared away.

"Thanks again Sophie. How can I ever stop saying thank you?"

"Please Verity. It wasn't me any more than it was you, or Nick, or things just aligning at the right time. So, is it really going OK?" I felt I knew Verity well enough now to probe a little deeper.

"Yes, amazingly it really is. Time, as they say, is a great healer and age has mellowed us all. The events of forty years ago, whilst traumatic at the time, are now in the distant past. Johnny has been amazing, and I swear it's brought Dad back to a happier place than he's been since our mother died. His rate of recovery has been marvellous since Charlotte came home."

"And what about Rob? How on earth has he coped with it all?" Verity was about to answer when there was a knock on the front door and he re-appeared with Sam, just as Charlotte and Johnny returned via the back door.

I was more than a little surprised to see Sam, but not as surprised as Charlotte. "Oh Sam, is it really you? How lovely to see you after all these years." She walked over to him but didn't try to hug him – she seemed to know instinctively how to be with him. She gently put a hand on his shoulder for a second before removing it.

Sam seemed overwhelmed with being in the midst of so many people and stood with his head bowed, wringing his hands, glancing up every second or so to steal a look at Charlotte. His face was flushed. And then Rob stepped in. "I'm not really one for making big speeches and the like, but I wanted to do my bit and I also wanted to say thanks to Sam for his part in all this." We all looked at Sam and I suddenly thought how significant his pieces of information had been and how we'd barely acknowledged it. Sam was squirming now, with all eyes on him, so Rob continued, to move the focus back to him. "Where do I start? Let's say it's been an interesting year. As you know, Sophie hired us to do up the house when she moved in last year, and that's when my life as I'd known it, started to unravel. First, there was dad's reaction to the project, which seemed a bit extreme to say the least." He smiled across at Johnny who was intently studying the floor. "I knew he'd never liked Woolacombe but then his reaction to this house, it just didn't make any sense. I, on the other hand, felt a real affinity with the place. Then, as you know Sophie, Sam had a couple of run ins with some of my guys. It was then that I got to know him. My boys didn't know how to behave around Sam and so I decided to see what made him tick." He gave Sam a friendly nudge and Sam returned a quick grin before lowering his eyes again. I remembered then the times I'd seen the two of them sitting together on the bench in the garden. I'd assumed they'd been discussing the altercations with the builders. "Sam told me about how he worked here in 1976 for a girl called Charlotte, how she came from Cornwall and had a sister called Verity. This got my interest, and I started doing some digging. Local papers from back in the day and the like. I could hardly believe what was unravelling before me. I'd always believed that Charlotte, mum, had been lost to the sea, but when Sam told me how he'd seen her leaving and then showed me the butterfly pendant and the letter.... well, you know the rest. When dad finally told me what had happened all those years ago, I was kind of prepared for it. In fact, I was steeling myself to talk to him and Auntie Verity about it when events overtook me."

There followed a silence while we all processed this final twist. But Rob wasn't finished. "I've got a couple of things here, hold on," and he retrieved two large packages from the hall. "Sophie, first of all – this is for you. Sam told me how you wanted to get it fixed up so this is my thanks to you for taking on Sam to restore the garden, without whom I wouldn't have found out about Charlotte, mum's, story." I was totally embarrassed and took the heavy package from Rob and unwrapped it. I gasped as I saw the exquisite mermaid weathervane, cleaned up and back in one piece. "I expect we can get that back on the roof for you at no extra charge!" Rob added.

"It's great, thanks so much Rob. Sam, you're a dark horse. You knew how much I loved this. Did you spirit it away for Rob? That'll spur us on to get the summerhouse sorted out. Fancy repairing the roof while you're at it?" I laughed.

"Ok, now for Sam. Sam, you've got something for Charlotte haven't you?" Sam hesitated for a moment, and I watched Rob, as a look of doubt crossed his face. "Are you OK with this Sam?" he added.

Sam gave a nod and then rifled around in his pocket for a moment, before pulling out a little packet. He thrust it into Charlotte's hand. "'Ere, this is yours. Don't need it now. Looked after it for you." Charlotte unwrapped the little butterfly pendant as her eyes glistened. "Sam, you kept it. All these years, you kept it. But I gave it to you as a present Sam. You don't have to give it back to me."

"Yours. Don't need it now. You'm back. Don't need it now," Sam replied.

"Sam, that's so kind. It's very special and lovely to have it back," and Johnny placed it around her neck as his eyes misted up.

"Right. Nearly done. Just one more thing and this is for Sam." He handed Sam an acrylic painting of the garden and the summerhouse, one which had been painted by Charlotte in the autumn of 1976 and in which she had perfectly captured the colours and light of the season. I gasped at its flawless portrayal of the garden that Sam had helped to create.

"I've never seen this one before," I said. "Was it in amongst the paintings we found in the summer house?" I asked Sam.

"No," replied Rob on Sam's behalf. "When you were away in Soctland, Sam showed me the ones from the summer house. I helped him to move them inside. But he also told me that Charlotte had stored some of her pictures in the loft and I took a sneaky peak, not for a minute thinking I'd find anything. And there it was with a few others, all acrylics, wrapped in cardboard right under the eaves." He smiled and tapped one side of his nose. "Easily missed if you didn't know where to look, eh Sam?" He nudged Sam again and the two of them gave a conspiratorial grin. I'd hardly ventured into the loft; only part of it had been boarded and I had shoved a couple of boxes up there during the move but hadn't explored further.

"Well, that's me done," said Rob, and suddenly there was a burst of spontaneous applause. To this day I'm not sure who started it, but it was quickly followed by laughter and then Nick made everyone a cup of tea.

***

Later, after everyone had gone, Nick and I took Smudge for a run along the beach. We mulled over the events of the day and concluded that it had been a success and the Tremayne/Penrose dynasty seemed to be on track for a brighter future. Back at the house, Smudge headed straight into the kitchen to check out his bowl, while Nick and I stood in the garden, as we often did before going indoors, for one last look at the view, Nick standing behind me with his arms wrapped around my middle. After our time together on Arran, we had given up on the long-distance relationship and Nick became a permanent fixture at the Sea House, renting Will's spare room in London when he needed to. It suited us well and, with Nick's fairly regular work away from home, kept our relationship fresh and we savoured the time we spent together. My working arrangement at Devon Dwellings allowed me to take time off when he was home and so we had the best of all worlds.

I shivered in the cooling March air. It had been one of those crystal-clear days that only seem to happen right on the coast, where the air is pure and the sky is endless, but now, as evening approached, the temperature was dropping quickly.

"Come on, what we need is a nice glass of red," said Nick, as he kissed my neck, unfolded his arms from around me and headed indoors.

I glanced once more towards the sea and glimpsed a middle-aged man, as he turned away from the Sea House and set off along the Esplanade. As I turned to follow Nick inside, I could've sworn I caught the aroma of Gauloises cigarettes, carried towards me on the evening breeze. I turned back but the man had disappeared.

Acknowledgements

This is my first novel and without the belief, encouragement and support of my family and friends it wouldn't have happened. I want to thank my youngest son, Jack, who set me the challenge of writing in the first place, 'just a paragraph to get started'. Eventually, feeling bored in my lunch hour at work one day, I typed that first paragraph. He continued to encourage and cajole until my creative juices were well and truly flowing and I was consumed by the writing bug. That doesn't mean it was all plain sailing – time constraints, self-doubt, and an inherent knack for procrastination, meant it took some years to complete The Sea House. During that time trusted friends and family have read various drafts and provided invaluable comment and reassurance, inspiration and support. Lizzie, Sarah, Jane, Claire, Ruth to name a few.

I particularly want to thank the multi-talented Helen Jarvis who has been my greatest cheerleader, and, more than that, proofreader extraordinaire (she's not known as the Grammar Queen for nothing!), and, even more than that, created the perfect cover illustration. She has kept me on track when self-doubt and procrastination threatened to win out and set achievable and completely necessary deadlines to get me to this point. Thank you Helen.

The 'research' for the book comes mainly from an inherent knowledge of my much-loved Devon and Cornwall (so I apologise for any inaccuracies, purely my own!). But I want to thank Mary Fardon, who provided an insight into maternity services in North Devon in the 1970s. By pure co-incidence she also knew of the original 'Sea House' and was able to give me some background information to its dilapidation, which is how it was when I first saw it and was the overarching inspiration for the book. Also, thanks to my friend and work colleague for many years, Jo Wayborn, who checked my attempts at Devon dialect, and Sue Walsh and Liz Liversage, who cast an eye over my (very schoolgirl!) French.

And last but not least, thanks to my husband Blake who has been on this entire journey with me, no doubt despairing of my sporadic stalling tactics but encouraging me, nonetheless. He was the first to read The Sea House and has believed in it from the start.

BV - #0039 - 111223 - C0 - 210/148/12 - PB - 9781913675400 - Matt Lamination